
"We've received no answer as yet to the message we sent to England," Salah informed her. "And, under the terms of that communique, we were obliged to kill you if our demands were not met. Of course, it's in nobody's interest to kill you, yours least of all."

"I'm not so sure," muttered Susannah.

"So we thought what a good idea it would be if we could have another little hostage of fortune, your child. We thought you should be given the opportunity to have one. But we were afraid you might not see it our way, so we just went ahead. It was, after all, done in your own best interest."

"My best interests?" Susannah's voice hovered on the brink of inaudibility. "Rape was in my best interest?"

The Rabbi's Wife

a novel by

David Benedictus

A FAWCETT CREST BOOK

Fawcett Books, Greenwich, Connecticut

THE RABBI'S WIFE

THIS BOOK CONTAINS THE COMPLETE TEXT OF THE
ORIGINAL HARDCOVER EDITION.

A Fawcett Crest Book reprinted by arrangement with M. Evans
and Company.

Copyright © 1976 by David Benedictus
ALL RIGHTS RESERVED

ISBN: 0-449-23394-4

Printed in the United States of America

10 9 8 7 6 5 4 3 2 1

To David Berger, Ze'ev Friedman, Joseph Gutfreund, Eliezer Halfin, Joseph Romano, Amitsur Shapiro, Kehat Shorr, Mark Slavin, André Spitzer, Yaa Kov Springer and Moshe Weinberg, who died at the Munich Olympic Games, 1972. And equally to the Palestinian refugees of Jordan, the Lebanon, Syria and the Gaza Strip, who live on.

Acknowledgements

My thanks are due to John Reddaway of
U.N.R.W.A., and my gratitude to
Jeanne La Chard, who was kind.

Part One

Eve of Atonement

‑‑‑‑‑‑‑‑‑‑‑‑‑‑‑‑‑‑‑‑‑‑‑

She had offered no defence. There could have been none. They had found the diary—though it was only scraps of paper torn from a student's exercise book—in a polythene bag tucked inside her trousers. Doubtless it was innocent enough—the romantic dreams of a young girl, that sort of thing—but it contravened the regulations, and that was why she offered no defence. Khalil thought it strange that anyone should be prepared to risk their life over something so trivial, but it endangered the lives of all of them, and could not therefore be overlooked.

Alia and the boy had dug the grave, and they had brought the girl to it, and shot her through the head. She had made one request before the execution, and Khalil had granted it. Consequently she embraced each of her comrades in turn, before standing, with head

bowed and hands by her sides, conveniently close to
the hole. It was sometimes considered best in such cases
for each of the group to fire simultaneously, the responsibility for the execution being equally shared, but
on this occasion Khalil, as the senior member of the
unit, carried it out alone. A single shot might suggest
a sportsman or a farmer or even a child; a volley of
shots could not be so easily disregarded.

The diary, which was no more really than a few jot-
tings, was thrown into the grave along with the girl's
clothes. She had no personal possessions, and such
money as she had left was distributed amongst the remaining members of the group.

They numbered seven. And now they sat hunched
around a table. The remains of a meal had been pushed
to one side. Those without greatcoats were huddled
under blankets, but still you could have seen the white
gusts of their breath. The room was cobwebbed, both
dusty and dank. The youngest of them was sixteen, the
oldest thirty, and, now that the girl was dead, Alia was
the only female. Some were scarred, though the scars
had not been inflicted in battles, but in intensive training sessions in the hills. Khalil lacked two fingers of
his left hand, but this was an old injury, and the skin
had long since grown over the knuckles. For a week
they had lived on tinned provisions and the carcase of
a sheep, which had wandered away from the flock to
receive a bullet between its silly eyes. For a week they
had slept on the floor without heat or light, lest their
presence in the remote hideout should be remarked,
owning only what they wore and what was with them
in the gloomy room, and what they had brought from
London in the brown van. Their rifles contained live
ammunition even during training exercises. They carried no identity papers, no discs, tattoos, bracelets, dis-

tinguishing trinkets of any kind. They did not even know each other's real names. Some of them had held their fingertips over a naked flame in the hope that their prints might be expunged; whether such a drastic measure was effective or not, there was no question but that it was impressive evidence of their dedication.

Their meeting had lasted for some hours. At one end of the table lay a Geographia Street Map of London, a motley collection of tools and electrical equipment, a loud hailer, rolls of wire, and a Junior Chemistry Set. Also a battered transistor radio, an old typewriter, some rolled-up flags, and a set of London telephone directories. They didn't shift around much in their seats. A single candle, set in its own wax, provided the illumination. Once the sixteen-year-old adjusted his position slightly to ease the cramp in his leg. Once somebody stifled a cough. They were recapitulating their alternative plans. They did so every night.

A shepherd's hut in the Welsh mountains was all it was. And in a week's time there would be nothing left in the hut, no signs of human habitation in that bleak fold of the Welsh hills. Only two graves—one containing the body of the girl, her clothes and her diary, if it could be dignified by such a description, the other the carcase of the sheep—indicated that visitors had dropped in. And within a month, you wouldn't have been able to distinguish the graves.

Committee meetings! Israeli sherry, because gestures must be made and be seen to be made, cheese straws and bacon-flavoured potato crisps. Was it possible some-one had blundered? Squiggle pads in front of each place, beautifully sharpened pencils, HB. Who sharpened them, Susannah wondered. All these minutiae that one took for granted, yet without which the running of

DAVID BENEDICTUS

our society would falter and fail. One must take *nothing*
for granted. Susannah frowned with the seriousness of
her new resolve, as she began with her sharpened pencil
to doodle Concorde mysteriously piercing the clouds
into a sunlit world, symbolic perhaps of a Better Tomorrow. She wrote the words 'Better Tomorrow' under
the doodle, and embroidered them with curlicues. Concorde didn't look quite like Concorde, and when
Susannah tried to improve the contours of the elegant
machine, the tip of the pencil-lead crunched off. Bloody
pencils! Everything fell to bits; Concorde probably
would.

"You want to borrow mine?" Hattie asked, smiling
her infuriating smile, so full of goodwill that it made
one want to go into the street and kick small animals.
Susannah shook her head.

"Is it a fish, dear?"

"No." And she tore the doodle off the pad, and
crumpled it up.

From the walls of the library pictures of the Foun-
ders of the Movement, looking less Liberal and
Progressive than earnest and gloomy. Also, in his academic flim-flam, the President of the Synagogue, and,
on a horse, Her Majesty. Plenty of oak, which was
safe, and books, unread and therefore safe as well.
Susannah, arriving early for the meeting and browsing
amongst the shelves had uncovered, between a biogra-
phy of Maimonides and *The Jew in the Mediaeval
World: A Source Book*, a copy of *Goldfinger*. Odd,
that.

"Just because," Old Jacob Kestelman was saying to
her, "the Minutes have been detained by a puncture
that is no justification for assuming that there will be
no Matters Arising. If we take the Minutes as read
without reading them, we might just as well disregard

the Agenda entirely, and then where would we all be? Judith will be here soon, my dear Susannah. I suggest we contain ourselves in patience. More sherry? So."

Susannah divined that Old Jacob's aggressiveness was little more than magisterial flirting. She had displayed no undue impatience beyond doodling, and certainly deserved no reprimand. She had nodded her head when Jamie suggested taking the Minutes as read, but Jacob said nothing to Jamie. It was "my dear Susannah" which rankled. Jamie pressed her knee under the table but, crossing her legs, she rejected the intimacy. She could handle Old Jacob without Jamie's support.

She took out her cigarettes, and, before Old Jacob had a chance to remonstrate, remarked "The meeting is not yet officially open, is it, so that's all right."

Unfortunately she had to turn to Jamie for a light, which was the last thing she wanted to do, since it would force him to take sides, and somewhat diminish her nicely calculated gesture. The cigarette tasted vile anyway. Tobacco clung to her tongue. The muck I put into my mouth, Susannah thought. Still Old Jacob was flapping his hands at the smoke, so something had been achieved.

An unexpected shaft of sunlight irradiated Old Jacob's pinched face with its bony nose, bristle moustache, sarcastic eyebrows; a dignified face, nevertheless. The President of the Synagogue looked resentfully back at the sun, and asked Hattie, the Synagogue Secretary, if she would mind drawing the blinds. She seemed not to notice the imputation that she might have minded, and did as she was told with good grace. Susannah couldn't stand her. The *minyan* was completed by Jack Cowan, the Treasurer, who spoke seldom but was a witty, musical man, and Judith, the recently punctured minute-taker.

The Minutes were read, found to be unexceptionable, and approved. There were no Matters Arising. Jack gave the Treasurer's Report and spoke of burial funds and tardy subscriptions. With a regret which surprised and a nostalgia which alarmed her, Susannah recalled her father's Synagogue. It had been Orthodox, with much chanting and muttering and prayer shawls and dim lights. Business deals had been done to the accompaniment of the cantor, but in an atmosphere like that one could believe in the efficacy of prayer, the uniqueness of the Jew. Susannah found the Blackheath and District more than a little fly. Not that she'd said so to Jamie—he'd agree with her, which would make any further discussion redundant. But she wished that the services had more fervour and fantasy, that Messianism and Zionism had some place in the dry rationale of their observance. But fervour had gone out of fashion, and religion nowadays seemed little more than social sellotape. Jamie would not accept that definition, but there was no question that he enjoyed his dinners and his charity do's and his luncheon clubs and his Ask The Rabbi talk-ins—particularly when they enabled him to show off his tall and elegant wife.

They were discussing the arrangements for the Holy Days now.

"Judith will be in charge of the Young People's Group, and you'll be taking the Infants again this year, Susannah. No need to discontinue a successful line."

"That'll be fine, won't it, Susannah?" said Jamie.

Susannah said nothing.

"Splendid. Then all that remains is to make the final decision regarding the Day of Atonement Appeal.

Jack has drawn up a short list . . ."

"What did you say, darling?" Jamie's private voice, snug and sexy.

"I didn't say anything. Should I have done?"

"You're content to take the Infants then?"

Susannah was morally pole-axed. She had no stomach for a public row in front of Jacob and the rest, and Jamie must have known it. Why then was he nudging her into one?

"I'd rather take the Young People this year," she said in a matter of fact voice, but loud, "if Judith doesn't object to the Infants."

Judith, agreeable as ever, began "Not at all, I—"

"Are we to take it, Mrs Arnatt"—and Old Jacob's brows lowered which, when it happened in New Broad Street, caused sterling to shed a point—"that you would prefer not to take the Infants, or are we to take it that you won't take the Infants?"

"You must take it as you find it," Susannah replied. "I'm just pointing out that I'd be better with the older ones. I've nothing against the Infant Samuel and Moses in the bullrushes, but—"

"I always used to take the Infants," said Judith, picking unhappily at the sleeve of her patched and recently oil-stained cardigan. "They're most of them Young People now." But Judith knew that she hadn't been good with them, too gushing, too eager to be loved, too tense, too physical. What she didn't know was that she frightened them—something about her, her smell, her rattling ribs, her bony fingers like the bony fingers of the witch in Hansel and Gretel, something of the sort frightened the more nervous of them.

"I see," said Jacob, "a monstrous regiment of women ranged against me. What should I do? Bow my head, and await the blow of the rolling pin? Or are the

weapons of the Libbers more up to date than that?"
And he managed enough of a laugh to suggest that he
was not entirely in earnest. "So you don't feel, Mrs
Arnatt, that the Young People's Service would be beneath you? Or would you care to have a stab at reading
the Law and the Prophets, and opening the Ark, and
blowing the *shofar*, and—"

"I'm sorry if I spoke out of turn," said Susannah,
surprising herself by her mildness, "but it seemed best
to let you all know my preference." She had suddenly
felt a little ashamed on Jamie's behalf, and, after all,
she had got her way and could afford to be generous.

"It's best, isn't it, to be frank?" she inquired, confusing them further by another swerve.

"Oh yes," trilled Judith, anxious that everyone
should be friendly, and handed round a bedraggled bag
of peppermints. And everyone was friends.

Susannah was an elegant wife for Jamie, or for any
rabbi. Although there had been times when she had
feared that she might grow up big-boned and horsey,
her adolescent gaucheness had given way to an in-
triguing kind of beauty. At the age of thirty she was
not the sort of woman to make heads turn in the
street; she looked best under artificial lights which
made more mysterious her pale skin, dark hair, thin
nose, deep-set eyes and wide mouth (exaggeratedly
bowed and turning up slightly at the edges as if she
were constantly on the point of smiling—false: she
rarely smiled, but those who looked at her mouth
wanted sympathetically to smile themselves). She could,
and did, wear vivid colours—deep greens, purples,
aquamarines, rich oranges and lemons. Her long legs
seemed even longer when booted and trousered. Her
tennis was powerful; she could look after her elegant

self. And it was the confidence which this strength and beauty had given her which enabled her to outface the Old Jacobs of this world. But Jamie, who knew her better, was another matter.

"Well, that was fun," he remarked, emphasising the verb, as he backed his Volkswagen into the main road. He drove a Volkswagen for two reasons: it was his symbol of forgiveness to the German people, and it was so damn reliable.

"Moses in the bullrushes!" she exclaimed in disgust.

"You got your way though."

"I don't really care." Which was the truth. Infants or Young People, it didn't matter twopence to her now.

"Old Jacob's enormously fond of you. He looks forward to your little sessions together."

"Little sessions! You're as bad as he is."

Married four years, she was constantly bewildered at the aggressions which were beginning to float to the surface of her agreeable marriage like bloated, white whales. Jamie adjusted the rear-view mirror into which Susannah had been staring defiantly at her big, defiant eyes.

"God, Jamie, sometimes I'd like to put a bomb under Old Jacob, and Hattie, and Jack Cowan, and Judith, and you!"

"Why Hattie?" asked Jamie. "That's a lot of bombs."

"Don't worry, the bombs wouldn't be the problem." And indeed Susannah had seen an underground newspaper a few days previously which, in the name of freedom, had published a detailed cartoon-strip on do-it-yourself bomb-making. A straightforward process, it seemed. A child could handle it.

"I do worry," said Jamie. "If only the Synagogue could give some sort of a lead."

"With Old Jacob in charge? He's about as progressive as a tortoise. Evolution moves faster than he does."

"He's a force to reckon with though," said Jamie. "He could be Lord Mayor one day."

"Big deal! Why don't you shake him up a bit, darling?"

"Because you do it so much more charmingly."

A Morris stalled in front of the Volkswagen, and Jamie had to brake sharply.

"Bloody men drivers!" Susannah was working herself into high spirits. She felt she was a match for any man in the world, and consequently would cook the dinner for Jamie quite happily, while he put his feet up and read the evening paper. Making concessions from a position of strength. And then they could watch the Olympic Games together on the recently installed colour television.

Evidently Jamie's mind was running along the same tracks as hers. "Do you know what Noël Coward called the Olympic Games? He said they were a rehearsal for the next war."

"Fantastic!"

"Yes."

"I wish they still had naked discus throwers."

"No doubt."

"Do you think if they were to shoot the last three in each heat, they'd run any faster?"

"I think the world needs games."

"More than religion?"

The gunmen moved in. Nothing could have been easier. And nothing more deadly. Although two men gave their lives, one standing spread-eagled in front of a door while the bullets tore into the fibres of his flesh, nothing was salvaged. The gunmen had moved in.

Intense activity in the television tower allowed the

anxious millions to share the thrills and spills of a sport which had not been scheduled by the Olympics Committee, and which was not for amateurs. Diplomatic activity (old men hustled out of bed, standing dry-mouthed by telephones, baggy pyjamas, slopped cups of coffee, wives packing overnight cases, political and diplomatic careers at stake, 'planes and boats and trains, cuff-links left behind, the most *appalling* rumours which turned out to be true, opportunities for the younger men if the nerves of the older ones cracked under the strain) between Bonn and Bavaria, between Tel Aviv, Cairo and Beirut achieved nothing. It was a fiasco, or a triumph depending . . .

The German government was to report that all that should have been done had been done, that no one was to blame, that it couldn't have been avoided—as though piles of bodies and pools of blood were the natural consequences of the natural order of things. And such bodies! The gunmen had been directed towards the living quarters of the weight-lifters and wrestlers, as though their bodies would be able to withstand bullets and wrestle with ballistics. They went down in all their glory; in their prime.

The gunmen had moved in. Those who died were hailed as heroes when they returned to Libya and their triumphant coffins were bedecked with flowers in a festival of celebration. They danced too in Cairo, Damascus and Baghdad as they had not danced since the massacre at Lod Airport. But there would be many opportunities to dance again.

The gunmen who lived were shut away in separate prisons and in solitary confinement; for the time being. Dressed as athletes, and trained to the minute, they had competed for their medals on a floodlit military airport runway, while other young men, also trained to the minute, were trussed and blindfolded for all their speed and strength. So many years of dedication for this! So many years of preparation for that!

And the old boys bumbled and struck attitudes, and dressed in their darkest suits, and stuck cotton-wool on to the places where they had nicked themselves shaving; and bleary-eyed musicians found themselves on an overcast morning playing Beethoven to an audience of billions. And the old men went into committee and hummed and ha'ed, then cleared their collective throats and said that on the whole it would be better if the games went on—after a short interregnum —so that the world should learn that there was something more important than terror and dying, trussed and blindfolded, because you were young and strong and came from Israel. Consequently the Olympic runway was floodlit once again, and the lucky young men and girls who had survived showed just how alive they were (although the best swimmer the world had ever known since men crawled out of the sea, a Jew who parted the water like Moses, was threatened with death, and flew over, not through, the water, back home where the killing was less discriminating), and the television royalties continued to pour in, which was just as well for those who had to foot the bills.

And all of that took place in a country which was not England, although bits of people, usually arms and legs, sometimes just hands and feet, were being hurled through the air in a country that *was*—most people said—England, and that was worrying, although the sea did not turn red and no governments, except that little one at Stormont, fell. But Englishmen, secure within the bullet-and-bomb-proof jacket of the sea, carried on somehow, for a little longer at least. After all, one does, doesn't one?

And on Blackheath model boats whizzed and whined around the pond as usual, football players with their hair tied back in ponytails hurled obscenities at one another on Sunday mornings, and stray dogs fought for the supremacy of the manse. Even at the Blackheath and District Progressive Synagogue along Lee Road people managed somehow. A memorial service to the dead was held, a modest affair, without sermon or moralising of any sort. Two psalms, the Amidah, Memorial Prayers, the Kaddish of course, and the Adon Olam. Old Jacob had wanted to say a few words, but Jamie persuaded him that Rosh Hashanah would be the proper occasion for that. The less emotional atmosphere of the New Year would enable him to take a more rational and pragmatic line. Old Jacob could never resist anything described as "rational", and if people called him pragmatic he took it as a compliment. But his sermon on Rosh Hashanah Eve came as something of a surprise to Jamie and Susannah. Old Jacob was moved:

". . . the birthright of our peoples. The Wandering Jew, his head hoary with frost, his heart sore, his shoes worn through, wherever he settles, my friends, wherever he rests, the crows, you may be sure, will come and peck at him. In the words Tevye uses to God in *Fiddler on the Roof*: 'Why don't you choose somebody else for a change?' "

From the gallery Susannah looked down on the congregation. She counted sixteen bowlers, rather fewer embroidered *capels*, and the odd top hat. The women's hats were formed from what looked like blue osiers, or pink turbans, or fruit or flowers or feathers. The gallery was intended less for the congregation than for the convenience of cleaning the interior of the building,

but Susannah liked it there. Superior and alone she
felt as though she were filtering the prayers of the ungodly, censoring them for unworthiness before passing
them on to a higher authority. From above, the scene
was almost surreal; so many hats! Cows on the ceiling
or burning giraffes would scarcely have seemed out of
place. A croquet game with hedgehogs and flamingoes.
Tallis in Wonderland.

". . . should we complain, should we beat our breasts
and rend our garments and sit in ashes and cry out
and cause our voices to be heard in the land? Not unto
us, not unto us, O Lord! And beg, as Jonah begged,
for the burden to be taken from our shoulders? But
who gave us the burden? In whose name do we carry
it? By whose will? Are we not to be tested, as Job was
tested, and shall we curse and deny our birthright? Or
should we not rather resign ourselves to the will of
the Almighty, and with clean hands and a pure heart
dedicate ourselves afresh to his service? Do with us as
you please, O Lord, for our life is but a span, labour
and sorrow, but in the life to come everlasting peace.
Renew a right spirit within us, O Lord, for He is our
God and we are His people, the work of His hands . . ."

The words floated up to Susannah like soap bubbles.
They refused to join into sentences, remained devoid
of sense. And what were all those people *doing*? Organised religion seemed to Susannah as hopeless as
sex education, making public confusion out of private
doubt and anxiety. All those men in bowlers, those
women with cherries on their hats, how did they per-
sonalise the Lord to whom they prayed so freely? As a
sort of Old Testament radio announcer? A white-
bearded Prince Philip? A haughty professor? Or did
any of them grasp the need for an abstract divinity?
As for the Bible, they could neither bring themselves

to believe it, nor dare to refute it, so their God remained enthroned—not to say 'marooned'—on high.
Perhaps one day scientists, biologists, space observers
or astronauts would locate Him, isolate Him, plant a
flag on Him, but until such time Old Jacob would
drone on about accepting the will of the Almighty—
which in his case was not so very malignant—and she,
Susannah, would sit and listen and remain uninvolved.

She had not always been that way.

She had first been attracted to Jamie simply because
he was a rabbi. She had passed through, as what
privileged English girl, Jewess or *shiksah*, did not, the
ballet stage, and the horsey stage, and the film-star
stage, and the Beatles stage—with a marked preference
for George, the quiet one, almost spooky at times,
whose music had a plangent longing which accorded
well with her—oh, but a long way back!—ghetto inheritance. And from all this, and between each stage,
she had turned to God, as she turned to her father, a
universal provider, a kindly critic of her foibles, a
trustworthy if somewhat distant friend.

There were not many Jewish girls at her elegantly
private school, and the ones who were there she found
a bit—well, it would be hypocritical not to confess it,
to herself at least—'common'. But the visiting rabbi, in
spite of his Birmingham accent and his habit of pulling
at his beard when the femininity of the company became overwhelming, was something else entirely. Who
could fail to be impressed with the dark intensity of
his eyes, the profundity of his learning, the whiteness
of his teeth?

"He's like Omar Sharif."

"Don't be ridiculous, Beth."

"I tell you he is, Susannah, and I can quite understand you being jealous after this evening's class."

"I don't know what you mean. And anyway if you think I intend to spend my entire summer poring over the Ethics of the Fathers in order to be rewarded by one of his famous smiles . . ."

Beth was wrong. The rabbi was not at all like Omar Sharif. And Susannah was a hypocrite. She set a great deal of store by the rabbinical smile. The only question was, whether her intense religious activity—and that summer, her sixteenth, and an unusually hot one in Weybridge, she did become exceedingly intense—was due to the influence of the rabbi, or whether her interest in the rabbi was due to her deeply felt religiosity. The same question, differently phrased, was to trouble her years later when Jamie entered her life, but this summer religion was everything to her. Hebrew classes by post and a visiting rabbi once a week were scarcely enough, no matter how white his teeth, and she found more fuel for her flames in the school chapel where the image of the Crucified Christ in the big East window was full of pathos for her. He was a rabbi too, she thought, and a good pupil of the great Rabbi Hillel, so it couldn't be wrong to worship Him as well. When the other Jewish girls pointed out that she was bowing down to a graven image, she told them, and meant it, that they were being absurd, and her voice rang out, loudest of all the school, when they sang about the water and the blood and the riven side to a tune that might have been composed especially for romantically-minded pubescent girls. (And Jesus on the Cross wore only that stained glass loin-cloth which sometimes in the mornings when the sun was low . . .)

The headmistress wrote to Susannah's father to warn him that his daughter was embracing Christianity with disturbing fervour, and she hoped that it wouldn't be at the expense of the religion of her ancestors, and her home. (The headmistress was proud of her Jewish quota, and had no wish to lose any of it.) Susannah's father, finding Susannah's empirical devoutness impressive—for he was that rare and almost extinct old bird, an intellectual without dogmatism, but with strict moral standards nonetheless—let her get on with it, which she did, going so far as to accompany one of her Christian friends to Midnight Mass on Christmas Eve.

One reason for Susannah's passionate involvement in things spiritual was so obvious that no one ever thought to suggest it to Susannah, and Susannah chose not to suggest it to herself. Hillel, Jesus on the Cross, God, so rumour had it, and the visiting rabbi who pulled his beard, were all male, and, in the steamy atmosphere of the school, Susannah's body had begun to cry out for satisfaction. Between her legs all was confusion. She was devout!

And many years later she had her rabbi—a superior model at that—and a Victorian brass bedstead in Blackheath, and striped sheets, and a Dunlopillo mattress, and an electric blanket. Between her legs now all was ordered and immaculate, and the lubricious appeal which religion had made to her adolescent self had gradually given way to a stony cynicism in which nothing could flourish, and little grow.

"What did you reckon to Old Jacob's sermon?"

"Safe." Jamie was reading a mordant novel about smart British Jewry by Brian Glanville and didn't wish to be disturbed. Nonetheless . . .

"And that's good?"

"It's safe."

"As safe as those eleven coffins?"

"Oh come *on*, Susie, you know Jacob. He lived

through a pogrom. Can you blame him if he wants to play it a bit close to the bat?"

"I'm not blaming him."

"He said to me once that the greatest danger to modern Jewry is the lack of anti-semitism."

"Fantastic! From a man who lost a father and a sister . . ."

"He thinks we're in danger of losing our identity."

"How ridiculous!" Susannah replied after a brief pause.

"When you've lain awake at night waiting for the hammering on the door . . ."

"From what I hear he does the hammering these days. Or at least his bailiffs do."

"That's quite unfair."

" 'Do with us as you please'—well really! The man's a millionaire."

"It won't bring his family back though. And he's not just a talker, Susie. He does wonderful charity work—Jewish Blind, Friends of Progressive Judaism in Israel, Jewish Welfare Board, Oxfam . . ."

"You didn't find anything inappropriate in his sermon?"

"I wouldn't say that necessarily."

"What would you say?"

"Wait and see."

"Your sermon tomorrow?" Jamie didn't answer. Susannah put her hand between his legs. Down in the forest nothing stirred. She took her hand away. "Are you going to be long?"

"I'll just finish this chapter."

Susannah burrowed lower in the bed. The room was papered with soft reds, mellow yellows and greens. The curtains were slightly apart. A huge elm tree in the garden swayed gently in the breeze between Kid-

brooke and the moon, and cast spectral shadows on the
eiderdown. Although Jamie's body was hunched and
tense—he was a messy lyer, an uncomfortable bed-
companion when he was reading—she felt wonderfully
secure. The room, Jamie's broad back, the solid house,
the tree (they said it had Dutch elm disease, but surely
not, it was so thick and strong), Blackheath itself with
the monstrous lorries thundering to France across a
heath where translucent highwaymen waved their invisible blunderbusses in vain, as though anything could
change Blackheath, a great baffle around London, so
safe. To be the smallest of the tiny Russian dolls,
screwed securely inside eight of your big sisters, though
some might have felt suffocated, to be playing sardines and to have found the airing cupboard, in which
the clean smell of the fresh sheets and towels and the
heat from the boiler combined to create a sensuous
smog into which one could sink, to be. . . .

"He's got a keen satirical mind," said Jamie suddenly. Susannah, her mind awash with blunderbusses,
baffles, Russian dolls and airing cupboards, was confused. Conveniently Jamie continued. "He's really
sharp, is Brian," and Susannah smiled, sleepily secure,
amused at Old Jacob and Jamie, and with nothing personal against Brian Glanville.

Soon enough the book would be discarded and Jamie
might—he was unpredictable, which was nice—agitate
a bit, and she would wecome him into her, like a good
hostess should, putting him at his ease, offering him
slices of strudel, smiling sweetly, and maybe this time
. . . It was all a matter of luck, everyone said so,
except those who still believed in prayer.

It didn't do to recall that hot summer, that rabbi,
that Christ on the Cross, that riven side, that Midnight
Mass, that confusion between her legs. People only

made themselves miserable by harking back, one couldn't change what one had been, was, and might become. Things happened to you, you didn't happen to things, at least that was how it seemed to Susannah lying in her Blackheath bed on the eve of the New Year. And then she thought that that was wrong, that that was what Old Jacob had been saying and what she had taken such exception to, and then she thought she really must make an effort to *do something* with her life, maybe learn Italian by Linguaphone while she washed up, or buy a book on Buddhism, or take up part-time teaching, or . . .

Then Jamie put down his book, switched off the light, and turned towards her in a meaningful sort of way.

Blackheath's position is psychologically important to those who live there. From Blackheath the residents look down on the London basin and cannot help but feel themselves superior to those who live in the smoke and the smog to the North and the West. There is a haughty kinship with the residents of Hampstead and Highgate and the fortunate few who set up their sub-urban castles on the elegant slopes of Richmond Hill.

It's a hard slog across the ferry and up the hill from the East End of London, where the tradesmen and tailors from Poland and Russia had settled in the early years of the century. But they had earned their promotion. Long hours in the sweatshops and tough bargaining in the synagogues had seen them thrive when others failed. Many had fought in the first Great War to protect the British way of life, something as yet quiet alien to them. But they would be rewarded. When the blackshirts marched along the Commercial Road, truncheons flailing and bawling about racial purity, the survivors of the pogroms began to feel at home. And many fought in the second Great War to protect something more important than honey for tea and rural deans. But the ones who stayed at home were not protected from the deadly downpour of the bombs. Not many homes were left down among the docks, not many communities survived. The Yiddish Theatre went, and the language too in due course, and most of the Jews dispersed North and West to the lush suburbs of Edgware and Hendon, where there were Vauxhalls and privet hedges, Conservative Members of Parliament and trees in the streets. Just a few moved South, isolated souls in New Cross, Camberwell, Peckham and Bexley, Catford, Lewisham, Woolwich and Charlton, and it was from these conurbations that the Blackheath and District drew its membership, from the inhabitants of these unspectacular places, small professional people, office workers, market traders, bookmakers, chemists and drapers, that it drew its subscriptions.

Architecturally the Synagogue was a compromise. A compromise between the site as it was when bought by the Building Committee and the site as it formed itself in the architect's imagination. A compromise between the Territorial Army Drill Hall, which had stood on the site for the last hundred years, and the Synagogue, which should stand there to all eternity. A compromise between the fantasies of the Tsarists from Eastern Europe who felt that God would best be served by something which could clearly indicate to Him and His servants that He had chosen well to choose the Jews. "A touch of style," they instructed the architect, "some fancy features," they added, handing him a dish of asparagus rolls, "marble pilasters, mosaics, electroliers, you know the sort of thing"; and the dreams of the Utility Boys, whose instructions tended more to-

wards "simple and clean lines, only the best materials,
nothing vulgar, oak's always nice, can't go far wrong
with oak". The architect, an obedient little chap, who
specialised in service stations and crematoria, did his
best to please everybody and succeeded in pleasing
himself and his family, who formed a large and vocal
section of the congregation.

Consequently the completed Synagogue was neither
one thing nor another, but something in between, like
a small-scale public baths (marble *did* figure here and
there) with an elegant niche for the scrolls, greenish,
subtly concealed neon lighting, provoking wrought
iron, gentlemanly oak, and seats that combined an attractive veneer with a notable degree of discomfort.
This was deliberate. To sleep during the services was
both disrespectful to the Synagogue and a wasted opportunity to learn a bit of Torah. The restlessness of
the congregation at the dedication distracted Old Jacob
who in his closing remarks inveighed against inatten-
tion, but seldom had to sit in the seats himself.

Around the main hall were a number of additional
chambers, a library, a study centre, a social centre, a
music room, offices and so on. The whole structure was
on two floors, but the main hall with its narrow, almost
concealed gallery took up the full height of the building.

And so the members of the Blackheath and District
sat fidgeting in their five-year-old Synagogue on the
morning of New Year's Day, 5733, while Jamie, nice
and warm in his prayer-shawl, and anxious to follow
Jacob's traditional *cholent* with a rather spicier dish of
his own concocting, preached, not resignation, passiv-
ity, the blind acceptance of divine displeasure, or the
sanctity of study, but . . .

" 'Blessed above women shall Jael the wife of Heber

the Kenite be, blessed shall she be above women in the tent. He asked water and she gave him milk; she brought forth butter in a lordly dish. She put her hand to the nail, and her right hand to the workman's hammer; and with the hammer she smote Sisera, she smote off his head, when she had pierced and stricken through his temples. At her feet he bowed, he fell, he lay down: at her feet he bowed, he fell: where he bowed, there he fell down dead . . . So let all thine enemies perish, O Lord: but let them that love him be as the sun when he goeth forth in his might. And the land had rest forty years'.

"Revenge. Revenge against the Canaanites. Revenge against the Canaanites in God's holy name. And the land had rest forty years. Revenge, my friends, is a human instinct. Revenge, my friends, is a basic reaction to an outrage committed against one's person, one's property, one's tribe, one's race. Animals will go to any lengths to defend their own. Read Lorenz. Men living in jungle-cities remain tribal animals. Read Desmond Morris. There is nothing unnatural in revenge if it is seen in the light of a warning to the offender not to repeat the offence. And so we must not be shocked or alarmed or confused by any reprisals that Israel may decide to take against her Arab neighbours, those good neighbours who have repeatedly stressed their intention of driving Israel into the sea. Reprisals in these circumstances are perfectly proper, so long as those responsible for them are inspired by the necessity for the deed, and not by the deed itself. When the debt is paid, the eye plucked out for the eye plucked out, then and only then is a reprisal not a reprisal, but an outrage against humanity. When the children of Israel smote the Canaanites, and Jael, the wife of Heber the Kenite struck off Sisera's head,

the country had rest for forty years. Forty years' rest
. . . that for a country worn out with fighting is no
small prize. And so we should not be apologetic in
defence of Israel or our Israeli friends. We should not
say: 'They are at war, and in times of war the rules
are changed', for, although they are at war, the rules
have not changed. The rules are the same. An outrage
will be followed by retribution. Let the biter beware
lest he be bitten back so badly that he may not bite
again. No, we should not be apologetic, but proud,
proud and fierce in our defence of that small, brave
nation, which we English did so much to create. Proud
and fierce in our words, fierce and proud to dig deep
into our pockets . . ."

After Jamie's sermon the closing hymns and the
benediction—in which Jamie blessed his congregation
with the promise of peace—mitigated somewhat the
fervour of his sermon. At the door of the Synagogue
he shook hands with the congregants, and on his face,
thought Susannah, was the smile of a schoolboy about
to receive a prize.

Jamie sliced the silverside of beef, pierced a dump-
ling on the end of a fork, handed a plate to Susannah.
  "So?"
  "There's mustard or horseradish, darling, if you'd
prefer it."
  "I hope you weren't shocked."
  "Carrots?"
  "What did you think—really?"
  "I thought you looked very handsome."
  "Do be serious."
  "I wasn't joking."
  "And that's *all* you've got to say?"
  "No."

"Well?"

"Do animals kill each other out of revenge? But my main criticism is just that, well, you didn't mean it."

"Of course I meant it!" Jamie was so appalled that the slice of beef, which he had so carefully spread with mustard and mated with a carrot, was returned to the plate. "Do you think I'd stand up there . . ."

"What has your standing up to do with your sincerity?"

"Susannah!"

"Well, why bloody ask me then?"

"I don't understand you sometimes. First you attack Old Jacob for being what you call 'safe', and then you turn on me—"

"I'm not turning on you. Either my opinion is worth something, in which case allow me to explain it, or it's worth nothing, in which case there's no point in discussing it."

"So explain it." Anticipating an explanation, the beef and carrot at last found their resting place.

"I think you're handsome. And I think you're a hypocrite. You don't really believe in revenge. If Jack Cowan burst through that door and raped me, would you go round and rape Mrs C? Of course not. I wonder what you would do. Nothing violent I'm sure."

"I was talking about attitudes. I was talking about influencing events. I was talking about money."

"And if it came to fighting?" Having feinted with the left, Susannah threw a mean hook with the right. "What about the Six Day War?"

"I'd have gone if they wanted me. I volunteered my services. Nothing to be ashamed of in that."

"Of course there isn't. Are you ashamed? I hadn't realised. No, Jamie, all I want from you is an admission—it wouldn't go beyond this room—that reprisals against the Arab States would be morally despicable."

"Well, of course, one wants to protect the innocent—"

"Thank you. And one more admission, if you feel up to it. You do? Good. That is that you, Rabbi Jamie Arnatt of the Blackheath and District Synagogue feel no compassion for the dead athletes, not really, none at all."

"But, Susannah, I do."

"All right then, you do. Inquisition over. More carrots?"

"How did we get into all this? I thought you'd approve of my sermon."

"Did you write it so that I should?" Susannah pushed her plate away. The food had merely been regrouped on her plate. Her hands were trembling.

Jamie refused the lemon tart, and said he was going for a walk. Susannah watched him go, wiping away the condensation on the kitchen window, steamy from the washing-up water. Poor Jamie. He had given his congregation what they wanted, and they had lapped it up. If only he would blind them with scholarship. She could feel some pride when he did that, when they trotted out into the sunshine, looking dazed and groggy. Revenge! A battle-cry from the Blackheath and District! What a ludicrous way to start the New Year!

He strode out of her view. He'd forgotten his overcoat; that meant that she'd got through to him. Poor love! She didn't mean to upset him, but he'd never discuss things with her, not like he would with Jacob and Jack, and she was his wife! In an hour or so he'd return, frozen stiff but pretending not to be, and he'd sulk for a bit, or go and work—or pretend to—in his study, and she'd make a tiny gesture of contrition, hot buttered toast perhaps (the lemon tart would keep),

which would allow him to 'forgive' her, and then, after
a required hour or so he'd cheer up, and they'd watch
television together over some sherry, and he'd be particularly nice to her. And she'd suffer it.

He was weak. She knew it now. But this weakness
had not been apparent when they had first met. And
Susannah, dry and tense with guilt in the aftermath of
her father's death, had been so susceptible, and Jamie
paradoxically had been impressed by her strength.

Jamie's first task after his induction had been to
bury Susannah's father, and the moral certitudes which
figured so prominently in the syllabus of the Leo
Baeck College still shone from his eyes. Yet he was
accessible.

"Would you like me to say a few words about his
life, his career?"

"For whom? For him?" (She was such a gracious
young thing then, so serious, so slender, such a sheen
of hair, and a face so full of possibilities.)

"You know, mention his childhood in—where was
it now?"

"Krakow."

"Yes, of course. And his distinguished work as an
archaeologist—"

"Antiquarian."

"Surely, Susannah, he was an archaeologist first and
foremost. I've read his books. I wish I'd met him."

The reproach was justified—she hadn't really known,
had been arguing for the sake of it—and the use of her
name in that soft voice justified it again. Her response
to his voice had been shattering; it had shattered her
determination to forbid this clean, young man access
to her grief. He seemed so . . . unstoppable.

"You'd like me to speak about him?"

"You must do as you think best. But that's what

you're trained to do, isn't it?" Then the tears. He put
an arm around her.

"He lived his life. He died in the fullness of years.
If anyone's life had a meaning, your father's did. He
made a contribution to scholarship. He'll be remembered after the captains and kings. No reason to cry,
Susannah." (Again! Had he no idea of the effect it
had? And on such an occasion!) "Should I have a talk
with Mrs Klein, do you think?"

"No. Better not." The wind dried the tears on her
cheeks. She had been determined not to brush them
away.

And then he had spoken eloquently back at the big
house in Finchley . . . charitable endeavours . . . distinguished scholar . . . generous patron of the young.
All undeniably true. But he should have checked with
Susannah's mother. It would have avoided an embarrassing scene. The anguished widow with her hair hanging loose, and no control—none—over what she was
saying. He couldn't have known about the jealous an-
tagonism between mother and daughter, their hostili-
ties across the death bed. Susannah hadn't warned him;
nobody had. But when at length he left, thinking that
for all its merits the College had not fully prepared
him, the girl followed him to the car and apologised.

"You were wonderful with her. I should have told
you. But I'd hoped . . . You haven't any family, have
you? And you're not married, so how could you have
guessed?"

"I wasn't wonderful with her. I must have said
something to upset her."

"It wasn't you. She hadn't been consulted, you see.
Well I couldn't consult her. She locked herself in the
bedroom."

"You shouldn't blame yourself."

"Two neurotic females buzzing around a great man —he was, wasn't he, *really*? I'm afraid we didn't make his last years very happy ones."

"The survivors always inherit the guilt."

"May I tell you about it? I need to tell someone." And close up in the open air he looked much older— there was even some grey around his ears—and capable.

"Yes, of course, but not here." It was coming on to rain. Odd relatives were looking oddly at them. Susannah had run coatless out of the house after Jamie.

" 'Phone me," said Susannah breathlessly. Which, incredibly, he did.

And now the following morning and six years— God!—later, here he was reappearing from the bathroom with the words: "I sometimes believe I shall never be able to make you happy." Jamie usually became soulful and occasionally maudlin around the time of the Days of Penitence, and this year was no exception. His beaky face, in public view so scrubbed and shining, was covered with shaving soap, and his wavy, raven hair, scarcely greyer now than then (surely he wasn't a secret tinter?) was uncharacteristically upstanding. Susannah considered his remark carefully. Did it relate backwards or forwards? Was it accusation or confession? She concluded that, although intended as an accusation, its effect was confessional. The conversational tone of the remark made it possible for her to avoid any serious confrontation—it was too early in the day. They were both accustomed to leaving hatches open in this way, always had been since the honeymoon. Their bottoms were shiny from sliding down shutes.

Jamie had left the radio on in the bathroom and a

jolly old fellow was babbling about his tomatoes.

"I'm happy enough," said Susannah, somewhat bleakly, "but could we take a holiday when Yom Kippur is out of the way? I'd love to go back to Cerne Abbas. We haven't been there for so long."

"Lyme Regis is nice too," said Jamie.

It was time for the eight o'clock news. The announcer's neutral voice reported, stumbling over the unfamiliar names, unable at such an hour to contact anyone from the pronunciation unit, that Israeli forces had carried out a series of reprisal raids (the word revenge was not used) following the massacre in Munich. Lebanon had been the chief target, it seemed. Refugee camps were smoking ruins. Pause. The industrial outlook was bad. The weather forecast was good. An articulated lorry had shed its load near Workington.

After the headlines there was a report from Michael Elkins in Jerusalem, but as yet no eye-witness reports from the Lebanon. Then a man spoke about Britain's lack of success in the track events at the Olympic Games. He sounded very angry, as though there had been a conspiracy to upset him, as though no one had been trying. Later in the morning there were harrowing reports from the targets of the attacks; troop activity, it appeared, had been on a sizeable scale. There were conflicting reports as to whether terrorist headquarters were contained within the refugee camps.

"Somebody's been taking your sermon to heart," said Susannah over breakfast. Jamie went off to an FPJI meeting in Hendon, but Susannah could settle to nothing.

She had letters to write, an appointment with the hairdresser, fruit and gossip to take to a hopeless aunt in a mental condition. There was the Tutankhamen Exhibition—she had been meaning to go to that; every-

one else did. How her father would have loved it!
Instead she wandered about the house aimlessly, half-
dressed, half-hearted. She dialled a poem, but the line
appeared to be out of order. Just have to do without
poetry. She ate a ginger nut and glanced at the
Guardian. An article on Anorexia Nervosa. A comical
piece on sponsored walks. She threw the paper to the
ground. Repellent, smug, have-it-both-ways liberals.
She took her flute from its case and screwed it together,
but, before she had played a note, she knew that she
couldn't play a note and wouldn't play a note and
didn't play a note, but returned the instrument to its
case. Flutes!

Dusted the living-room, which didn't need it. Sat in
a chair. Stared at the wall. Eyes ached. She despised
the furnishings and fabrics upon which they had lav-
ished so much time and money. They seemed intoler-
ably sunny and bright. Marigolds! How pathetic! She
cried a little, but quite dispassionately, not feeling
particularly wretched. Made a cup of coffee, forgot to
drink it, remembered it, drank it cold, got a piece of
skin stuck to her lip.

Then the images came. Eleven coffins. Ruined Arab
villages, painted blue to keep the evil spirits away, and
camps. Why did her imagination have to keep lifting
the lids of the coffins, turning over the rubble, moving
masonry from a severed arm? She had only seen one
dead body; her father's, both before and after the un-
dertakers had finished with him. It had been as though
he had been brought back to life. Not for years had she
seen so much colour in his cheeks, such an expression
of satisfaction on his battered, old face. Victims of
violence were permitted nightly on television, the zoom
on to the pool of blood in the gutter, the heads twisting
on the stretchers to gaze balefully at the camera, oh

yes, all that was permitted, but it was a world away from . . . Once, when Jamie was driving her along the motorway to Birmingham, they had passed what appeared to be an alarming accident. Susannah had craned to look, but Jamie said not to—the accident was on his side of the road—and accelerated past the corpses. They heard on the radio that three teenagers had been killed; one, a drummer in a pop group, had been decapitated. Images, images, morbid, obsessive, prurient.

She telephoned for a cab.

"The Israeli Embassy, please." The driver was obviously Jewish, but not the kind of Jew with whom Susannah readily identified. Rough trade. She was fascinated by his vulgarity, his choice of adjectives. His hair shone. He questioned her about her business at the Embassy, but, before she could answer. . . .

"It's these fucking Arabs shitting themselves in the desert, that's what's fucking wrong. Why don't they get themselves fucking sorted out? Dirty, lazy sods! I could tell you things . . ."

At the Embassy she dismissed the cab. She would have kept it on until her business was completed, but the man's exuberance unnerved her.

"Keep the change, keep it and go!" Throwing a couple of pound notes at him. But he wouldn't go.

" 'Ang on."

"What is it, for heaven's sake?"

"Do me a favour, lady. I'm not a fucking charity."

She passed a handful of coins to him and ran towards the building. Her hands were shaking, her heart pounding. Where was she? What had she come here for? A woman took her arm, an unbelievably awful woman who did things with cakes somewhere in Highgate and who wanted Susannah to accompany her to

Peter Jones. But first they had to sign the book.

"I'm so enormously glad you came too. I do think that gestures are all-important, don't you?"

"I don't know," cried Susannah, her voice shrill with bewilderment.

"You may borrow my pen."

"But I came here to protest."

"Well, of course you did, my dear. Now come along." And they both signed their names with a rolled gold Parker pen in a large Morocco-bound volume. "Why, Susannah, you've signed your maiden name. Look, 'Klein'. There's nothing wrong, is there?"

"Silly of me."

"I simply *have* to take you to Peter Jones. I won't take 'no' for an answer."

"No!" cried Susannah and, running into Kensington High Street, tried to hail another cab, only they were all full, and this Mrs . . . Mrs . . . Lorna Something Or Other followed her, extending her talons again, and suggested Harrods first for a bite of lunch, and then Peter Jones.

"Some other time. Some *other* time," Susannah shouted even more rudely, and ran across the street in front of a bus, whose driver let her have the full flood of his invective.

"And sod you!" she replied, using one of the taxi driver's words, not hers, and then a taxi did come by with its flag up, and did agree to take her to the Lebanese Embassy (an older, quieter driver, not unlike photographs of her grandad, only he had worn rimless glasses, but otherwise the resemblance was striking) but when they got there a cordon of police wouldn't let her through. Young policemen, but quite implacable. Where did they find them? How did they train them?

"Where now?" her grandfather asked.

"Blackheath?"

"I'm afraid not, Madam. It's too far."

"Oh *please*"—and her tears did the rest.

She reached home eventually, tumbled into bed without undressing, and dreamed of a high cliff on the South coast somewhere, ever so high, and birds, only the sky was pitch, and the birds were not singing, but croaking.

It was Kol Nidre, the Eve of the Day of Atonement, a solemn and awe-inspiring moment in the Jewish Calendar. Those of the congregation of the Blackheath and District who considered themselves to be *frumm*— and of course the term was only relative; to the ortho-dox these progressive congregations were irreconcilably heretical, some even (it was rumoured) keeping their heads uncovered—had started their twenty-four-hour fast with the highest of high teas. Others less austere fancied that the willingness of the spirit would com-pensate for the weakness of the flesh.

The mood in the hall before the service began was almost cheerful. Cheques had been paid into the *Jewish Chronicle* Fund for the families of the eleven murdered athletes, impressively generous cheques. All that could be done had been decently done, and, when you've buried six million, you cannot mourn eleven for ever.

But the 'cello sobbed, and the ravaged beauty of its melody recalled all victims everywhere, in Belsen and Buchenwald as well as in Munich, in Berlin and War-saw, in Syria and Russia and all over the world, and not just in the Holocaust and the Pogroms, but in all holocausts, all pogroms. And not just Jewish victims but all victims, all of us. And not just all of us, but the unborn as well. And not just the human race but the natural order of things, so vulnerable to disorder.

The 'cello sobbed for those who had died before their time, and for those who would. The 'cello sobbed, and now it sobbed quietly to itself, recalling personal loss. Some of the congregation sobbed with the 'cello, some dabbed with their handkerchiefs, and a few lips murmured the words of the Kaddish. There was a powerful aroma in the air; after-shave, toilet-water, and scent.

In the body of the hall, forsaking the gallery, Susannah mourned for a huge man, whose picture had been in the papers. She saw his face creased permanently by laughter into lines of good humour. She saw him standing spread-eagled, barring the door, while the bullets thudded into the straining muscles of his superb body, severing the delicate membranes. And in the distance the noise of running feet, and cries in the night.

"Excuse me, *please*." A purple lady pushed past Susannah, took her seat, and proceeded to powder her nose.

"Our God and God of our Fathers, as evening casts its shadows over the earth, ushering in this most solemn of days, we join with our fellow Jews throughout the world in prayer and meditation. This night, hallowed by sacred memories, unites us with the generations of the past. Recalling their piety and devotion, we stand before You, humbled. Stripped of all pretence and revealed in all our weakness, we seek Your pardon. Lord, often we have been faithless to the heritage of our fathers. Their passion for learning and justice has burnt but dimly within us; their teaching of mercy and peace we have much neglected. We have fallen far short of what we might have been.

"We aim for the heights, but our footsteps falter. Greed and vanity blind us, envy and arrogance consume us, selfishness dwarfs our souls. Unsteady, we

stumble and fall; unsure of the way, we lose our
bearings . . ."

Jamie's gentle voice, and the scented ladies, and the
dark-suited men, and the music, and the singing of the
small choir, and the dusk, and the candles either side
of Jamie, and the scrolls behind their curtains, almost
compelled Susannah to surrender. Why hold back?
What was it within her that plunged and squirmed at
the end of the line? She was being reeled in. Why not
go with it gracefully, let him, let God, let Jamie, ease
out the hook? But still her soul flipped and jumped in
the bottom of the boat. In the past there had been
times when she had envied women in closed communities, and those whose marriages were like closed communities; she had envied them, feared them a little, and,
terrified of being trapped, despised them. Where did
this contempt come from? Why could she not powder
her nose and say 'Amen'?

"Remember us this day for well-being. Amen. Bless
us this day with Your presence. Amen. Save us this day
unto life. Amen."

She kept the commandments, except for a little covet-
ing now and again, not because they were commandments, but because she was not very sorely tempted to
break them. She had always honoured her father (that
had been simple) and, now that her mother had moved
to Hove, it was not difficult to be at least civil to her.
She had no other gods, that was for certain, and had
never committed adultery. Never even considered it,
despite all those television plays. She worked quite
hard on Saturdays, but chiefly on Synagogue work and
on feeding her rabbi. She hadn't done much wrong.

"Purge me with hyssop, that I may become clean;
wash me till I am whiter than snow. Let me hear the
sound of joy and gladness, so that the bones which

You have broken may dance again. Turn Your face
from my sins, and wipe out all my iniquities . . ."

Measured against those solemn words, his insinuat-
ing Edinburgh voice is almost irresistible. A strange
clash of cultures, the pinched Presbyterianism of
Jamie's accent, and the overwhelming heritage of
Mosaic tradition. He's undeniably attractive too, and
he looks his best tonight, sleek, intelligent and spry.
Modern. By tomorrow night, after the fast and the
strain of eleven hours in the Synagogue, reading and
singing and praying, his eyes will have sunk a little, his
skin will be waxy, his shoulders hunched. Not to matter. A slap-up meal at that cosy Victorian-style Greenwich restaurant (hope the service is quicker than last
year), plenty of wine, and he'll be ready for anything.
Good news. There was an asterisk against the date in
Susannah's pocket diary.

"O Lord, open my lips, and my mouth shall declare
Your praise."

All around her the scented ladies and sober-suited
men murmured the responses, stood and sat, humbled
themselves and prayed for guidance. She should have
seated herself in the gallery as she had done for Rosh
Hashanah. She felt stifled by the overwhelming pressure
of communal piety. It was all very well for them.

That night in bed Susannah lay awake and watched
as Jamie threw his limbs around, and grunted and
twitched under the influence of some malignant dream.
She felt very calm and very superior. When she reached
out a hand to try and pacify him, Jamie hurled it off.
He never referred to these dreams in the mornings and
she didn't mention them either, all those demons; yet,
when awake, Jamie was more than a match for them.

The van brought the gunmen along the M4 from Wales to London. On the journey Abu Khalil had a few words with each of his six colleagues, distributed money (for in Wales they had carried none, carried nothing) and embraced each one. Although the group was generally little concerned with views from the motorway, one of them caught a glimpse of Windsor Castle and remarked that it would make a suitable target for future operations. Although intended humorously, the remark evoked few smiles. Such an idea was too momentous for laughter. When they reached London they scattered, according to a prearranged plan.

The boy of sixteen signed in at the YMCA in Great Russell Street. He gave his name as A. Mahmoud. He watched with amazement the gymnasts bending away from the parallel bars and curvetting through the air. He had not expected the British to be so supple. He gazed at the floppy-haired squash-players, who measured up more precisely to his preconceptions. They were heavy-footed and yelled. A balding paederast offered him a cup of coffee and a piece of pie in the canteen, but the lad shrugged and moved on. He slept soundly, one finger in his mouth, and dreamed of machine-guns and the mutilated corpse of the sheep.

One of his colleagues, who had shaved his head and walked with his arms stiffly by his side, sat through a late-night programme of films from Latin America at the Electric Cinema Club. The films presumed that their audiences would identfy with the proletariat, and so this shaven-headed revolutionary did. He seemed not at all dismayed that each film portrayed a radical movement which was doomed to fail against the ruthless efficiency of right wing régimes hand-in-glove with the CIA, and indeed in each case the closing titles were set against a symbol of the continuing revolution: a corpse's arm raised in an eternal gesture of solidarity; blood from a dead comrade's side trickling towards a field of young wheat; that sort of thing. When he left the cinema he was approached by a boisterous group of expatriate Greek Cypriots who took him to their 'cell' in Camden Town, and shared Retsina and Ambelopoulia with him.

The third of the seven spent the night in a Turkish bath, the fourth in the waiting-room at Waterloo Station, huddled in a duffel coat, occasionally blowing on his hands, moving when the drug addicts moved, at the approach of the police (only some of the drug addicts were too far gone to move), then moving back, surly and uncommunicative when anyone tried to engage him in conversation. And the fifth made his way to Covent Garden, where a charitable lady handed him a cup of milky tea and a sausage sandwich. He had to move swiftly to avoid being filmed by a television company making a documentary on down-on-outs, but the bustle of the market and the smell of the fruit made him think of home. His father had been a fruit trader. He sat on a box of oranges until the sky grew light, then followed a crowd of porters into a pub, where he was handed a pint of beer. He drank it and put coins into the juke-box.

Alia went window-shopping in Oxford Street. In one window she saw a pair of black leather shoes with the most elegant buckles and straps. A year ago she would have given all she possessed for just such a pair of shoes. But in any case the shop was shut. While she was staring wistfully at the shoes, a kerb-crawler stopped his Cortina and took her to a hotel room in Victoria. In the early morning, while he lay asleep, she stole her pick-up's brief-case, which contained stale sandwiches and racing notebooks, took the wallet from the hip pocket of his trousers, and walked into the street. The money from the wallet she pressed upon an alarmed cripple who had been asleep in the doorway of a large office building, the stale sandwiches and the racing notebooks she left on the plinth of one of the Trafalgar Square lions.

Abu Khalil, a tall man, impressively moustached and of imposing build, sat up all night in a room in Charlotte Street. While checking the electrical equipment, double-checking the small armoury of weapons, and making notes in a Baberton notebook, he worked his way through half a dozen bottles of Coca-Cola. The sounds of human neighbourliness—a distant quarrel, plugs being pulled and cisterns emptying, intimate murmurs, raucous shouting from the street, a jammed car horn, a noisy gear-change—died gradually away to nothing, until the silence was audible to him, to Abu Khalil, as a distinct hum, as something which threatened to grow louder and deafen him. From time to time he moved to the window and looked out. The enormity of the Post Office Tower winked down at him, part of its foreskin torn off by local revolutionaries.

Abu Khalil remembered walls of corrugated iron and petrol tins, floors of mud and duck-boards, roofs covered with rags weighed down by stones. He yearned to see a shanty-town London, a London of rubble and smoke. Once, of course—in the year before the year in which Khalil was born—there had been such a London, but he knew little or nothing of that.

Now for the first time Khalil saw that mountain range of influence and privilege as brittle, as no more than painted canvas on a wooden frame. He thought, with a kitchen knife I could rip it to shreds. He took a knife from the pocket of his jeans and dug it deep into the window-sill. The wood was damp and rotting. The knife went in—deep.

Part Two

Day of Atonement

———————————————————

"Good Yom Tov!" cried Susannah enthusiastically to her twelve golden candlesticks which would illuminate the world. "Happy New Year, and well over the fast!"

It was early afternoon. The day, as Days of Atonements go, had gone well. Attendance was up on previous years. Old Jacob had preached a safe sermon, neither too scholarly nor too bland, and appealed eloquently for funds for Leo Baeck College and Sightless Jews and War on Want. The choir had been in good voice, and Dr Raizman less inspired than usual— which was as it should be—on the organ. They had been at it four and a half hours and were over the hump.

And now the Young People, ill at ease in their best clothes and the Study Centre but glad to be out of the stuffy atmosphere of the Synagogue proper, were hop-

ing that Susannah wasn't going to be too earnest. A
small, blond boy named Simon, with straight hair and
National Health Service specs, removed much chewed
pink gum from his mouth and stuck it under his chair.
Chewing gum, he had concluded, only broke the fast
if you swallowed it.

Susannah, like so many people who have none,
fancied herself to be 'good' with children. This implied
a brisk tone of voice and a concentration on the more
positive aspects of life and living. One musn't conde-
scend; nor must one defer. Susannah looked forward
to a lively discussion in which she would learn as much
as teach.

Jethro, aged sixteen, tall for his years and bony,
only son of honest and industrious parents, the apple
of their eyes, shy, self-obsessed, lonely, serious, bright,
agnostic, guilt-ridden and, as he thought, over-sexed,
stared at Susannah in fascination. He felt ridiculously
ill at ease with the other Young People who seemed
so much younger than he was, but wonderfully warm
and protective towards this long-legged goddess. Oh,
how he would amaze her with his sophisticated philo-
sophical aphorisms!

"First of all let me introduce myself. My name is
Susannah, like the Susannah I'm sure you've read
about in the Bible, and I'm married to Rabbi Arnatt,
whom you've all seen and heard in the Synagogue this
morning."

A hand went up. "Please, Mrs."

"What's your name?"

"Jack."

"What do you want, Jack?"

"I want to wash my hands, Mrs." Giggles from a
few of the children.

Jack, in his grey flannel suit, white shirt, woollen tie

with dogs on it, lank hair combed but recalcitrant, spotty face, irritated Susannah. He had interrupted her flow.

"Well, of course, you can wash your hands, Jack, if that's what you really want to do, but if, as I suspect, you want to use the lavatory, then you'd be better advised to say so. The whole purpose of this afternoon's service—only it's more of a discussion really—is to give ourselves a chance to be absolutely honest with one another, because that in a sense is what Yom Kippur is all about, honesty with one another, and honesty with God, only now that I've mentioned God, perhaps the time has come when we should think a little about defining terms—"

"Please, Mrs, I want to use the lavatory."

"Oh very well, off you go, Jack, but don't be long." Off Jack went. "And now that I've introduced myself to you, it would be a good idea if you introduced yourselves to me. We all know Jack, of course"—pause for laughter—"but perhaps the rest of you would be so kind as to name yourselves as I point at you."

Six rows, eight oak chairs to a row, had been optimistically provided by the caretaker. The front row and the second row were empty. In the third row Patricia and Hannah, fourteen- and twelve-year-old sisters, with olive complexions and olive-shaped faces; in the fourth row Jethro—subjecting Susannah to a baleful stare, little blond Simon who looked so much wiser than his eleven years, and Ruth, who was fifteen and very much the beauty of the party, with huge eyes under a fringe, and a mobile expression which reacted to everything about her; in the fifth row Maurice, a fat, glazed-looking ten-year-old, the seat which Jack had occupied, and Pippa, twelve years old, rose-cheeked and eager; and in the back row Jonathan, who had—now Susannah noticed it for the first time, why hadn't she been told, why hadn't someone warned her? —no arms, thanks to Thalidomide, the Wonder Drug. Also in the back row two extrovert brothers, Harry and Gerry, thirteen and fifteen respectively, and Alison, a solemn sixteen-year-old with straight hair over one eye and a heavy social conscience.

"So. Now that you know my name, and I know your names, let's get back to that all-important subject of definitions. Alison, you start us off. What do you understand by 'God'?" She looked, with her long neck and mournful eyes, an interesting sort of girl, Susannah thought. It was tremendously important, she knew, when time was so short, to get off to a lively start.

"Well that depends, Mrs Arnatt, on what you understand by 'understand'. Surely if we could 'understand' God, he would by definition no longer be God. Isn't it the very fact that we can't define Him that gives Him His godhead?"

"Good, Alison, very good, go on"—As though this was just what Susannah had been angling for!

"Well, I'll tell you what God isn't, not that that will narrow the field much. He's not an old man with a white beard who lives on mountain tops and rides around in clouds and chariots and burning bushes."

"Was there anyone who thought that He was?" Shakings of heads and murmurs of dissent, except for Maurice who was rather confused.

"Furthermore," said Alison, tossing her hair out of her face, "I don't think we ought to talk of 'Him' at all."

"What would you like to talk about then, Alison?"

"You misunderstand me, Mrs Arnatt. What I mean is that this suggestion of, you know, the masculine principle in talking about the Creator, that's what leaves such a nasty taste in the mouth."

Startled, Susannah commented briskly: "Isn't that interesting? Perhaps it would be a good idea to canvass somebody else's opinion. Gerry?"

Gerry, with his happy, rectangular face and large, flat ears, just smiled merrily back at Susannah. Harry, who was topped off with the same thatch of light brown hair, but with a more inquisitive expression (as though the older boy had found what he was looking for, while his brother was still searching) spoke instead.

"Gerry's a bit shy, Mrs Arnatt. If you come back to him later, he'll probably have more to say."

"What are your views then, Harry?"

"Oh me, Mrs Arnatt, I don't know. I've never really thought about it."

"Jethro?"

Much confused, Jethro blushed. He was desperate not to waste this opportunity of making an impression, yet what could he contribute that she might possibly want to hear? Browning came to his rescue. Jethro had been studying Browning for A Levels.

"God is the perfect poet," said Jethro (and Browning), "Who in his person acts his own creations."

Susannah smiled nervously, as she tried to work it out. Failing, she improvised swiftly. "Well, that's certainly a conversation-stopper!"

Jethro was disappointed that his beautiful quotation had plopped so sadly into a murky pool of embarrassed silence.

Ruth came to the rescue. "Surely what matters is whose side He's on."

"No, I think you've raised a fascinating point there," said Susannah, sounding rather as though Ruth had happened upon it by accident, "because, you see, in the early years of Jewish history there was no doubt

at all in people's minds. He was our God and we were
His people. That implies of course that other people
had other Gods, but that ours was the best and that's
why the Jewish tradition survived where others did not.
Now, with the Jewish God adopted by the majority of
people on this globe—" Susannah paused suddenly,
hoping that she'd got her statistics right, then soldiered
on—"the situation frequently arises where the same
God appears to be on both sides at the same time.
Wasn't there a Bob Dylan song about that?" Blank
stares. Was Bob Dylan *passé* already? "I mean, take
the trouble in Ulster for instance."

"That's not the same God," said Alison. "It's the
Queen's God against the Pope's God."

"The Queen and the Pope should fight it out in
single combat," said Harry. "Don't you think so,
Gerry?"

"Yes," said Gerry, smiling happily.

"Anyone else have anything to add? Speaking purely
for myself—"

The door was hurled open, and Jack flew horizon-
tally through the air, thudding against the leg of the
table upon which Susannah was leaning. Pippa
scream shrilly once, then put a hand to her mouth as
though to muffle any further screams, and all faces
turned towards the open door, through which six headless figures marched, carrying shotguns at the ready,
and taking up positions along the walls. One remained
on guard outside the door.

In the Synagogue Jamie was preaching the afternoon
sermon. Always a problem, the afternoon sermon. The
faint-hearted had left at lunch-time, and would not be
back until the Memorial Service, when they would pay
their death-duties to the dead. The ones who remained

throughout the day, the very old for whom the Synagogue was simply the warmest and most congenial place
to be, the very lonely, and the dedicated ones, deserved
something rather special. Jamie gave them some nice
scholarship; a sermon that contrasted with the subjec-
tive tone of much of the liturgy. The topic was an interesting one: 'The Jewish Sources of the Sermon on
the Mount', and offered a good opportunity for some
sly jokes at the expense of Anglican smugness and
Orthodox Jewish hypocrisy. Scholarship, Jamie called
it, with the crust off. Pity Susannah wasn't there to hear
it. Still, he'd give her a potted version of it over dinner.
She'd be bound to find it interesting, for, if it could be
shown—and he could show it—that the central body of
Christian faith was little more than an anthology of
contemporary Jewish scholarship in the first century
CE then it stood to reason that Christianity was less a
new religion than a somewhat heretical branch of the
old one. A new religion had been invented, yes, one
that was not based on Jewish tradition, but that was
St Paulity rather than Christianity. Paul owed little to
Hillel, and—

It was at this point in the sermon that there was a
considerable disturbance, off-stage as it was. It was
created by Hattie, bustling her way past the steward,
and scuttling up the aisle pursued by hostile looks from
the thirty or so faithful, and the scent of eau-de-
cologne. Her face, normally highly-coloured, had a
waxy appearance and pearls rattled around her neck.
Jamie frowned at her disapprovingly over the reading
stand, but on she came unerringly and whispered her
urgent message. And then scuttled back.

Jamie was not sure that he had heard her correctly.
His mind had been so full of Hillel and Shammai, St
Peter and St Paul, Canterbury and Jerusalem and

Rome, that he had trouble making room in it for gunmen. Gunmen! In the Study Centre of the Blackheath
and District! Of course he was excited. Of *course* he
was. Then he realised who was in the Study Centre,
who and who. And refused to believe it.

But believe it or believe it not, some sort of announcement had to be made to the small congregation
—by now buzzing like a rotary hoe.

"Ladies and gentlemen"—and his voice was curiously listless—"the news I have to pass on to you is
grave indeed. But I must beg of you to remain seated
until I have finished speaking and then to leave the
building in an orderly manner." And he told them
what Hattie had told him, a most unlikely story involving gunmen, the Study Centre, and the Young
People's Service. And he added that this year the
Service was in the charge of Susannah, his wife Susannah. And then, in the main body of the Synagogue,
quite improperly in the circumstances, it began to rain.
Hattie, having delivered her message and scuttled
bravely back to her office, which was already a cramped
headquarters of operations, 'phone ringing, security
men knocking things over, had pressed the sprinkler
button, meaning well.

Susannah closed her eyes and clung desperately to
the vision of Dorset, as they had seen it that spring six,
or was it seven, years ago. The gorse had been in
flower, also bouquets of primroses and some late daffo-
dils growing wild. It had been a yellow honeymoon.
Aconites and kingcups and narcissi—oh, the vision of
all those yellow flowers!—dandelions and celandines
and buttercups. The insides of daisies. Good to eat.
All that had been real. But none of this could be. What
was the reality of this grey depressing room, compared

with those yellow spring flowers growing wild in the hedgerows of her mind? The past has a permanent reality. When this is a memory, Susannah thought, then I shall believe it. Not now. Not now. And the sea had been so lethargic in Lyme Regis, the plashing of the water against the sides of the boats so pleasing that she and Jamie had hardly needed to talk at all. They had shared the reality. They had read Jane Austen together.

"This is better than any Synagogue," she had once said, spreading her hands wide and indicating a soporific village which had everything a village ought to have. And Jamie had agreed, but added a rider.

"Man has always been a property developer. He takes what is formless and gives it shape, he humanises his environment. In the countryside change is all around us just now. You can almost hear things growing. And things being destroyed. But in a Synagogue nothing need change. The peace and security of four familiar walls gives a man confidence. This *is* a pretty place, Susannah, but it has no permanence. When people talk of worshipping God in a garden, they mean that they're worshipping a garden. God has no seasons. God cannot be developed. This may be 'better' than a Synagogue in the sense that it's prettier and pleasanter and smells sweeter, but it won't last. It can't. A Synagogue is more than its bricks and mortar: And therefore it will."

He'd taught her so much on the honeymoon, and she, being sexually the more experienced, had taught him a thing or two.

One day, when they were climbing this rather stark, flat-topped hill—quite a high one, but they both agreed it must be climbed, no question about that—he had said something that had showed such understanding of her that it was quite uncanny—what was it now?

"I told you not to move. You must do as we say." That wasn't Jamie's voice. Snatched rudely out of the real past, which she and Jamie had shared, Susannah reluctantly entered the unreal present, which they couldn't. Had somebody moved? Who had moved? Jack, here at her feet, blubbing and sniffing, had pulled himself a few feet along the ground. The leg which had crashed against the table seemed to be very broken. Susannah bent towards him, but a blow from the butt of a rifle upon her shoulder sent her to the floor.

They were not headless. They had sacking draped over their heads, with slits for the eyes, which had the effect of making them appear extremely sinister. It was this which, as much as anything else, had frightened the younger children, who feared witches more than guns. Their education had trained them to.

The gunmen had made their separate ways to Abu Khalil's room in Charlotte Street. They had packed themselves and their equipment into the van in a state of high nervous tension. They had covered their heads with the sacks in the gloom of the Blackwall Tunnel and, as they re-emberged into the daylight, had recognised themselves for what they were. Their fingers trembled on triggers as they piled out of the van and clattered into the foyer, so it was as well perhaps that the security men had been having a cup of tea in Hattie's office. These security men had been totally at a loss. Not that they could have done much. Trained thirty and more years ago to obey orders, to fire, if at all, in short bursts and at moving targets, up against an enemy as anxious in many cases to be taken prisoner and to sit out the rest of the war securely behind barbed wire as they were themselves, these old boys would have been no match for the gunmen. They didn't even carry firearms, just truncheons. When their tea-drinking was so rudely interrupted, one of them choked, spraying tea over his trousers, another shouted: "Hey, come back here!" as the last of the seven vanished up the stairs to the Study Centre, a third just sat, liver-spotted hands on thighs, gaping.

Susannah crouched on the ground as pain ran riot in her shoulder. She looked up at the gunman who had spoken, then at the others around the wall. Their headlessness contributed to the unreality of the situation, but Jack's blubbing was real enough. She felt no anger and no fear, only pain and excitement.

At a word from the large man, who had struck Susannah with the rifle, the other invaders got busy. One broke up the chairs. Another unrolled wire from what looked like a fishing reel. One knocked the glass out of the two windows, and checked angles of fire. One remained outside the door. The other two were guarding the children, who, with the exception of the unhappy Jack, were clustered together in a corner of the room under a map of Israel and an El Al poster, showing a jet flying over a lake, on the shores of which fishing nets were hanging over poles—the nets in the foreground so that the jet appeared to be enmeshed, an artistic touch certainly, but not, Susannah thought, the right sort of image for a state air line to project. What was needed was something to symbolise the *freedom* of air travel. She had seen Pan Am commercials on television which suggested all that was effective, the power and thrust of the engines set against the available-looking stewardesses, well, that was only to be expected perhaps, but then came the moment—the jet slicing, sluicing its way through the shimmering heat at the end of the runway towards a spectacular sunset, up, up and away! Oh, and there was the pain again, oh, *oh*, and she couldn't help a small strangled yelp, which, as soon as it escaped, resulted in another blow to the side of the head, knocking her unconscious.

Jethro too had been aware of an exhilaration, a heightening of the faculties when the gunmen burst into the Study Centre. He imagined himself describing the scene at school (his final year began the following week), and hoped that it would have a heroic outcome so that, when he told it, he would be able to dismiss his own courageous part with a shrug and a blush, reluctantly confessing when pressed that yes, he had disarmed two of the gunmen, turning their guns upon themselves, and yes, if you must know, he had—

But then the tallest and most authoritative of the gunmen began beating Mrs Arnatt about the head and shoulders with his rifle butt, and Jethro's emotions became rather confused. He hated to see her hit, and winced as if it were his shoulders receiving the blows, but a part of him exulted in it, and longed for more blows, and harder ones, to rain down upon her. And then, almost at once, a more common, Jethroic sensation, shame and self-detestation, put all else to flight.

Susannah could not have been unconscious for long, because, when the mists cleared, the view was exactly as it had been before, only someone, the one who had spoken, the one with the eloquent rifle butt, was speaking again. His English had an American accent, but was serviceable. He was telling the children to sit on the floor back to back, so that they could be tied up. He hoped they wouldn't be floolish enough to attempt to escape. If they didn't sit on the floor back to back so that they could be tied up they would be shot. If they attempted to escape they would be shot. And they would do well to keep quiet.

The news of the continuing drama at the Blackheath and District was brought to the Prime Minister, who was thumbing his way through the *Oxford Dictionary of Quotations*, preparatory to Question Time in the House. He was tempted to use the occasion for a personal intervention in the manner of Winnie at Sydney Street (it would be particularly nice to teach the Germans, who had bungled that Munich affair most deplorably, a thing or two) but wiser councils prevailed. The Home Secretary should be given a watching brief. He was utterly reliable and, moveover, he was not one of your death or glory boys. The Prime Minister would make an announcement to a hushed and solemn House, and the rest could be left to the Commissioner of Police, who was on the telephone. The Prime Minister did his best to impress upon him that whatever happened the lives of the unfortunate hostages must come first. The Commissioner, wondering what other priority there could possibly be, agreed. The Prime Minister inquired whether the gunmen had made any specific demands; the Commissioner thought not. Then the Prime Minister opined that it was a most terrible business, but was reassured when the Police Chief advised him not to worry. Thus matters rested between them.

The research had been thorough, the training comprehensive, the planning extensive, the briefing exemplary, and yet, when the gunmen saw Jonathan they hesitated, confused, and not without a twinge of that most bourgeois of sentiments, guilt. Had they been warned in advance about Jonathan, they would not have been fazed. Taken by surprise, they were much troubled. Even with sacking over their heads, they appeared doubtful.

They had wired the two sisters, Patricia and Han-

nah, together, back to back. They had wired Maurice
and Pippa, both short and plump, together, back to
back. And then they had seized Jonathan to tie him to
Simon, and, grabbing hold of his arms, had discovered
that he hadn't got any. They stopped, let go of Simon,
turned to Khalil, and muttered to him. He replied
sharply, whereupon they overcame their qualms,
whether moral, practical or aesthetic, and continued
to wire up their hostages, Susannah to Alison, Gerry
to his brother, Harry, and Jethro to the beautiful Ruth.

Although his leg was still causing him pain, Jack
had cried himself out; his nose was running and he was
sniffing. Patricia and Hannah were being very brave,
although you could see how the wire was digging into
their arms, and Gerry and Harry and Ruth were watching in silence. Alison, looking bleak and terrified, was
not the crying sort. Jethro, wrestling with his guilt, felt
himself to be isolated from the dramatic events being
enacted in the Study Centre. He'd let them batter
Susannah with rifle butts—he'd revelled in it; how
could he ever live with himself again? Maurice, Simon
and Jonathan were gulping and gasping, and Pippa was
wailing. One of the masked figures stepped over to her,
stuffed a rag into her mouth, tying it round her head
with a length of wire. It stopped the wailing all right,
but it must have touched off real panic in the girl, because she thrashed around with her limbs, giving the
unfortunate Maurice an extremely bumpy ride. Then
they tied her legs to the radiator, which was hot but not
scalding, so that she was sandwiched between the hot
pipes and Maurice.

Susannah's head was throbbing and the pain came in
rhythm with the throbs. She had to direct all her attention towards isolating the pain, and then eliminat-

ing it. All this pain, she thought, and not even a baby at the end of it.

The tying-up was completed ahead of schedule, and the gunmen waited, shifted their weight, breathing with discomfort through the sacking, anxious to get on with things.

Sitting on the edge of his seat, the chauffeur-driven Home Secretary swept across Waterloo Bridge, a police-escorted St George in search of dragons. Like an old-fashioned fire engine, the car had a bell on it, which clanged away all up the Old Kent Road.

"Is that quite necessary?" the Home Secretary plaintively inquired, but nobody could hear him for the ringing of the bell.

An Indian greengrocer came to the door of his shop, terrified lest the authorities had come for him at last.

The Home Secretary was a reluctant St George. He could not see what anybody would gain from his participation in these sorry events, but the PM had asked him to put in an appearance and implied that he was lucky to be going, although for the life of him he couldn't see what was lucky about it. He was off to Washington the following day, and had particularly wanted to buy some drip-dry shirts for the visit, the sort you could hang up overnight in the—what did they call it? ah yes, *closet*—and wear the next morning over your, um, *sweatshirt*. As it was, he'd feel hot and grubby in the usual old, frayed shirts and be bad-tempered because of it, and people would get offended, and everything would be ruined. If one travelled, one needed new clothes, and now he wouldn't have any. Things like shirts *mattered*. It was as simple, and as irritating, as that.

The cavalcade reached Blackheath, where girls with

mottled legs were playing an aimless game of lacrosse,
encouraged by a PT mistress with mottled legs. Where
stray dogs scavenged for the remains of last night's
finger-lickin' fried chicken. Where post office workers
were laying cables, and a boy flying a recalcitrant kite.
Turning right, it crossed the Heath and startled shop-
pers in the village, and women doing their wash in the
laundromat. It drew to a halt in Lee Road, where fire
engines, armoured cars, black marias, motorcycles and
ambulances littered the highway, and officious policemen berated the onlookers.

A messenger stepped up to the Home Secretary's
car, and handed an envelope through the window, before being hustled away by Special Branch men. The
Commissioner of Scotland Yard held open the door,
and helped the unhappy Minister out.

"Everything in order? Anything you need?" inquired
the Home Secretary, smiling a shy smile at the crowds
and automatically signing his autograph on a shopping
list that was thrust in front of him.

What intrigued him was that there were so many
people dressed so smartly on a weekday in Blackheath.
Many of the men were in bowlers and, good lord, some
were wearing white scarves. And then it occurred to
him that, of course, they must all be Jews from the
Synagogue. My goodness! And apart from their clothes
they looked normal enough.

"All these people. . . . You managed to get them out
safely then? Well done."

"No, sir, I'm afraid not. These are the congregants
from the main hall. The gunmen are in the Study
Centre on the first floor with the children. You can see
the windows there and the Palestinian guerilla flag.
And I'd be grateful if you'd withdraw out of range, sir.
The building's surrounded and we've reinforcements

on their way, but we haven't made any move yet."

"Good show," remarked the Home Secretary, impressed with the policeman's confidence and wishing that he too could be as decisive in moments of stress. Then he glanced at the note he had been handed. He read it twice with growing excitement, and passed it to the Commissioner without comment. It was printed in capitals on cheap typing paper.

"WE DEMAND THE RELEASE OF THIRTY-SIX FREEDOM FIGHTERS IMPRISONED BY IMPERIALIST LACKEYS IN ISRAEL"—here followed thirty-six names headed by—"KOZO OKAMOTO, RIMA ISSA TANOUS, THERESE MALASEH"—the first responsible for the Lod Airport massacre, the others for the Sabena hijack attempt—"THESE MUST BE SENT TO DAMASCUS AIRPORT. FOR THREE OF OUR MEN WE SHALL RELEASE ONE OF YOUR CHILDREN. IF NONE ARE RELEASED ONE YOUNG ZIONIST SHALL DIE EACH HOUR ON THE HOUR. ANY VIOLENT ATTEMPT TO TAKE US, ANY TREACHERY OR DECEIT, WILL PUT AN END TO NEGOTIATIONS AND THE LIVES OF THE CHILDREN, FOR WHOSE DEATHS YOU WILL BE PERSONALLY RESPONSIBLE. LONG LIVE PALESTINIAN LIBERATION, DEATH TO ALL ZIONISTS!"

On the bottom of the paper was written in a sophisticated holograph the following:

"The Israeli Embassy was closed for Yom Kippur. This message handed to me in Synagogue by a caretaker from the Embassy. I shall be on the 'phone to

Mrs. Meir for instructions." The note was signed by the Israeli Ambassador.

The Home Secretary looked at his watch which read ten minutes to four, then at the Commissioner.

"What do we do now?"

"You are a sitting target, sir."

"Am I? Oh lord, I suppose I am."

"If you wouldn't mind. . . ."

"I don't see that we can do anything until we hear from Israel. But you've done jolly well so far. You really have."

The Commissioner raised a sceptical eyebrow, and, taking the ministerial arm, escorted him out of range.

Jamie had stood watching his congregation leave— which they did with impressive calm and dignity, despite the water sprinkling down upon them—uttering the ancient benediction, calling for the God of their Fathers to bring them peace—and, after they had left, he remained standing, apparently impassive, in front of the closed ark. A policeman, awed by the solemnity of the hall and by the curiously clad figure standing behind the reading desk, approached him, taking pains to walk quietly in his heavy, gentile boots and carrying a gun. He escorted Jamie out and whispered to him that he was sure everything would be all right, adding that he had served with the army in the Holy Land. Jamie was shocked. Which was worse, a policeman in the Synagogue, or a gun in the policeman's hand.

The rabbi blinked in the sunlight for a moment, and then, recognising the Commissioner from his television appearances, and failing to recognise the Home Secretary, whose back was turned, walked over to the Scotland Yard man and grabbed his arm. The sight of the heavy and apparently unperturbed officer enraged him.

"How the hell did this happen? Surely after recent events the least you could have done would have been to take some elementary precautions."

"It's your Synagogue, sir. And I do assure you that all that can be done is being done. And in the meantime if you will ask your people to keep *well* clear of the building, it would help us all." As though to add weight to the Commissioner's words a warning shot was fired from one of the windows. No one in the crowd was harmed, but there was a general movement away from the Synagogue, and some gasps and cries. Simultaneously a police van drew up with a fresh contingent of special patrolmen. Armed with pistols and rifles, and protected by bullet-proof shields and visors, these men were swiftly deployed in a wide arc around the building, ensuring that the crowd—on the outside of the arc—was nudged away from the danger. An Inspector reported to the Commissioner, who nodded his approval.

"I say, that *was* well done," exclaimed the Home Secretary. Neither the Inspector nor Jamie had registered his presence. They stared at him in amazement. Jamie was the first to recover, and to return terrier-like to the bone he was sharing with the Commissioner.

"What requests have been made? I demand to know. My wife is in that room."

The Commissioner, who had recognised Jamie as a rabbi by his hat and *tallis*, but hadn't known that rabbis had wives, looked more sympathetic, but his attention was still directed towards the Home Secretary and the Inspector. Although the Commissioner was not a Jew, he was sometimes mistaken for one. His heavy jowls and pendulous nose flattered to deceive. He was Chapel, respecting the memory of his mother. A lonely, brooding, ambitious man, who had worked his

way up through the ranks with single-minded dedication. On the beat he had been sharp-eyed but surly,
with little time for fashion models who lost their
poodles or tourists who lost their way. He had distinguished himself again and again. The more vicious the
criminal, the more determined the pursuit; the wilier
the trail, the more conscientious the hunter. He was
powerful, with a back like a fork-lift, and arms like
mechanical cranes. Charmless, tireless and unmarried,
his enemies and some of his colleagues called him
'PC Plod', but not without grudging respect. He had
been outstanding in court too.

"All in good time," he murmured to Jamie, as the
Home Secretary was called to his car to take an important telephone call. But for Jamie there was no
more good time.

The kids were all paired off, and wired, with the exception of Jack, who no longer represented any sort of
a threat to anyone. The girl gunman set up a loud
hailer at the window, then, at a word of command from
Abu Khalil, fired a shot into the air, keeping her head
carefully below the window-sill. This was the warning
shot, but not in the sense in which it had been understood. The warning was not a generalised keep-well-
away warning, but a specific five-minute warning.

To everyone's surprise, and even in a way to Gerry's,
Gerry suddenly said, almost shouted:

"Has anyone got a pack of cards? Harry's terrifically
good at cards. He beats me at gin and cribbage *easily*."

The gunmen glanced curiously at Gerry, but it appeared that gin and cribbage were not among their ac-
complishments. Or at least none of them answered
him, and Gerry muttered:

"It was only a thought," a little resentfully.

Soon, however, Jack became the centre of attention as one of the gunmen grabbed the boy and carried him, hanging limply under his arm, to the window. There he was held aloft, his face streaked with dust and tears. The sun was low and its shafts illuminated his silver hair. There was a sigh that rose to a murmur from beyond the window—a murmur both angry and expectant.

Then Jack waved to them.

Somebody laughed. The crowd craned to see. Others laughed. If the boy was waving, he must be all right; if he was all right, everything must be all right, everything might be all right. Encouraged by the friendly response Jack waved again to the two groups, along the road to the left and along the road to the right. He waved, less tentatively this time, and Susannah was irresistibly reminded of a young prince acknowledging his subjects from a balcony, the flag fluttering above him, a young prince with silver hair, the hope of the nation. Young Moses, young Samuel, young Jesus, young Charles. The prince upon whom all their hopes depended . . . Jack began to speak, but his speech of accession was interrupted so rudely by the bullet that the assassination was high treason and *lèse majesté* too.

Still, shot he was, the pistol close up against his ribs, by the republican who held him, and he gave a bit of a gasp, and twitched, and his head slumped forward, and then he fell, defenestrated, eighteen feet to the ground.

And the leader of the gunmen read a message to his congregation, using the loud hailer so that there was no need for him to raise his well-modulated voice. The message was the same message which had been relayed to the Israeli Ambassador, and hence to the Prime

Minister and ultimately to the Home Secretary. It made its point with emphasis.

On the telephone to the Prime Minister of England, the Prime Minister of Israel said:

"They are not our children. What can we do but pity them and pray for them? Should we release these murderers? Would you, Prime Minister? They will slaughter others of our children if we do. It is a terrible thing, but we can no longer afford to be weak. When we were weak they led us to the gas chambers. We cannot turn the other cheek. We are no longer required to do so. Why should we? Weakness now will be punished later. Strength now—they will call us murderers, but we have thick skins—will save lives, our children's lives in the future.

"You know what my first memory is? But how could you? The pogrom in Kiev, that is what I remember. Many children died there. What promise would these killers accept that we could give? You tell me that. None! And when, heaven forbid, they have killed these children, the British will not allow them to go free. We must be strong, as you will be strong. You must be strong, as we have been strong.

"No. Tell the British we are sorry, but no. My people still mourn those who died at Munich. We have not so many children as you. Why should it always be ours who die? You must ask them that, Prime Minister. You must explain to them."

Jack's parents had been in the congregation, and, as his son fell from the window, Jack's father ran forward to break his fall. But the boy was either dead, or too far along that dark avenue to be recalled.

Two young policemen cleared a way for Jack's father to carry the boy to an ambulance, which set off instantly for St Alphage's Hospital. Jack's mother encompassed by the crowd, was left behind.

A television journalist in a recently purchased leather jacket and smart Wrangler jeans prodded his microphone in the direction of the woman.

"Are you the mother of one of the hostaged children?" he asked, smiling hopefully, and signalling with his hand behind his back for a cameraman and sound recordist to move in closer. But the woman looked bewildered and failed to answer.

"*Nationwide*," explained the young man amiably. "Do you have a child up there?"

"No," replied the woman, pale-faced and blinking.

"Oh, I see," said the reporter, "in that case if you don't mind . . ." and he pushed past her through the crowd, attached to his crew by wires visible and invisible, in search of someone more eloquent and more tragically involved.

In a state of shock, Jack's mother sat down on the kerb and ran her hands through her hair.

Jamie saw the reporter coming, and hurried over to him.

"My wife's in there," he remarked brusquely.

The reporter was impressed, and the head of the microphone in its wind-shield danced irresistibly forward, like the head of a cobra. "Are you worried about her?"

"Of course I am."

"How exactly do you feel at this moment?"

Jamie shrugged off such an insolent question and added: "What I wanted to say was this. I think it's appalling that the police should have been so lax as to allow . . . I'm the rabbi here . . . it's incredible that no one seems to have taken the most elementary . . ." (shouted) "why doesn't somebody *do* something?"

"A question that it's easy to ask," said the reporter, swinging round on his heels to face his cameraman and the whole of London and the South East, "but by no means so easy to answer. Jonathan Pearman, *Nationwide,* from Blackheath."

As he walked away in disgust from the interview, Jamie looked up at the window behind which Susannah must be undergoing who knew what torments.

"Don't worry, Rabbi,' said an elderly lady from the congregation, a lady whose name he should have known but didn't. "I'm sure she'll be all right." She had a powdered parchment face and a squint, so that Jamie was not at first certain that it was he who was being addressed. "Such a lovely girl, and a *most* distinguished father. I suppose you never knew him? Well, believe me, believe an old woman, you missed quite an experience. And little Susie, *such* a lovely girl. Why, when I saw her this morning, I thought it must be easy to be a rabbi with such a wife. God grant my son another such! And her hair! Believe me, the miracle of the ages! But what can I say? Me, an old woman, at a time like this? What indeed? Please God, we shall all see tomorrow."

"Amen to that, Mrs—"

"De Groot. Laurie's mother. You remember? Well, it has been a pleasure, this little chat. But what should you want to stand talking to an old lady like me, when you have a wife like that to go home to? Happy New Year, Rabbi, and well over the fast!" With which she clamped his face between two vice-like hands, and kissed it.

Running through Jamie's head while this embarrassing scene was being enacted—rendered the more embarrassing by Mrs de Groot's lips finding his mouth as he turned his head to avoid the embrace—was a passage from Bonhoeffer which he sometimes read to couples as they stood together under the canopy:

"Now, in the midst of demolition, we want to build up; in the midst of life by the day, and by the hour, we want a future; in the midst of banishment from the earth a bit of room; in the midst of the general distress a bit of happiness. And what overwhelms us is that God says Yes to this strange desire, that God acquiesces in our will, though the reverse should normally be true. So marriage becomes something quite new, mighty, grand, for us who want to be Christians in Germany."

The last three words would come as such a shock in the awed atmosphere of a marriage ceremony that the couple would look at him, at each other, in some surprise, and he'd tell them about Germany, and about Bonhoeffer, and about the power of marriage to change the world. Few of the couples he married these days had any memory of the War or the Holocaust. Few of them wished to know about it and at times he wondered if he did right to remind them. Was it morbid of him? But marriage, he liked to stress, was based on mutual respect, and respect based on a knowledge of the truth, about God, about the world, about one's own partner.

(Mrs de Groot waddled off—thank the Lord for that!)

But he was, had been, a traitor to these principles. He never talked to Susannah with respect, never attempted to discover how she felt about the world, about God, about himself. Indeed when she attempted to question him about his beliefs he would shrug her off as though a wife had no right to know about such things. He never even expressed his gratitude to her for her loyalty and beauty. He would do it now before it was too late. Perhaps ultimately the terrible afternoon would be the saving of their marriage, the start of a new era of love and comradeship.

Dodging between silent policemen, they in their bullet-proof vests, he in his rabbinical garb, Jamie crossed the road towards the Synagogue.

From a helicopter hovering overhead, a harsh and amplified voice ordered him to turn back, but he went on. When he reached the sanctuary of the main entrance, he didn't pause but continued up the stairs.

"Fucking suicidal maniac!" muttered the Commissioner.

"I beg your pardon, sir?" A young constable had thought for a terrifying moment that the Commissioner had been addressing him.

The Home Secretary returned from his car, smiling at the ground, and noticing that the toes of his shoes were badly scuffed.

"Nice to see you, nice to see you," he murmured vaguely at a couple of importunate admirers, but the Commissioner was no more pleased to see him return than to hear his news.

"The Israelis won't budge. They're being rather irresponsible."

Said the Commissioner: "A boy's dead."

"Yes, I saw."

The saturnine, heavy-topped man stood next to the slender one with dry hair. Between them they could command such power and such loyalty; yet both were at a loss.

"I think we ought to make a move," said the Home Secretary.

"What had you in mind?"

"We could offer them a free passage out of the country. And some money."

The policeman shrugged. "It's not what they're asking for."

The Home Secretary looked more cheerful. "And then you could pick them up at the airport." The Commissioner made no reply. "Could you handle that, do you think?"

"I doubt it."

"Well, I don't know what else to suggest." The Home Secretary sounded peevish. He seldom got ruffled, but when he did he had this ridiculous anxiety that he might burst into tears, and the fear of such an occurrence served to mollify his temper. "You accept my reading of the situation?"

"Of course, sir."

"Our world is changing. The old rules no longer apply."

The Commissioner adopted an unusually hearty tone of voice for: "Well, thank you, sir, for taking so much trouble . . ."

"You will keep me informed? Or the Prime Minister?"

"Of course."

A young, untimely constable arrived with a microphone on the end of a long lead, and handed it deferentially to the Commissioner.

"You wouldn't care to say a word or two on behalf of the British Government before you leave us? It might be quite effective."

"Really? You think so?" The Commissioner passed him the microphone. The Home Secretary looked at it suspiciously, but took it and held it at arm's length. The constable indicated by gestures that he should hold it closer to his face, then, moving in, tapped its working parts with his fingers. The effect was disappointing.

"Say something into it, sir, for level."

"Ah yes, let me see now. 'Mary had a little lamb, its fleece was white as snow'. Is that the sort of thing?"

The microphone had been working perfectly. Heads turned in some surprise. The Home Secretary continued in a more public voice:

"Now then, look here. I don't want there to be any misunderstanding about this. The thing is, em, that what you do in your own countries is your own business, but what you do over here is a very different kettle of fish. Now, I am reliably informed that a child has been killed and that is reprehensible, it's to be deplored. However—and it's the Home Secretary speaking, so mind you take note of what I'm telling you—I am prepared to offer you a safe conduct home, and that's a promise. Are you with me? But you really must, em, come down at once, and leave your guns and things behind you, and, if you don't, then I'm afraid I can't, em, be responsible for the consequences. Do you hear me? There are women and children involved in this outrageous business, and so we've got to be *very* careful not to lose our 'cool'. Was that the sort of thing you had in mind?"

This last remark was intended solely for the Commissioner, but was carried fortissimmo to the waiting crowd. The policeman hastily switched off the microphone and commented:

"Excellent, sir, but you didn't mention the money offer."

"No. No more I did. But it's my belief that in principle one should never pay the blackmailer."

Jamie heard the voice of the Government with incredulity. He had taken the back stairs which led to the choir loft and thence had made his way in stockinged feet along a narrow corridor towards the Library, Study Centre and main offices. From this passage a door gave on to the gallery from which Susannah had watched the Rosh Hashanah services. Jamie had written her a note in the margin of a copy of the Synagogue Newsletter. His intention was to push the note under the door of the Study Centre, or even march in and hand it to her if circumstances seemed favourable, but he had not reckoned on there being a guard outside the door. Rounding a corner he found himself face to face with this armed headless spectre, who waved a gun at him in a threatening manner.

Jamie put the note on the floor, and made gestures indicating that he desired it to be taken inside the room.

"It's for my wife," he said. "*Le lui donnez-vous.*" The guard failed to react. "*Geben es zu meinen Frau bitte*", and then the rabbi backed away until he was round the corner and out of range of anything but a ricochet. He sat down, unable to stand for a moment for the trembling of his legs.

The guard took the newsletter into the room and handed it to the guerilla leader, who studied it briefly, before crumpling it in his powerful hands and ordering the guard to resume his vigil outside the door.

Susannah craned forward—it was not easy with Alison on her back—but a kick from the smallest of the gunmen knocked her to the wall, where she vomited. Abu Khalil picked up the crumpled note and put a match to it. The ashes drifted through his fingers to the floor, leaving a grey stain on his skin. The Home Secretary's announcement had roused the children. Jethro was playing an invisible chess game in his head,

and it was Hannah with the dark clown's features, who
shouted in outrage:

"Don't do that!" as the kick landed in Susannah's
face, and spat as best she could—she wasn't the greatest of spitters—in the direction of the nearest gunman.
At once most of the children turned spitfires, with the
pitiable exception of Pippa, gagged and limp, who
seemed unaware of what was taking place around her.
One of the masked figures had raised his arm to strike
Hannah, when, at a word from Khalil, the arm was let
fall. Wiping her mouth against the shoulder of her
dress, Susannah said:

"Let the children go now, *please*. You've proved
how serious you are, and everyone knows you mean
business. You can do what you like with me, take me
with you as a hostage if you want to. They'll give you
safe conduct if I'm with you. They said they would.
They'll have to. What do you need the children for
anyway? Oh *please*."

At which the guerilla leader took off his head, his
hood, and put his face so close to hers that she could
feel its warmth, smell its odour.

"No."

She said again, trying to hold his gaze, determined
neither to blink nor to look away:

"Please, if you have children of your own, let these
children go."

"I had a child," he said, "until you Jews killed him."

His face. Heavy and swart and square with a seedy
moustache under a prominent and slightly curved nose.
The mouth grey, the teeth broken, the hair dry and
split, but cut quite short and neat around the ears. A
very tired sort of face, in which the eyes still danced
and flickered. Small pupils, small irises swimming in a
bubble of bloodshot white; Susannah took encourage-

ment from those eyes. She looked steadily into them. They were not the eyes of an enemy.

"I didn't kill your child. These children didn't kill your child. How could they? They were born, their mothers and fathers were married, after the end of the Mandate, long after the establishment of Israel. They know nothing about Palestine."

"I had a child," the gunman repeated, "until you Jews killed him. What did our children do in this world, what crime have they committed so that they are deprived of everything, even life itself? We searched the rubble for twelve hours. We never even found the body."

"Perhaps he wasn't dead?"

The man's voice remained quiet and steady.

"You think you know about my son? You think you are not all dead too? I tell you, you are dead already, you Jews. The sins of the fathers shall be visited upon the children, so don't talk to me about Mandates and Palestine."

"What about the Jewish children in Belsen and Dachau? They died. What about them?"

"Death to all Zionists!"

"But the *children*. They just wanted to live. And they took them from their homes and they put them in camps and they killed them."

"Exactly. And with our children also."

"It's not true."

"Listen," said Abu Khalil, "if you wish to learn. In 1948 in a Palestinian village 430 villagers, women, men and children, our children, were killed by bullet and bayonet thrust. With the pregnant women the soldiers say: 'Is it a boy or a girl? Let's see this way', and they use the bayonet. You never knew that. Nobody told you. Sure, sure. We have much to do and no more time to talk. We have talked too much already."

Then he moved to the table and gestured towards one of the gunmen who produced a pack of cards. They were shuffled and dealt. Gerry's face lit up at the prospect, and he called to Harry: "They have got cards!" but it was apparent even to Gerry that no one intended to play gin or cribbage.

Across the road and a hundred yards or so from the Synagogue, under the umbrella of a fine horse-chestnut tree, an impromptu committee meeting was taking place. Old Jacob, Jack Cowan, Judith and Hattie stood together amongst the conkers. An orange sun declined behind Lewisham. A beautiful evening, but chilly.

Hattie, small, round, characteristically red in the face now that the initial shock was wearing off, had been describing details of the gunmen's irruption into the Synagogue, as seen from her office. At first she had thought them—irrationally, but then who could blame her for that?—to be children playing a cruel game, but the masks were not children's masks, she soon realised, and, well, one never expected that sort of thing to happen to *one*, did one?

Hattie took it as a personal affront that such a thing should have happened in her Synagogue.

"These people!" she exclaimed. "If I could get my hands on them . . . They just marched straight in without so much as a by your leave."

Hattie had a strict sense of the proprieties. Because of this, she had become a secretary, and being a secretary had made her more than ever conscious of the need for order in a world of muddle and indiscipline. She lived alone in Shooter's Hill Road in a flat which was immaculate, but inside her head her emotions were as jumbled and disordered as any junk room. Nobody had ever come along to card index *those*, and that was not a job St Godric's had trained her to undertake for herself.

"It should have been me taking the Young People's Service," remarked Judith, and not for the first time. "I should have been where Susannah is now. Why is it her and not me?"

It sounded almost as if she were jealous of Susannah, which she wasn't. Nonetheles she was becoming increasingly aware as the years passed that, although she had lived through momentous times, she had remained shadowy and peripheral. She had once set out on the Aldermaston march, but had developed blisters, and had had to return home. And now that she was truly near the centre of things, nothing was required of her. She would have given her life willingly. Instead she stood amongst the conkers. But she had no reason to reproach herself. When the storm broke, she had led her Infants' class to safety in the Health Department of the Local Council offices with the greatest coolness and efficiency. She had left them busily occupied with slates and chalks, drawing Moses in the bullrushes, and had returned to the Synagogue, impelled by a sense of duty and overwhelming curiosity. While she was away Jack died.

Old Jacob stood erect but with his head slightly bowed, as though at a funeral. Judith noticed how his carefully tended veneer had begun to crack; his eyes were quite yellow when you got close to, and the skin was crumbling around the eyes. The moustache remained perfect, unchanging, no matter what happened to the face behind it. Judith wondered what it would be like to live within that body. Very cold and lonely, she fancied. She ought to offer to cook him a good meal one night. It was absurd that they only ever met on Synagogue business. As for Jack Cowan, well the poor dear was obviously deeply embarrassed by the whole thing. He kept biting his lips and pulling at his ears and clearing his throat and picking up conkers and throwing them down again, and humming consoling snatches of music, and stopping himself when he realised that they might be considered inappropriate. He ran a wholesale business in Deptford called Sabrena Contemporary Knitwear, and in Deptford where he and his wife were liked and respected, he never knew a moment's embarrassment.

"These poor children!" said Judith, and Jack wished she would not say such things. "When this terrible business has all blown over we must give them a party. Something to take the taste out of their mouths, as it were. To remind them that they are still children after all. I might ask Mrs Levy if the Women's Group would provide an entertainment, or, maybe we could hire some nice nature films. Why, only last week—"

From the Study Centre another shot rang out, and Patricia flew through the air, and landed with such a crack on the tarmac forecourt that there was actually an echo from across the road.

And yet it didn't immediately kill her, any more than the bullet had. She lingered there, an uncomfortable place to die, moaning and crying and haemorrhaging, and the police couldn't keep the crowd back. They formed a circle around Patricia, watching her life dribbling out of her mouth, until ambulance men lifted her on to a stretcher (carefully holding her skirt in place to preserve her modesty) and hauled her off. Somebody picked up a single red shoe and bustled after Patricia, carrying it so carefully that it might have been the shoe not the girl that was bleeding to death.

The crowd was angry now. Some shouted rude things to the policemen, others proposed outlandish courses of action. We must . . . light a fire and smoke them out. We must . . . call the fire brigade and climb their ladders and hose them out. We must accept all their demands. We must pretend to accept all their demands, and then move in. We must move in on the Embassies of the responsible Arab States, and take counter-hostages until they are responsible. We must . . . we must . . . we must . . . *do something*!

The Commissioner of Police determined to clear the area. He had resolved on a course of action, and it was essential that his men be free to operate, pointless that more lives be put at risk. But when the police attempted to move the crowds on, the crowds dug in their heels, and, ironically, a second struggle broke out, which threatened to become as violent as the first.

The Commissioner retired his men to Florian's Delicatessen, where temporary headquarters had been set up, and there, amidst sour cream, Polish sausage, artichoke hearts and cream cakes, men were issued with tear gas rifles, mortars, gas canisters, and so forth. Several hundred policemen were now involved and, while the helicopter continued to hover overhead, the Commissioner outlined his new plan, a desperate one at best, to save the lives of the remaining children.

Jamie sat on the *almena* before the open ark. Since delivering his message to Susannah he felt more at peace. If she had received the message—and it was in no way a dangerous or compromising one, they could see that—all would be well. He had put into that brief note much that he had been wanting to say to Susannah for some time and already by now she would be reappraising him, and them together, and what the future might hold. She would be making plans. A visit to Israel. That had always intrigued her. They could go there in the spring when Galilee was at its most colourful. Or he might agree to take that post at the Reform Temple in Philadelphia. The Reform Temple . . . oh yes, anything would be possible now. If they came through this thing together, alive.

Jamie set about finding words which, when strung together, would make a worthy prayer to the Almighty and Most Merciful Father who would surely intervene on an occasion such as this. A prayer for Susannah and the children, but chiefly for himself. Such a task did not come easily to Jamie, who prayed so eloquently on behalf of his congregation.

The children, Susannah, and even the gunmen had been quiet since Patricia's departure. Killing a girl had been an unnervingly different sort of enterprise. Hannah, who had been untied from her sister when Patricia's number came up, blinked back her tears and said in a hoarse and weepy voice:

"Please, I've got to go to the loo. Please." There could be no doubting that she meant it.

"Me too," said Harry.

"And me," said Simon, "I really do have to."

The gunmen conferred. The request seemed to have taken them by surprise. Susannah was hopeful. Once the children were out of the room, once the door was open, anything might happen. And if she could get near the window she could shout down to them: "Now!" just at the right moment, and they would force their way up the stairs, and some of the children would be saved. If . . . but it was cloud-cuckoo-land beyond that window, and she could never reach it with Alison wired to her back. How different it was in films and on the television! There in that plastic world the villains could always be relied upon to be stupid or to over-reach themselves, or to brag away their advantages. Children would be held as hostages, but never killed. Help would come from the most unlikely quarter, after which psychiatric evidence would be called, deviation from the norm blamed, treatment prescribed. But what if there were more deviants than norms, if the psychiatrists themselves ran amok? What if Gods proved fallible, the laws of nature mutable, the sky as brittle as best porcelain, the sea canvas painted green?

"No," said Abu Khalil, "that is not permitted."

"Oh please," said Hannah, "honestly, it's not a trick or anything. It's really urgent."

Said Maurice sadly: "Pippa's already gone. She keeps on going. It smells awful."

"Not permitted. Not permitted."

But ten-year-old Maurice with his curly hair wasn't taking no for an answer. His small voice husky with emotion, he continued:

"You're rotten, that's what you are, rotten bullies. There's absolutely nothing worse than a bully either. You've got guns, and we haven't, and you hit women and you shoot children and you've gagged Pippa, and she's only twelve, and it's a rotten shame."

Simon, a year older than Maurice, his legs pressed tightly together to relieve the strain on his bladder, picked up where Maurice left off. "And it's awful not to let us go and make water. If I make water in my pants, it'll be *your* fault, so there! And don't blame me."

Jethro said quietly and a little pompously: "I was sympathetic towards the Palestinians until today. I'm still sympathetic towards their cause. I think they've had a raw deal."

The guerilla leader turned to Jethro, whose serious face didn't flinch when he was asked:

"You're sympathetic, are you?"

Jethro, a little less confidently: "To your aims, yes, but never to your methods."

"Maybe you tell us how we should proceed?" (He had an American accent, Susannah noted, yet his voice was not that of someone born and bred in America. Unlike an English voice, it gave nothing away.)

"Democratic means."

"Oh yeah?"

"The United Nations."

The gunman allowed himself a laugh. A shocking sound in that room on that afternoon. He translated to the others. They may have smiled within their masks.

"You think we didn't? For twenty-two years we say, give us our rights, give us our human dignity, in the UN, in the conferences, in the councils of the reactionary Arab régimes. We are sick of charity. We want what is ours."

"You could hold demonstrations like we do in Britain, have articles in the paper, educational lectures, advertising. I could think of a hundred—"

"Advertisements? You think that would be a fancy idea?"

"Well, yes I do. You could put your case, and—"

"And what do you think this is? What do you suppose you are to us if not an advertisement? The front page of every newspaper in Fleet Street, however would we find the money for that? Shit! We're not a nation. We have no resources, no exports, no tourist industry. The Americans give us nothing, the Russians give us nothing, our own governments give us nothing. Old clothes, old toys for our children, a bowl of pig-food. They'd like nothing better than to get shot of us."

"They do," said Jethro. "They give money to Al Fatah, and Al Fatah gives it to you."

"You know all the answers, do you?" Abu Khalil came so close to the boy that Jethro shut his eyes tight. "Lod Airport, right? The hijackings, right? The kidnappings, right? Isn't it all advertising? Who had heard of us before? Who cared then? Once we were terrorists, now we are revolutionaries, superstars. Now they care. Some of them may hate us; tough. But even your Zionist newspapers now recognise that there is some justice in our case."

"If you murder us, what will they think of you then?"

"They will be scared," said the bland voice, "as those who know that they are losing a war. In due course they will fear us so much that they will do what we say."

"A rule of terror."

"There are two kinds of terror. Reactionary terror and that is against humanity and that is Zionism, and Revolutionary terror and that is for humanity and freedom."

"You're more afraid of us than we are of you," said Jethro, opening his eyes again and staring first at Khalil, and then at the others.

"How so?"

"Otherwise why should your men wear those hoods?"

"I've wet my knickers," whispered Hannah, ashen-faced.

The Commissioner let fly at a young constable, when he noticed the lad helping himself to one of Florian's chocolate éclairs. Then with a physical effort—tightening his fists—he restrained himself. Two children were dead already, and, within forty minutes, unless he put a plan into operation, a third would die. He gave

instructions to his armed and armoured men to sur-
round the Synagogue. He had the helicopter direct
operations from above. He had a marksman, with a
silencer fitted to his rifle—an obvious refinement which
those inept Teutons had overlooked—take up his position on the roof of a block of flats most nearly opposite
the occupied building. When a flare was released, CS
gas and smoke bombs would be lobbed into the window
of the Study Centre, while special patrol officers
stormed the stairs, shooting to kill. As he outlined the
plan, the Commissioner, celebrated for his dispassion-
ate temperament, was not entirely successful in keeping
the excitement out of his voice.

In the early evening the Prime Minister called an
Emergency Cabinet Meeting.

He was the first in the Cabinet Room. Mahogany
and green leather; that monstrous table, upon which
were laid—as if for an amazing bureaucratic meal—
the place settings of blotters, paper racks and ink-
stands. Walpole keeping a gloomy eye on things, like a
disapproving nanny from above the grey, mottled
marble of the fireplace. Rows of reference books like
reservists who know their services will never be required, and, beyond the windows, the trees which
waved ever so discreetly. It was all too good. The
Prime Minister was aware that the only imperfections
in the room entered with him. He was not badly main-
tained for his age, but teeth, hair, and skin, bulk and
belly were not good enough for that cream-panelled
mausoleum. Nonetheless he would connive at the de-
ception. When his colleagues arrived they must, and
would, see an immaculate man, architect-designed to
go with the room, a perfect embellishment, a symbol of
all that was most perdurable. As he thought of Glad-

stone and Palmerston, so his colleagues must think of him. Not the office, as in America, nor the man, as in so many sad countries, but both together, strong, indissoluble. Let mayhem rage abroad, in the badlands of Blackheath and beyond, nothing should threaten the serene sanctity of this place and all it stood for, nothing could. . . .

Entering the room the Home Secretary put an arm around the tense shoulders of his senior colleague, who was startled out of his reverie.

"It's all right, old chap," murmured the Home Secretary, "we've weathered worse than this in our time."

The Prime Minister managed a January smile. "I don't think people realise."

"Oh yes, they do. Why don't I get you a bloody big whisky?"

All over London the sun was setting on the Day of Atonement. In friendly East End Synagogues, exclusive West End Synagogues, exotic Spanish and Portuguese Synagogues, liberal Liberal Synagogues, suburban 1930s Synagogues, and stuffy traditional Synagogues, the last prayers were being intoned, the last anthems sung, the last resolutions made, and stomachs rumbling. The man with the *shofar* was nervously awaiting the cue to blow his horn, the congregations counting the pages in the prayer book before that light-hearted moment of release, and throughout all these Synagogues, the whispers were spreading, the rumours sprouting.

For some in the congregation the rumours came as no surprise. These were the men and women who had seen it all before, whose lives had been wrenched apart, and who had never learnt to accept that there could be a country in which the fist, boot, brick through the window, shout at the door, could be contained by

calmly considered arguments and the proper process of
law. These were the men and women who still awoke
in the night and sat straight up, staring, who *knew*,
who were branded subcutaneously with that most
shameful of marks, the mark of the victim. Their
prayers in the dying moments of Yom Kippur were
"not again, Lord, not again".

And for the others, those who felt themselves to be
secure, who accepted freedom from fear as their birthright, as something they paid their rates for, as something as natural as the progression of the seasons and
the cult of the equity, did they believe the whispers,
and was their faith shaken? Yes, they did; it was. They
were amazed at the rumours, and as amazed at their
reaction to them. They felt terrified, bewildered, inadequate, betrayed, persecuted, excited. They felt—and
some of them for the first time in their lives—Jewish.

The sound of the *shofar* on the hilltop, a call to
prayers, a call to arms, or a tocsin?

The rest of the gunmen had removed their masks. It
was extraordinary the difference their faces made.
Susannah felt the shock of a child who had walked
behind the Punch and Judy tent. Except that as a child
she had learned that what she had taken for reality was
mere puppetry, and now she knew that those she had
considered puppets were human beings, capable of
anything, even free will. One of them was not even an
Arab, one of them was quite a pretty girl, one of them
was no more than a boy.

"You should be out playing football, not involved
in something like this," she said severely. "It's a shame
at your age."

The boy didn't reply. He understood no English.

But it was Jethro who remarked to the guerilla leader:

"That one isn't even an Arab."

"You better believe it."

"Yes, but I mean . . . If he's a member of the revolutionary left, and not a Palestinian, well then it seems to me he's little better than a mercenary."

"Our struggle is the struggle of all liberation organisations. We have allies all over. There are Jews, born and brought up in Israel, who fight on our behalf."

"There are traitors everywhere."

"Yes, but traitors to what? You're sympathetic to us, right? So you're a traitor too."

"Nobody pays me."

Khalil translated Jethro's words into French, and the white-faced gunman spat on the floor and replied in French and at some length.

"He says," Khalil reported, "that nobody pays him. He says that his comrade's revolutionary struggle is his own. He is angry at the imputation that he can be bought. He's right to be angry."

"As to your payment," Jethro continued, wanting to glance at Susannah, wanting to make sure that she was attending, but scared to look away, "nobody's going to tell me that you pick up the bill. No, it wouldn't surprise me at all to learn that you've all got private accounts in a Swiss bank. It's common knowledge what the Japanese gentlemen got for what they did."

"You are a remarkable boy. You know so little, and you talk so much. As a reward you shall be next on our list."

Even then, to his own and everyone's surprise, Jethro stayed cool and continued his argument.

"You'll do whatever you're paid to do, and if beating

women and shooting kids is in your contract, then I'm
sorry for you, *but* there's no more to be said. But as far
as this Palestine thing goes, our deaths won't achieve
anything. There must be a better way. Your grievances
lie in the past. But if you kill us, those murders will
remain fresh in the minds of your enemies long after
your struggle has been lost. As to dying, no doubt you
are going to kill me, but you'll die today too, unless
you surrender. I don't much want to die, but I shan't
die angry and frustrated as you shall. I wouldn't wish
that on anyone. So go right ahead, you idiots, but it's
not Marxism, nor Maoism, just masochism."

Now Jethro could look round at Susannah, a phrase
like that would surely get her going—it was wonderful
the way it had just come to him, whoomph, like that!
—but, dammit, when he looked, Susannah was talking
to one of the girls. Not fair!

And a bomb bounced through the window.

Words hadn't come, wouldn't come, to Jamie. When
he prayed for others on Saturday mornings, it was not
hard to trawl round the Synagogue for their unexpressed
hopes and anxieties, and offer up a netful of little
wishes to the austere but benevolent wishmonger in
the sky. But now it was different, now when he cast
his net, it blew back and entangled himself. He tried
again, hauled it in; it was empty. Tried again.

"Please God, God of our Fathers," but the word
'God' was like a steel bolt in his head. "God of Abra-
ham, Isaac, and Jacob," and he could see the old
patriarchs with their shovel beards, looking piously up
to heaven where their Father lay, like Martin Büber,
or, um, Orson Welles in the big family bed with all his
—No! He could conjure up only banalities; there was
no comfort to be had that way.

Perhaps an old formula would be best. Familiar words. Words which had worked for thousands of years for millions of men might just conceivably work for him. A magic carpet of friendly phrases which would fly him up to God. Familiar, good words. Softly he sang a psalm.

"Deliver me, O Lord, from the evil man, and preserve me from the wicked man.

"Who imagine mischief in their hearts, and stir up strife all the day long.

"Keep me, O Lord, from the hands of the ungodly; preserve me from the wicked men, who are purposed to overthrow my goings.

"The proud have laid a snare for me, and spread a net abroad with cords; yea, and set traps in my way.

"I said unto the Lord, thou are my God: hear the voice of my prayers, O Lord . . ."

Nothing. Nothing, nothing, nothing, and then, for a moment, something. At least he was no longer aware of the weight of his own body, it was as though he were rising, as though . . .

Two large policemen had taken hold of him, lifting him by the elbows from his sitting position, and walking him away from the ark.

"Beg pardon, sir, but we must ask you to leave now. We have a job to do, know what I mean?"

Jamie was dazed. The noises from upstairs, the shouts and shrieks and bangs, returned to him as though they had been recorded on tape and someone was turning up the volume control . . . Soon he was in the open air, blinking and shivering with cold.

The bomb did not explode, but sat hissing venomously on the floor and exuding an evil-smelling smoke. Jethro, edgy from his argument with the guerilla leader, was the quickest off the mark. Concentrating all his strength, he leant forwards, lifting Ruth, who was still wired to his back, into the air, and began lurching and trundling towards the window. Ruth, taken as much by surprise as anyone, was too startled to cry out, and the unnatural pair had almost reached the window by the time one of the gunmen, the twelve-year-old whose re-actions were swift and whose gun was light in his hand, got in his shots. The first tore trouser and flesh from Jethro's upper leg, the second grazed Ruth's temple, and the third only managed to connect with the window frame, since Jethro and Ruth were through the window by then and halfway to the ground. One of the gunmen, not the boy, dashed to the window to finish off the job, but, surprisingly, sank to his knees, while blood dripped from his hair. The police marksman with blackened face on the roof of the Span flats across the road, finding a target at last, had earned his com-mendation; it had not been easy, his fingers being cold with the wind and the waiting, head aching, eyes run-ning, and great caution essential if he were to avoid shooting one of the captive children, which he almost did when Jethro and Ruth sailed through his sights.

"Never mind, lad, you did all right, you got him."

"Thank you, sir."

Nevertheless the memory of this moment, so utterly removed from the clinical sessions at the rifle range, first the unlikely bundle falling to the ground, then the man at the window frozen in an attitude of amaze-ment as the bullet struck silently home, was to haunt him night after night. He was only twenty and had never even been with a girl.

The helicopter reported that it had seen—well, it wasn't exactly sure what it had seen—a body or two bodies flung out of the window—but the Commissioner with a detachment of his men was already in the building.

Jethro landed on his wounded leg, and with Ruth's weight (thought the girl was light for her fifteen years) on top of him, he landed badly. He landed only a few yards in front of the emerging Jamie, and lay unconscious on the tarmac with Ruth winded and stunned at his side. The blood from Jethro's leg mingled with the blood from Ruth's forehead, and the blood of both of them trickled to where some large brown horse-chestnut leaves stemmed the flow. Jamie looked sadly down at the two children, and then up at the window from which Jethro had jumped. He bent down to minister to them, then changed his mind, and re-entered the building from which he had so recently been escorted.

Up in the Study Centre, confusion was doubly confounded. The bomb came in through the window, then Jethro and Ruth went out through the window. The gunman ran to the window, then sank down by the window, and, no sooner had his soul left his body—though this was not visible to the onlookers—than the door was broken down by invading policemen. The room was full of noxious smoke. The children had been appalled by the bomb, amazed by Jethro's opportunism, startled by the death of the gunman, and thrilled by the arrival of the police, although they didn't look like policemen in all their gear. Hannah, untied since her sister's death, ran towards the policemen, arms outstretched, but was grabbed from the side by the girl gunman who stuck a pistol into her ribs.

The girl gunman shouted to the police to stand still or else Hannah would pay the penalty. She shouted this in Arabic, but her meaning was clear enough. One of

the policemen—the first through the door—had reached
the blond brothers, Harry and Gerry, and had been on
the point of untying them, the Commissioner and several of his men had been about to shoot, everyone was
coughing and spluttering, eyes sore and streaming,
when the Arab girl's shrill voice was heard. At a word
from the Commissioner all activity from the police
ceased, and the Arab girl led Hannah before her into
the corridor unopposed. The twelve-year-old gunman
untied Pippa from the radiator. Poor, limp Pippa. The
gag and the gas had together done for her entirely—
such a cheery, plump, little thing too. The other gunmen pushed the remaining children in front of them,
Simon and Jonathan, then Harry and Gerry, then
Alison with Susannah, then Maurice, and finally the
young lad with his booty. The policemen could do
nothing but fret as the procession set off. The Commissioner bit his lip until it bled.

Jamie stood on the stairs. They passed him. Susannah passed him. He stretched out a hand to her as she
stumbled down the stairs, walking backwards and wired
to Alison, and would have touched her arm, had not a
rifle butt descended on his knuckles, causing him such
pain that tears filled his eyes. Susannah, pale and
bruised, was crying too, and Jamie didn't realise that
her tears were induced by the gas. He gave her the
nearest he could manage to a smile, and wasn't sure
whether or not she had noticed it. He meant to speak,
but could think of nothing to say. Then the moment
was past. She gave no acknowledgement of having seen
him, but surely she must have done, despite the tears.
He was grateful for the burning pain in his knuckles.
He felt that it helped him to share, however insignifi-
cantly, in their ordeal.

The Commissioner was tempted to rush the bandits,

but there could be no doubt that the little girl would die if they did, and others too most likely. That was the irony of his position. He could not sacrifice a single life wittingly, yet, if he took no action, he would assuredly sacrifice many lives unwittingly. But by the time he had deliberated, it was too late, the gunmen and their hostages having penetrated the main body of the Synagogue, which they entered from the bottom of the stairs.

Already calculating his next move, hopeful that such a depleted group of desperadoes couldn't hold a room as large as the Synagogue for long, the Commissioner's planning was interrupted by Jamie who, much excited and waving his arms about, ran up to him.

"You did nothing! You had the opportunity—I was here, I saw it—and you bungled it. Now are you pleased with yourself?"

To which the stressful Commissioner replied, not tartly as he was tempted, but politely, because the man was a rabbi and subject, no doubt, to strange pressures.

"Believe me, we shall do all we can to save the lives of these unfortunate children—"

"The ones who are left!"

"Indeed yes."

"And my wife."

"And your wife, but you must do what you can to help us. Send your flock home"—was 'flock' right? it sounded undeniably odd—"and our job will be a great deal easier. Oh, um, and, um, pray."

It wasn't easy for Alison, back to back with Susannah, to communicate with her. Nonetheless, as they entered the Synagogue proper, she whispered:

"Did you see Rabbi Arnatt on the stairs? I think he was trying to say something."

"I expect he was," Susannah replied quite loudly.

The gunmen were spreading themselves around the hall, looking for trouble, finding none.

"I know how you must feel. He looked so sad. It's awful, isn't it? Awful for us all."

Awful? Yes, it was. But contempt was the emotion Susannah was feeling most powerfully just then, contempt for Jamie. Pathetic! Stretching out an arm to her like a beggar; go on, rattle your little tin! And all of them, faffing around, just standing there, allowing it to happen. Wasn't it typical though, wasn't it just typical of their way of doing things? Others had been prepared to fight, in Warsaw they had fought, in the Middle East against all comers, but what had Jamie and his pals done? In six days, the time in which it took God to create the world, and the Israelis to win a major war on all fronts, Jamie had come to the conclusion that it was his duty to volunteer.

"I think I *will*," he had announced to the blare of trumpets.

"Too late," said Susannah. "They've just announced it on the radio. It's all over."

Before they married Susannah had asked: "Why don't we go to Israel then?" She knew all about the nagging guilt, the arching ambivalence of the diaspora Jew.

Be realistic, Jamie had instructed her. We're no pioneers. Besides, Jamie pointed out, now that Israel existed it was even more of a fantasy. All those dreams of a democratic socialist kingdom of God on earth, a peace-loving nation of dedicated artisans, artists, and chess-players, had dissipated with the smoke from the first shot fired in anger on the new soil. They had killed Eichmann, Jamie pointed out, when they could have put an end to the Atreus-like sequence of murder and revenge.

"What should they have done with Eichmann?" Susannah asked. "Now who's being realistic?"

And Israel, Jamie confirmed, had never looked back since then, and was rapidly approaching the status of another spiteful, little nationalist state, a bit too big for its boots and a danger to shipping.

Susannah had ignored the mixed metaphor and the extremism of the views expressed (Jamie's opinions had moderated in the years since they had married— these days he was continually encouraging people to "plant trees for Israel") and had argued ferociously that on moral grounds there never had been a state run on such high principles, so that, when Jamie mentioned Cuba she laughed in his face. Cuba! My life! Didn't he *know* what went on there?

"Just because Castro doesn't wear a tie," Susannah had said, "you mustn't assume that he's always right."

"Nor you with Ben Gurion," Jamie had retorted. A fine return of service, on the backhand, and most unexpected, Susannah had had to admit. Besides which, secretly she admired Castro no end, not just a doer, but powerfully erotic, actually smoking a cigarette, whilst leading his men to victory in the Bay of Pigs . . . So she narrowed the argument to Israel . . .

That Israel had survived was no small miracle, that it had survived with any morality or culture left intact was a big miracle. What did he expect? In post-revolutionary Russia the purges had continued for generations (still did). What purge did Jamie know of that could be laid at the door of Israel?

Susannah's blood was up. She was flinging her arms about, knocking china ornaments to the floor. Jamie stopped plying her with brandy and suggested they go to bed.

"All I'm saying," Susannah had murmured, snuggling

up to him, "is that if you want to go to Israel to live there, that's okay by me. Let's go."

But he didn't take her to Israel, not even the Sharon Hotel, Herzlia-on-Sea, only to Dorset, which was pretty, but . . .

He had strange tastes for a rabbi. He was crazy about Cilla Black . . . old idiot!

"Yes," said Susannah to Alison, "it is awful for us all. And what makes it worse is that I haven't a lot of confidence in that load of old bunglers out there."

There was no reply from the sad-eyed, doomed young lady, to whom she was temporarily, but genuinely, attached.

Dew had fallen in the Synagogue when the guerillas, with their seven living child hostages, and their rabbi's wife, took up their positions, guns erect, on the *almena*. Everything was damp from the sprinklers. The hostages were encouraged into the front two rows of pews, while the guerilla leader, flanked by his five remaining disciples, delivered his sermon on the mount. He spoke little of love and charity, this self-ordained Palestinian rabbi, nor had he much to say about the meek and how they were to inherit the earth, although the earth (or a small strip of it) and its inheritors did figure in what he had to say. His sermon was more belligerent than the usual run of sermons in that Synagogue, and he punctuated his words by glancing apprehensively around him, thus conveying to his congregation doubts about the divinity of his message. The burden of his sermon was that certain demands had been made of the authorities concerning Palestine and some notorious Palestinians, that these demands had met with contemptuous indifference, and that—in spite of a change of venue necessitated by an ill-advised and murderous intervention—the policy of bringing all possible pressure to bear on those responsible for decision-making would be continued. He reprimanded his congregation on their past behaviour. He advised his congregation that passive obedience would be in their best interests and that bids for freedom would not be sympathetically considered. And his words, transmitted to all parts of the building by the sensitive microphones in front of the lectern, were monitored by the Commissioner, by Jamie, and by all the policemen and detectives. Also faintly audible via the loud speakers was the distressing sound of Hannah weeping, for Hannah was suffering a reaction to having a gun in her ribs—and to witnessing all that she had witnessed during the last three hours.

The sobbing added urgency—although the situation could hardly have been more urgent—to the Commissioner's plans for salvaging something from the havoc all around him. But these plans must have been sketched in invisible ink on imaginary paper, for the Commissioner could think of absolutely nothing to do.

The gunmen had been flushed from the Study Centre into the Synagogue; Jethro, who would recover quickly, and Ruth, whose fractured skull would take more time to mend, had been saved; one of the guerillas had been killed, and yet the situation remained as desperate as ever. In time of stress the Commissioner cracked his knuckles—he did so now; it didn't help. It was hard to see how the terrorists could be disposed of without their first disposing of the hostages. The Commissioner called for a ground plan of the building. Twenty bad-tempered minutes passed while one was procured and studied. All around him were the buzzing and twitching of those who thought that they knew best—chief amongst whom was Jamie.

The Commissioner's face showed no sign of his impatience, but his knuckles cracked away. When he finished studying the ground plan, they showed him the body of a plump, curly-headed girl lying on the ground. Fucking hell! A police surgeon murmured that the girl appeared to have suffocated, and had probably swallowed vomit. She had been gagged and tied up, but there seemed to be no bullet wounds.

"You know what has to be done, so do it!"

The smell of the body was disagreeable, as disagreeable as the prospect of delegating to a young constable the job of breaking the news to the family. (Oh, as a young man, the Commissioner had had to do it, a boy victim of a hit-and-run accident. And the family had seemed better able to cope than he was, had offered him a cup of tea. He was very close to the public in those days; young coppers were. Now he hardly ever met anyone you would call ordinary. Were there still men in Clapham omnibuses? God, those endless nights on the beat! The tranquillity of them! He stalked the streets like a God amongst mortals then— nobody could touch him, he could do no wrong.) Somebody took the child's body away.

A troublesome fellow in a funny hat was hopping about at the edge of his field of vision. Oh yes, of course, the rabbi, and the woman's husband. A time-waster. No time for him now.

With the ground plan before him and, in his mind, the memory of a successful siege in—where *was* it now? couldn't remember anything these days—the Commissioner had an idea. The Synagogue had four doors. It should be possible, with perfect synchronisation of watches, to burst open each door simultaneously, and, with his men shielding behind their visors, pick off the gunmen before they had a chance to kill their hostages.

The plan was crude and, depending as it did on the marksmanship of nervous officers, only too vulnerable. But it was the only plan he had.

No sooner had he started briefing his men than he was once more interrupted by the rabbi. Evidently there was nothing for it but to threaten to take him into custody, unless he was patient and quiet.

The children were still now, and it was growing dark, and they were cold. The corners of the room had retreated into impenetrable darkness; the centre of the room, lit only by the everlasting light, was gloomy, and the gloom had infected the fervour of the gunmen. They, like the children, felt their teeth chatter. With the gloom and the chill and the lull, they had time to reflect; the prospects were not bright. If their bluff were called and all the children killed, what then?

Arms supporting the guns grew stiff, but never wavered; fingers curled cutely around the triggers ached but never weakened, as the minute hand started its inexorable ascent towards the vertical. The girl terrorist held a knife in the hand which held no gun, clutched it tightly, like a crucifix, as though it were a weapon of defence, as though it would ward off vampires. Then, when she shifted her position, the light caught it, and, glinting, it became sharp and provocative once more.

Susannah could not believe that they were all going to die. To her, too, it was illogical to kill one's hostages, who were valueless dead. But she feared for the children, as she did not for herself. Death held no terrors for her; never had. In her experience it was women who were scared of ageing, men of dying. She was in awe of Death, slightly embarrassed by him when as now he came close, but the prospect of his vanishing for ever

was far more terrifying than his contiguity. When she
tried to imagine herself dead, she visualised a tiny
milky way of particles floating through space, and the
particles would collide with others, be broken down
into components, reassemble in new and beautiful patterns in some other part of the universe. There was
nothing sacred to Susannah in human personality, a
quirky, unreliable thing at the best of times. But the
melding of all human personalities, herself and this
stern revolutionary in front of her and a Sioux Indian
and a Bengali beggar, for example, into a lump of
coal, the tail of a comet, or the Marxist President of
Chile, was not unpleasant. Indeed quite the reverse,
and she smiled at the thought of conjoining after her
death with someone whom she might never have cared
to meet socially before it.

No; thoughts of death and dissolution were a comfort to her during this difficult time, but what was so
galling, so cruelly ironic, was that just now a damp-
ness on the inside of her leg indicated the premature
onset of her period.

"Synchronise watches. It's now—" and the Commissioner tapped his pencil on the table-top—"precisely twenty minutes to eight. In ten minutes, that's at
precisely ten minutes to eight o'clock we will make
our strike through each of the four doors simultaneously."

He was not going to permit his men to be outnum-
bered—as the German police at the airport had been
—by the terrorists. He allotted two police marksmen
(they were marksmen, the others gunmen, a nice dis-
tinction!) to each gunman.

"Aim for the head," the Commissioner continued,
"the middle of the head, and pull your gun well into

your shoulder as you aim. Remember the description of your man. Each door will be opened for you, all you have to do is spot your man quickly and fire. You'll only have one opportunity. If you bungle it, children will die. The whole plan depends on perfect timing to the second. Synchronise your watches once again."

They did so, then looked back at him with faces like plates. His men! Some of them looked younger than his nephew at Westminster School.

"Any questions?"

A very pretty pink-and-white boy, far too pretty to have life and death at his fingertips, asked:

"Will we be eating afterwards, sir?"

But the Commissioner did not lean too hard on him. If there was leaning to be done, he would lean later, though, please heavens, there'd be no need. What were they feeling, these boys, about to kill? Himself, in all his career, he'd never fired a gun in anger, but times had changed. They'd probably be feeling a little sick, shivering a little, wishing it were over, imagining it was over, anticipating the discussions in the canteen.

"Will we be eating afterwards, sir?"

Would they have appetites? He sent them to take up their positions.

"How about a prayer, Rabbi?" He spoke flippantly.

"I can do better than that," said Jamie, "if you'll only give me half a chance. I've been trying to tell you about the gallery."

The Commissioner was generous enough to admit that the rabbi's suggestion (shooting from above, as well as from the horizontal sounded as though it might be conclusive) was indeed helpful, but was it workable? Jamie explained how it could be worked. And there was just time to recall four of his men, and to despatch them upstairs.

"Shoot them all if necessary, then yourselves. There is no big difference between your life without dignity, without freedom, without your people's dignity, without your people's freedom, and your death. Except that your death will be one step along the pathway back to the homeland, one small victory in the struggle of your people, in Palestine, in Vietnam, in Latin America, and throughout the world. You shall die as martyrs rather than live as slaves."

At training sessions it was not too hard to fancy that there might be glory in it, although no one could really believe that the bluff would be called. Not where children were concerned. Everybody knew about Jewish sentimentality in these matters. But now it seemed as though the children might have to die and, if the children died, might *they* not become the martyrs? In this chilly, gloomy room, in front of these pampered brats and this absurd woman, the issues were not as clear as they had seemed under the bright Middle Eastern sun. The overcast Northern skies bred alarm and confusion; it was better to think of other things; rare, happy times, womenfolk, the hospitable security of a bed. Better, but difficult, because, in this curious hiatus, in which all were aware of a sudden self-consciousness, it occurred to several of them at once: they are not going to give way; we shall die; we shall die tonight, in this hostile room, far from home; we shall never see daylight again. But then the thoroughness of their training, their inherited dedication took over, and they thought: we are the ones! Meaningful or not, our actions have been foretold. They have been planned for, they are necessary. We have been chosen! We are the ones!

Did the Jewish children, brought up also to regard themselves as the world's élite, and constantly reminded of their special relationship with God, share such emotions at such a time? Did they consider themselves to be honoured to be where they were and in such peril? Wired together like bunches of watercress, they felt nothing of the sort.

Harry and Gerry, for instance, were spending the time as they spent the long, miraculous nights in their shared bedroom when the lights had been switched off, playing an elaborate and sophisticated form of word-cricket, in which one would think of a word or sentence, the other interpret each letter as a ball being bowled to his team. Gerry, being the elder, captained the England team (as well as opening the bowling with Snow, the batting with Boycott), while Harry led the Australian side. They conversed in whispers. The fraternal intensity of their game—Gerry was really too old for it, and liked to imagine that he still played it for Harry's sake, which Harry realised, and realised also that Gerry enjoyed the game even more than he, Harry, did—which, when they played it at night, grew more desultory as they grew sleepier, now kept out thoughts of the gunmen, the smell of pee, and the terror. Harry had been a bit anxious about playing the game in the Synagogue on the Day of Atonement, but Gerry had said that it was all right because the sun must have gone down by now. Yom Kippur was officially over. And so they played on, uninterrupted because no one had a reason to interrupt them, and England's early collapse was remedied by some stout knocks from the middle-order batsmen.

The other children were almost entirely silent. Curly-headed Maurice with his moon face and his starry eyes, sat on his bench-pew with the wire still dangling from his upper arms. They had released Pippa from him when they discovered that she was

dead, and pushed her body out of the main doors.
Now, though free to move his arms around—and the
wire had cut so sharply into them that his fingers had
gone quite numb—Maurice didn't stir a muscle. He
stared at the wall and tried to pretend that it was the
wall of the playroom at home. If it had been, he could
have studied the chart of British birds, chiff-chaff, pee-
wit and magpie, and, sure enough, there it was, there
they were, all in order just as they should have been.
Nice. All those birds. Good. And, if he imagined hard
enough, maybe he could imagine those birds right off
the chart, right off the wall, then he could watch their
pretty plumage as they soared and dived, hovered and
fluttered around the playroom. The swallows darted
from the bedstead to the window-sill under which they
were constructing a nest. The heron dropped to the
floor and plucked a fish from the fast-flowing current
of the carpet, the woodpecker chafed at the leg of the
table, and the sparrows perched all around the bed, on
the rail, on the knobs, on everything, tweeting the
night away. (Because of course being only imaginary
birds they couldn't be expected to distinguish between
artificial daylight and the real thing.) So many birds,
such a friendly rustle of wings all around him, and in
the morning he would have to get all his football things
together for the start of the new season . . . Maurice
was happy.

Simon wasn't; no more was Jonathan. Simon was
furious. His anger throbbed inside him, and blazed
from his eyes. He discovered that *they* didn't like to be
looked at. And he thought of all the things he would
like to do to them if he had them in his power. That
big, hefty one, who spoke English with the moustache—hey, that was really funny, just think, speaking
English with a moustache, that would make them fall

about in 3A—he would like to tie him to the kitchen chair and dip his fingers into a saucepan of boiling water. The girl, well, he wasn't really sure that he ought to do anything too awful to her, but he could take her knickers down and . . . As for the others he imagined them hanging from a hook which went right through their chest-skin like Richard Harris in that film which they wouldn't take him to see even though it wasn't an 'X'—and then he would put his new studded boots on and hack away at their shins—that would serve them jolly well right. That anyway was what he'd like to do, but of course he couldn't manage it just at the moment, so probably the best thing to do was just to sit and glare at them and continue to try not to disgrace himself by peeing. It wasn't *too* bad, this pressure in his tummy, so long as he sat still. The only problem was that Jonathan would keep fidgeting so, and bustling him about.

"Do stop fidgeting, Jonathan," the little blond chap hissed, "you really are a fidgety Phil."

"I'm not Phil, I'm Jonathan."

Jonathan wasn't furious as Simon was, but sad, and a bit scared.

He had always been proud of his disabilities. It was only when they took him to the clinic and fitted him with awful metal and plastic arms that he became gruff, self-conscious and ashamed. He couldn't wear *those*; and it wasn't long before he learned that they couldn't make him. He knew why they wanted him too, of course, it was because then, in shirt and jacket, he looked, in the street, in the shop, to the casual observer, much like anyone else. But was that good? Once he had watched Kenneth Clark on television discussing the Venus De Milo. There she was, stumps like his, and nothing was said about them! All Sir Kenneth said was something about "the perfect proportions of feminine beauty", and the words astounded him. That night in front of a mirror he posed with his stumps at the same angle as Venus's. One out, one down. It didn't look bad. He didn't look as smooth or as white or as shiny as Venus had in the telefilm, but he didn't look bad.

On another occasion he read in one of Josie, his sister's, magazines, an article entitled: 'Why you should worry about your hands'. The author of the article, who seemed very expert, had given it as her opinion that "only one person in a hundred has hands to be proud of", and from then on Jonathan used to look hypercritically at the stubby, coarse and unkempt hands he saw everywhere about him. There were compensations.

Only once, when some well-intentioned Lady Something gave a Christmas party for Thalidomides (he had been seven at the time) and he looked around him at all those freaks, did the burden seem more than he could bear. At least he was able to run on his own two legs to the lavatory where he sat huddled in a corner until his face was smudged with snot and tears, even his hair was soaked, and they came to tell him how ungrateful he was, and how much more many of the others had to put up with, and to take him home.

There were things he couldn't do, of course, but being a positive fellow, he tended to concentrate on those he could and applied himself with such tenacity that he became captain of the school football team.

His best friend was his sister Josie, who was an exchange student in Chicago. The University was called North Western and in his mind it was a wild place, all wind and rain. His delight was evident when a postcard from Josie referred to Chicago as the "windy city". In his reply, dictated to his mother, he warned Josie to be careful not to blow away, but his mother said not to put that, it was silly, so he didn't.

But it was to Josie, not to his mother, that he had once said:

"Do you mind, Josie, honestly, Josie, tell me honestly, do *you* mind?" And Josie had said no, she didn't mind, and, because Josie was special, and because she meant it, he no longer minded—much. He learned earlier than most that other people's burden's weigh the heaviest.

But he couldn't understand why his Dad got so worked up about the "compensation money", because, after all, Josie didn't mind, and he didn't mind, much, and money couldn't make any real difference, not really.

Something else about his stumps. As seaweed tells weather forecasters whether rain is on the way, so his stumps told him whether people were going to be friends or enemies. He knew immediately from how they looked at them, and he had known to expect the worst from these gunmen people, even though their eyes had at first been hidden behind masks.

So he waited with the others in the Synagogue, and he was sad because he couldn't tell Josie all about what was happening, and, if he was going to be shot— and he was a bit scared of that—he would have liked Josie to be there to see how brave he was. If Josie was with him, it would have been *wonderful*. His mother would tell her all about it of course, whether he was shot or not, but she would get it all wrong.

And yet in one way he was not sad or scared at all. Now, as they all faced being shot, and after all they had been through together, he felt more than ever that he wasn't a Thalidomide at all, that he was a person, and that nobody proper thought of him as anything else.

Hannah had had a row with her sister, Patricia, that morning, as the family prepared to leave for school. It was a silly row, over who should sit in the front of the car with Daddy, and during the Morning Service Hannah had resolved that she would apologise to Patricia on the way home. The row had only been settled when Daddy lost patience with both his suitors, falling out of love with them, he said, as the brawl continued, jutting out his lower lip, until it was agreed that Patricia would sit in the back with Mummy on the way there, and in front on the way home. But now she, Patricia, would never have the chance to sit in the front, and she, Hannah, would never have the chance to apologise.

Guilty feelings tormented Hannah, about Patricia, about her wet knickers, which were making her bum itch, about the row. And terror of the *noises*, the gunshots, the shouts of command, left her wan and withdrawn. She shivered frequently, and her nails left crescent marks in the damp palms of her hands. Her ribs were sore from the barrel of the gun. Untied since Patricia had been killed, there was no reason why Hannah should not now make a run for the door, except that she was totally incapable of movement. She sat staring ahead of her, as if mesmerised, scarcely blinking. Her cheeks felt cold where her tears were drying.

In spite of being wired to Susannah, Alison, at sixteen the oldest of the children, was thinking of her bloke. She always called him that, because everyone called him by his name and she wanted her relationship with him to be different from anybody else's. For a kick-off it was her bloke who had taken her to her first women's lib meeting. The Sisters in Deptford were very liberated in the sense that they welcomed men at their meetings. Occasionally there were joint meetings with the Rotherhithe Gay Libbers, at which motions were passed, calling for brothels for women, and brothels for homosexuals (only one must always be on one's guard, it was pointed out, against exploitation of the brothel-workers, who would have to be unionised) and so it went on.

Of course, Alison thought, they got carried away, but the important thing was that they were right, and anyway she owed quite a debt to her bloke for taking her along, so that now she knew all about the treachery that was likely to be practised upon her, spiritually, physically and vaginally.

Her bloke had said that Jewish girls were amongst the least liberated of all, so of course she had had to sleep with him. Himself, he wasn't Jewish, but a disciple of the Prince of Peace, who wasn't actually *that* hot on women's lib.

Her bloke hadn't been with her in the Study Centre, but as soon as they transferred to the Synagogue proper, she felt his presence very powerfully, and it was a great comfort to her. Invisibly he stood by her, and his dark eyes told her not to worry. What matter if she did die? Death was nothing. She thought of the beautiful Prince of Peace in his white-flowered bower in the Caxton Hall, and remembered how, with a wave of his etiolated but plump hand, he had dismissed the old, cloaked skeleton with the scythe and likened death instead to a beautiful hostess welcoming her guests at the door of a fabulous mansion, inside of which—his English was good but Americanised—were all manner of goodies, the rice of right-mindfulness, the onion of universal empathy, the poppadum of perfect repentance. (At which metaphor the Prince of Peace had smiled merrily.) Thus a natural death was something to be welcomed, a privilege, a treat. But what if the death were premature, would the guest still be welcome, the feast laid out, the hostess prepared? Oh yes, said her invisible bloke inaudibly, you needn't worry about that, Alison, the Prince of Peace will see to that, for he sees to everything.

What with her bloke, the Deptford Sisters, and the Prince of Peace behind and beside and all around her, it was wrong of Alison, ungrateful of her, to be so afraid. But she was afraid, desperately afraid, of being hurt. The Sisters couldn't suffer for her, though doubtless they would suffer with her, the Prince of Peace, who even at his tender age was a Swami of unmatched perfection, wouldn't understand why she should be so frightened of something as insubstantial as pain, so she asked her bloke, would he hold her spiritual hand and hold it tightly when anything awful happened, so that she could concentrate on him and his hand, and make the pain retreat beyond the magic circle of his love for her, and his spirit whispered: yes, he would, and then she felt that she could bear whatever was sent her to bear, no matter what.

She breathed out loud her thanks to her bloke and Susannah asked her what was the matter (having been lost in thoughts of her own) and Alison said that everything was all right, thank you, really it was, and said it in such a confident way that Susannah marvelled at the girl's placidity, the infinite resources of the young.

In front of the ark the gunmen murmured to one another disconsolately. They were anxious. They couldn't understand why not only were their demands consistently ignored, but no approaches were being made to them. Did the children mean nothing to their parents that their lives were sacrificed so lightly? In twelve minutes they would be required to shoot another hostage, and their bargaining power would be proportionately diminished. No one had imagined that the Zionist Imperialists would be so callous as to watch their children die. What to do now?

The girl Alia was for an altogether tougher policy. They might for instance mutilate one of their hostages and send an arm or a finger or an ear by way of encouragement. The doveish element wished to settle for an aeroplane and a safe conduct with or even without the children. The argument was pragmatic. Already the publicity would have justified the mission, and their survival, and the lessons they had learned from the undertaking would enable other yet more successful missions to follow swiftly upon the heels of this one.

But Abu Khalil was adamant. All debate was academic. No compromise could be entertained. They had been steadfast in the face of appalling pressures, one of their number had been martyred; did they now wish to jeopardise the success of the entire mission because they were growing a little impatient? The eyes of the more moderate peered around in doubt and dismay. A dove cooed in protest. Abu Khalil, who had previous experience of just such another situation, shouted that that was *enough*, there would be no further discussion. An authoritative arm was raised to emphasise the point. Enough!

And so it was.

The synchronised watches agreed that the moment had arrived. The doors were thrown open, upstairs and down, the lights switched on. The guns shouted. There was blood upon the Ark of the Lord.

The gunmen were hit, the children were hit. The bullets were like kicks from a horse. Bodies tensed, diaphragms tightened, muscles gathered around the torn fibres. Breath was expelled in gasps, air sucked in sharply. There were screams and groans; but not many.

Everything happened so fast that there was little time for terror. The flesh wounds were painful, but the internal haemorrhaging caused a flood of warmth that was not in itself unpleasant. However, blood pulsing into the mouth is alarming. The gunmen were hit, the children were hit.

As the police marksmen fired on the gunmen, the gunmen, taken by surprise and a little slow to react, fired on the children. It was almost as though the bullets had ricochetted off their primary targets on to their secondary ones, almost as though the bodies of the guerillas bent bullets, as a mirror bends a shaft of light. But the children were not dazzled by the flashing of the bullets, they were shot. And the bandits too.

After the first shot, others follow. A scream cannot be sustained under such conditions. Subsequent bullets cut off its power and purpose. Shock cushions a body in any case, and the brain protests and refuses to accept any more evidence of injuries and pain. Multiple wounds are confusing, and confusion is merciful.

Susannah was unharmed. When the shooting began, she ducked down behind the pews with impressive speed, despite the girl on her back. Then she curled herself into a protective tortoiseshell, hands covering her skull, eyes tight shut. Although swarming with molecular activity, she felt herself to be reassuringly solid and compact; the warmth and the darkness comforted her. But the price of her security was Alison's vulnerability. Up in the air, on her back, wriggling and shrieking, her skirt around her waist, what better target could there have been? It would have made the Sisters of the Deptford Chapter furious beyond invective to have seen Alison in such a pose, and the way the men were treating her. Her blood drenched Susannah, who curled tighter and tighter.

The children were not all killed. Simon was; a bullet through his thin chest. But his body was Jonathan's armour. Jonathan would survive uninjured to face the world without arms, but bravely. Maurice went down, and, as he did so, all the birds fell with him, fluttering down, turning somersaults as they fell, vainly trying to beat the air with their broken wings, bundles of blood and fluff; odd, loose feathers followed them down. And Hannah died, quite messily, from multiple wounds. An easy target since, panicking, and without the restraint of another body on her back, she ran this way and that, attracting bullets like a magnet, biting them out of the air, swallowing them up. Who would travel in the front, who would travel in the back, all that quarrelling and complaining, they would look back on it wistfully now, Hannah and Patricia's Mummy and Daddy.

But Harry and Gerry lived. A single bullet passed from brother to brother, rupturing Harry's spleen, lodging near Gerry's kidney where it was found to be a bullet from a policeman's gun. No one's fault, and in any case the brothers lived, and their beds in St Alphage's hospital were contiguous, and they played many, many cricket games that September, October and November. Four of the gunmen died within seconds of being shot. They had families too; some of them.

Ali did not die. A bullet knocked the rifle from her grasp and she received another through her thigh, and wept, not with pain, but with frustration. She staggered to her feet, held her arms wide, and shouted out in Arabic:

"Kill me! Kill me!"

But they could see that she was helpless, and grabbed her instead.

Abu Khalil did not, as his younger and less experienced colleagues did, stand blasting away with his gun as if rooted to the ground. Rather than draw attention to himself, he ducked off the *almena* and crawled to where Susannah and Alison lay. Alison was dying. He put a bullet through her head, then untied her from Susannah's back. Alison slumped to the floor, bled and died there, her bloke comforting her, her Sisters grieving for her, the Prince of Peace awaiting her.

To Susannah Khalil said, whispering in the ear which peeped out from behind her hand:

"You're going to stand up with your hands raised and walk slowly out of the Synagogue, right? I shall be behind you, with my pistol in your back. If I die, baby, I take you with me. You read me?"

Susannah was not reading him. She was under the sheets. By and by the storm would pass, and it would be quiet once more. You only had to stay curled up tight with your eyes really shut and then you wouldn't see the lightning, and, if you heard the thunder, you knew you'd be all right, because, if the lightning struck you, you'd never have heard the thunder. And in the morning she could laugh about it to her friends, about the amazing storm, and they'd go into the meadows and look for meteorites and blasted oaks. The night wouldn't last for ever.

"Stand up real slow," he whispered into her ear like a lover, "and tell them that if they gun for me or make a move or a loud noise, I shall kill you. No bullshit.

Tell them all that and stand up . . . now!"

It was time to get up. It was the morning. Last night there had been this terrible storm, and when at length she did manage to fall asleep, she had had these fearful blood-filled dreams. Someone was poking her in the back. Did she really have to get up? He was speaking to her. He had such a lovely gentle voice. She got up. Her shoulders were damp, the collar of her dress sticky, where it brushed against her neck. She was stiff, as one is after a restless night. Stiffly she began to walk.

After the shootings, which had reverberated in the Synagogue for several seconds, flooding back in waves of sound, then fading once more, the hall was quite silent. The dead were quiet, of course, non-committal, jealous of their newly-acquired secrets, and the wounded were busy communicating with their pain. Those who had escaped injury hardly dared to draw breath in case everything was spoiled.

His voice, the snout of his pistol in her back, his sour breath, gave her no choice. Nor were his words ambiguous.

She didn't look at the bodies on the floor. Trod on something nasty (cow-pats? in Dorset? had been, yes). Didn't look at the policemen (they would be wanting her to do something, make some decision, get them out of a mess, and she couldn't face it, they couldn't expect it of her, surely not after what she'd been through), so didn't see Jamie standing with them, but heard when she was almost at the door his urgent "Susie *darling!*", an endearment reserved for special occasions, anniversaries for instance, and immediate post-coital cuddles, and, hearing that "Susie *darling!*" with all the memories it conjured up, she twitched a bit, blinked, tensed even more tightly the fingers of her left hand, Jamie being on her right, but didn't for an instant break her stride. Obedient legs.

The guerilla leader had spotted the police marksmen in the gallery. Spotted one of them raise his rifle to his shoulder. "Uh uh," he said loudly, and the Police Commissioner, following the direction of his glance, added hurriedly: "Better not, Dick."

"Better not," repeated the gunman mimicking the policeman and smiling slightly, then walked Susannah unhindered into the foyer, and thence into the fresh evening air.

Jamie grabbed hold of the Commissioner's shoulder.

"You're not going to let him get away with it again? Surely? *Surely*?"

"If it weren't for your wife we'd have had him," the policeman replied with bitterness. His head was throbbing, and he screwed his eyes up for a moment. He went on: "What else should I do? Get her killed?" His voice was tired, and he emphasised the tiredness, producing an effect pioneered successfully by a television actor who played a policeman in a popular series.

"Am I supposed to feel guilty?" Jamie asked furiously. "Is *she*?"

"Really, sir, we have no time for all this."

Not far from the Synagogue stood the sightseers. A police cordon had been doing its best to encourage people to go home, but everyone had a reason for staying. There were the mothers and fathers of the children; the mothers had blankets around their shoulders, and cups of tea in their hands; the fathers strode up and down. There were the reporters, who were a pest. Several of them had hip-flasks which they passed around, wiping the necks with the backs of their hands. There were the inevitable kids, impatient and spreading excited rumours eagerly. There were the ambulance men, discussing the crossword in the *Sun*. There was the WVS immaculate in uniform. And there were the others, the ones who were always there. A submarine, drawn up at the entrance to Greenwich Park, a visit by the Queen to Merton College, a road accident, a pop star, a fire, they were always there. And goggling. And determined to stay.

Across no man's land the two of them walked, Susannah actually blushing, the first time for years, and prodded along by the erect assurance of the little gun, then her new friend, Abu Khalil, calmly and softly passing instructions into her ear. And the police emerging from the building, halting on the steps, as if to see the happy couple on their way, or to be photographed —as indeed they were. It *was* like a wedding. The Commissioner, in the role of best man, pushed his way to the front. He didn't congratulate himself on saving the lives of some of the kids, but reproached himself bitterly for permitting the gunman to escape with his hostage. He had a megaphone in his hand. He raised it to his mouth.

The groom took the gun from the small of his bride's back, and put it to her head. She turned away from the prod of the metal. It was strange how the crowd, which had lingered in the hope that it might see some action, and gasped with fulfilment when Susannah appeared drenched in blood, became diffident when they saw that Khalil had a gun, and backed into the shadows. "Give me that!" cried Khalil to the Commissioner, and held out his free hand for the hailer, "or she dies."

The Commissioner took the megaphone from his lips and handed it to the gunman, staring steadily at him as he did so. The Commissioner knew the look in the eyes of men who were bluffing. This one was no bluffer. Jamie watched incredulously.

The happy couple reached the kerb. Through the megaphone Khalil announced in his rough transatlantic voice:

"Okay. Now I need a police car and a driver, right? I want it to line up right here and I want all you guys to keep way, way back."

Susannah was partially deafened by the noise, but could not turn her head away. Whenever she tried to do so, the muzzle of the gun was in the way, forcing her to look straight ahead. She could see Old Jacob and the others under the horse-chestnut tree. She could not see Jamie, who was some way behind her, but she could hear his voice.

"Susie . . . Susie . . . ," he kept repeating urgently, "Susie . . . Susie . . . Susie."

What Susannah could not know was that Jamie was being restrained in the sturdy embrace of a bearded constable. A car arrived, driven by a CID man.

"Get back, get back!" cried Abu Khalil to the crowd, and to the driver: "Step out real slow, *real* slow, and open the door for us."

He was not keen, this CID man, and could not for the life of him think how he came to be in this predicament. The Commissioner strode over to a little group of police officers and said:

"Right, lads, who's it to be?" and nobody had answered, and the Commissioner had looked straight at him and asked: "You?" and he had nodded.

"He's a bloody awful driver," somebody had joked in relief, but already he was wishing that he hadn't nodded. If it were just him . . . but he had a wife and a young son. 'Oh my Christ,' he thought, 'fucking bloody Christ!' As he climbed out of the car, and approached Khalil and Susannah, his knees were knocking together. He never knew that people's knees really did that.

"Your car, sir," he said, touching his cap in a nervous attempt at irony, and was at once aware that the madman might take the gesture literally and imagine that he regarded himself as a chauffeur, nothing more, or that he was a chauffeur.

"I'm a police officer," he added.

"Open the door."

The rear door was opened, and Susannah climbed in. A despairing "Susie!" from Jamie, as Khalil climbed in next to her. Not without some stalling and grinding of gears, the car drove off in the direction of the heath, and the scene, which had been frozen as if in ice, thawed out in a moment, and people ran to and fro, grabbing children, congratulating one another, behaving in short much like wedding guests do when the principals have left the scene. Only the bride's husband looked despondent.

They drove South along the A20. Khalil instructed the driver to unplug his radio set, then gave him terse directions. Susannah sat patiently in her corner seat, arms on the arm-rest, feet on the foot-rest. Khalil tucked his pistol into his belt and lit a cigarette for Susannah, then one for himself. Susannah noticed for the first time his missing fingers.

"Hey, man, you smoke?"

"No," said the CID man, "me, I like to keep fit."

"Your poor fingers," muttered Susannah.

They were not intercepted, although once they heard a cacophony of sirens in the distance; at once Khalil's hand went to his belt. It came on to rain, light drips of autumn rain from fat, low clouds, rain insufficiently heavy to justify the use of windscreen wipers. Overcome with the heat and with exhaustion, Susannah had difficulty staying awake. The blood on her clothes was caking.

They drove for a quarter of an hour, and then Khalil gave the driver instructions to wing the car into a field. A helicopter was awaiting them there, rotor spinning, precisely as planned. The pilot had monitored the news reports on the radio, had listened in to the police messages, knew just when to be there, was there, perfect. The draught through the car window refreshed Susannah a little, disarranging her hair.

Abu Khalil reached forward and shot the CID man while he was still in the driver's seat and despite his pleading:

"Please. I'll say nothing. I don't know anything. Please." And, turning to Susannah: "You ask him." Too late. Bang. One shot was sufficient.

Hirsute arms hoisted Susannah into the chopper. Khalil followed. When they were in the air, Susannah burst into tears, which smudged the mascara around her lovely eyes. Khalil ignored her and continued his intense discussion with the pilot in a language which the English girl could not understand.

Part Three

Passover

━━━━━━━━━

"*Jiggaddal w'jis kaddasch sch'meh rabbo b'ol mo diw'ro chirusseh w'jamlich mal chusseh b'chajjechon nw'jomechon uw'chajje d'chol bes jisroel uw'chajje d'chol bes jisroel baagolo uwis man koriw w'im'ru omen.*"

Old Jacob chanted the words of the Kaddish, swaying slightly on his feet. Odd to see this powerful and sarcastic city man so transformed. His bowler hat suggested expense account lunches, dirty jokes, free masonry, charitable works and "what's-your-poison", but the prayer-shawl and the chanting and the swaying told other, older tales. It was as though he, and his congregation, were only recognisable as Jews when they mourned. But of course mourning was their inheritance.

The majority of those present at the Memorial Ser-

vice counted a young relative amongst the victims. But
without Old Jacob to lead them in mourning they
would have been hopelessly lost and pitifully embarrassed.

> "The Lord gave, and the Lord has taken away:
> Praised be the name of the Lord."

Once they would have rent the fringes of their garments, sat in ashes, wrung their hands, torn their hair,
beaten their breasts. Now Jacob swayed and chanted
for them, and the small choir sang as though *their* lives
depended on it.

Cool hands had buried and burned the bodies, soft
voices had murmured consoling phrases, and the families had returned to Greenwich, Woolwich and Lee
Green to sit guiltily in front of the television, unable
to laugh at the comedians or be concerned with debates
on the desperate state of the economy. And now they
had come together again for their grief to be shared
and given substance, shaped and dignified by the newly
rewritten old words in the sombre voice of Old Jacob:

"O Lord who heals the broken-hearted, and binds
up their wounds: grant consolation to those who
mourn, strengthen and support them in the time of their
grief . . ."

There had been administrative problems. Other
bodies to be disposed of besides the Jewish ones, bodies
whose presence was an affront but which in death were
as rigid and as torn as the Jewish bodies. They had not
been claimed, but might at any moment attract vio-
lently-minded claimants. So there they lay in boxes, in
cold storage, in the care of a funeral director and several meaty security men, whose presence in the funeral

parlour was embarrassingly bad for business, but then what can you do?

Old Jacob referred in his address to these naughty corpses, and called them misguided, the symptoms of a world-wide infection. Alone amongst the children, Jonathan was present at the service, and, when Old Jacob spoke in this way, he conjured up in his mind— as he had so many times in his dreams—those headless and heedless figures, who had been so cruel and so rude and so disagreeable. He didn't understand about symptoms and infections; he wished he could have been watching Millwall, who had started the season in such splendid style.

"The Lord God will wipe the tears from every face. Sorrow and sighing shall flee away. May the Lord comfort you and all who mourn."

But the world continued on its roller-coaster ride.

A Lufthansa 'plane was hijacked and a polite request made to the German authorities to release the three surviving Munich murderers in exchange for the lives of the passengers. No one seemed surprised. The Germans were happy to oblige. It had been bound to happen sooner or later; better sooner. The Israeli mothers of the victims couldn't appreciate this pragmatism, and made a fuss. The murderers were welcomed in Libya with flowers and dancing in the streets. They gave a press conference. And the story of Munich was concluded. Nothing more need be written about that one.

On television screens in the West, Palestinian revolutionaries continued to earn themselves air-time. Their public image was of immaculately groomed, polished, multilingual, attractive young men and women, arguing on behalf of a desperate, unhoused and unprivileged refugee generation. A bland television commentator

remarked that what troubled him was the "niceness"
of these militants; what he must have meant was that
what troubled him was that *he* liked them. When everyone is gullible, anyone is plausible. And they were
plausible. Other television journalists investigated the
rigorous training of the 'Lion Cubs', terrorists of the
future. Over those it was permitted to tut-tut.

And the British public tut-tutted over the Stoke
Newington Eight, who had also been protesting on
behalf of the homeless and desperate and were also
advocating violence against . . . property. Property!
Those who talked of international conspiracies and
stirred Al Fatah, PFLP, Guevarists, Renault workers,
Black Panthers, IRA, SLL, YSL, Bogsiders, Marxist-
Leninists, Maoists, Trotskyites, Hippies, Yippies, New
Leftists, Radical students, Revolutionary Socialists,
Social Revolutionaries, Red Moles, Black Dwarfs,
Young Communists, Syndicalists, Weathermen, 'do-
gooders', and the BBC, into a seething porridge of
dissent, must have been surprised when these angry
kids appeared so irresolute and lonely in the dock and
admitted attacking . . . property! At the end of a long
trial they were to be sent down for many years, to
languish in cells, where their minds, trained in witty
universities, turned inwards upon themselves and became deformed like foetuses in wombs from which
there was no escape.

Once more the English Channel seemed to most
Britons like a copper bracelet, warding off the painful
rheumatics of radical idealism; but to a few it seemed
more like a manacle.

The air-mail however is international. And Post-
man's Knock became the game of the season. Letter-
bombs were on their way from Amsterdam, from India,
from Singapore. At the Israeli Embassy in London an

expert on agronomy opened an envelope containing his own obituary. He reaped the whirlwind. There were those who claimed that the letters had been sent by Israelis in an effort to discredit their opponents. It was certainly a sophisticated argument.

And the arguments were tossed back and forth on the radio, on the television, and in the newspapers, but it sometimes seemed as though everybody was speaking on behalf of somebody else, that there was nobody left to say: "I believe".

On the night of Yom Kippur Rabbi Arnatt was taken home by a policewoman. When he saw Susannah drive off in the Wolseley, Jamie had leapt into his Volkswagen to follow them, but the dependable little bug refused to start. Much frustrated, he had sought the Commissioner, but that gentleman was back in Florian's Delicatessen barking out commands vigorously amidst the cream cakes and pâtés.

"Don't fret yourself, sir," Jamie had been advised by an inspector, "they'll not get far. It's a routine matter from now on. Everything's in hand."

And Jamie had been persuaded. What else was there to do? So this policewoman, Helen Somthing Or Other, who had foxy little eyes, took him home, made him a cup of tea, and talked to him, spacing the words out carefully, as if he were a foreigner, or an imbecile, or both. But the tea had been welcome, for he had fasted longer than he was required to, and had been under much strain, and was shaky in the legs.

He would have telephoned the bereaved families, he might have telephoned the bereaved families; trouble was, Susannah had the address book, and he scarcely felt up to directory inquiries, or grubbing through the 'phone books, or anything much. Instead he asked the policewoman to telephone her headquarters and find out whether there was any news. There should be something by now, shouldn't there?

"One way to find out," said Helen, and she tried, but there wasn't, and she told him so in her oh-so-soothing voice which Jamie was rapidly coming to detest, so he asked her to leave, and she said that she quite understood, and that it was perfectly natural at times like this to want to be alone, and he wouldn't hesitate to get in touch with her, would he, if he wanted a chat or anything, and he said, just go. But after she had gone the worst time of all began for Rabbi Arnatt.

The house was perfumed with Susannah's presence, infected with her absence. There was a casserole in the oven, which only needed heating through, a silly novel of the sort she preferred lying open on a coffee table, a pair of her shoes left in the hall. She was to take them to be resoled. Her only comfortable ones, she had said.

He opened a tin of sardines, cutting himself in the process, dripped blood into the tin, picked unenthusiastically at the little, greasy bodies, opened a can of beer, enjoyed that, rang the Greenwich police station, was told nicely enough not to keep troubling them, they would let him know just as soon as they knew, not to worry, only a matter of time, *not* to worry, goodbye now, goodbye.

And as soon as he had replaced the receiver on its cradle, the telephone bell shrieked at him, quite a shock, and it was a moment before he could recover himself sufficiently to lift the receiver once more.

"Rabbi Arnatt?"

"Yes, yes, have you any news?"

"This is Harry Liston."

"Yes?"

"Do you have any news about your wife?"

"Do *you*?"

"I beg your pardon. I'm from the *Daily* ——, and I was contacting you in case—"

"You've had an anonymous 'phone call? A tip-off? No?"

"I take it, Rabbi, there are no new developments?"

"No, no. Why do you waste my time? Get off the line."

"You wouldn't care to tell us about this afternoon's events?"

"Us?"

"Did you have any intimations that something of the sort might happen? Did your wife—"

"I'm putting the 'phone down." And did. It rang again shortly afterwards. Same fellow.

"There are rumours that a reward is being offered? Have you had any communication from your wife?"

"How can I with you on the line all the time?"

"Do you have any theories as to her whereabouts?"

"I'm warning you . . ."

"I appreciate that you must be feeling quite distraught. Would that be a fair description? Or is there any other phrase that would more precisely convey to our readers what it feels like to—"

Again he slammed the receiver down.

He went upstairs, looking for Susannah. Found on a shelf in the unused 'playroom' a pile of her school exercise books, flipped through them. An essay on: "Can a scientist also believe in God?" which had been marked 5/10 with the comment: "Your ideas are interesting, but your spelling needs attention. And why are you not using a fountain pen as requested?" There were pictures of earthworms and sticky-buds in the biology book, and some nicely laid out quadratic equations, with satisfyingly probable solutions. Also: "This book belongs to Susannah Klein, 47 Lansdowne Road,

London N.3., England, Europe, The World, The Universe, The Solar System". Also: "Black is the Raven, Black is the Rook, Black is the Thief who steals this Book." Also, mysteriously: "Rather that than Pat Boone ! ! !"

Wandering, aimlessly, into the bedroom, he sat at Susannah's kidney-shaped dressing-table. This was more recent, this was better, she was still here. Her hairs in the hairbrushes, her scent in the spray, and, opening the bottom drawer which served as a dirty clothes basket, the tights she had discarded the previous evening. He passed them to his face. He curled up with them on the bed. It was all right. She would be back. And fell asleep.

And woke a few hours later to think: 'What an evil, mischievous dream. Amazing. And how detailed the fantasies of the sub-conscious mind!' Only then he realised that Susannah was not with him, and, with this realisation, the full horror of it all. Not a dream, not this one. In the study the telephone was ringing. That was what had disturbed him. He untangled himself from the tights—what were they doing on the bed with him?—and staggered to the next room.

"Yes?"

"We've found the car."

"What car?"

"The police car."

"Oh. Yes?"

"And the detective who drove it. He's dead."

"And Susannah?"

"No."

"Not dead?"

"No, sir, we haven't found her. We have reason to believe she's been taken abroad. Helicopter to the continent sort of thing."

"She wouldn't go."

"There were no signs of a struggle. But—"

"Yes?"

"Some blood. Not much. Some."

"Oh."

"We're not sure. She had blood on her from the girl . . . We're analysing it. Some of it may be . . ."

"Yes, come on. *Come on*!"

"Menstrual blood. Would that make sense to you?"

"Nothing makes sense, but . . . yes, I suppose so, yes, yes."

Silence. Jamie searched for a question to put. The sort of question which afterwards he would wish he had put.

"Any trace of chloroform?"

"No, I'm afraid not."

"Nothing like that?"

"No, sir. But he had a gun, of course."

"Yes, yes, we all know that. What now?"

"We'll keep you informed. Don't worry, sir, it'll turn out all right, you'll see." And rang off with evident relief that such a distasteful job had been completed.

Looking out of the window at the mysterious heath —it was almost dawn—Jamie observed a lone runner in singlet and shorts leaning into the wind, stray dogs, seagulls squatting on the grass, the white lines of the football pitches. Somewhere out there was the invisible line to Greenwich along which there was no time. Time, Jamie deduced, was his enemy. Twenty-four hours ago he had had all that anyone could reasonably have asked for. It was time that was to blame. A vicious, evil-minded chunk of it.

"For now I should have lain still and been quiet, I should have slept: then had I been at rest . . ."

Job knew it all. His days were swifter than a weaver's

shuttle, but the Lord had blessed his latter end more than his beginning. Jamie prayed. For Susannah. But chiefly for himself. Then, somewhat revived, he fried an egg, and 'phoned the Synagogue to request a few days' compassionate leave.

Susannah lay on an old mattress in a corner of the cell—indeed the cell was so small that it was hard *not* to lie in a corner—shivering with fever, and staring at the corrugated iron roof. She had much with which to occupy her mind, yet she found it hard to concentrate on anything beyond her bowels. They were, as the Bible had it, melting. So long as she lay still, she could manage to control herself, but the effort was exhausting.

The temperature must have been in the nineties, yet she shivered constantly. The cramp pains in her legs and arms were painful and debilitating. The sweat trickled into her smarting eyes, but, if she raised an arm to wipe them, she payed the penalty on that chipped enamel bucket. The mosquitoes were attracted by the bucket. And the ones that were bored with the bucket turned their attention to Susannah.

Yet all of this she could have borne patiently enough, were it not for all those podgy, Levantine faces peering in through the chicken-wire, which covered the hole which served for a window.

"Go away, you, go away!" A mistake. It was better not to talk. Although it seemed as if they understood her—well of *course* they understood her—for "Mār-heba!" they mouthed with an inane grin, and "Kaifik?" with a deprecating smile, and "Mut' assif", as they wriggled away. One face particularly irritated her, a toothless, wide-open sort of face, stubbled and oily, which kept reappearing at the window; it must have been back a dozen times. There would be a shuffling noise, then there would be the face with the oleaginous grin. It would tilt itself a little to one side or another, move itself around musingly, then disappear.

And again the journey to the bucket, and a pointless attempt to cover the window with the blanket from the mattress, but there was no time for such fastidiousness, and even the blanket brought no release. She could hear the giggling of children as she stumbled back to her bed. Bloody Middle Eastern food! Well, she'd know another time. A cigarette would have been welcome; she had no cigarettes. But wasn't there a packet of peppermints in her handbag (to suck at surreptitiously during the long hours of the Day of Atonement services)? And, freakishly, she still had her bag. Let's see now. Her fingers closed around a plastic tube. Max Factor's 'Pastel Fawn'. The tears were uncontrollable.

The helicopter had taken them to a field north of Paris. Thence an executive jet to the Lebanon, where they had landed at Beirut Airport the previous evening. There had been no immigration formalities, no customs, and indeed Susannah had had no luggage bar her handbag. They had walked across the airport runway, the pilot and Khalil, with herself between them, away from the busy Arrivals Lounge, away from the bright lights, and tannoys, and magazine racks, and smooth-cheeked stewardesses. And towards a shantytown which seemed to spill over on to the very periphery of the airport. Before she had covered a hundred yards her stained and stinking dress was sticking to her back and sweat was dripping into her eyes. But worst of all was the blood on her legs. When she stopped, the two men stopped, and nudged her forward.

When she looked back at the bright lights of the airport complex, they looked steadily on to the shacks of the shanty-town.

"Keep walking, baby," Khalil said.

No immigration facilities, no customs at the entrance to the Burj-el-Barajneh Refugee Camp either. Only a barricade of truck axles, and a small reception committee which ran neither to uniforms nor to rubber stamps. But Khalil was embraced fervently and the pilot's hand enthusiastically pumped.

A small group of well-wishers clustered around smiling and laughing with evident glee. They were obviously well-satisfied with the turn of events. But a wider circle of onlookers, including veiled women and naked children, stared sullenly at Susannah, at Abu Khalil and the pilot, from between the square blocks of tiny houses, from windows and roofs.

Susannah had demanded the use of a lavatory, which request created amongst the reception committee something of a panic. Arms were flung into the air, and voices raised, but eventually a girl in denims was procured, who took Susannah to a lean-to and slouched by the wall, pistol in stubby fingers, while Susannah performed the most intimate tasks.

Strange to treat her thus, since shortly afterwards she was required to play the role of honoured guest at an open-air banquet.

The table had been laid in the nearest thing the camp could offer to a market-place. Susannah was seated centrally, Khalil opposite her. A breeze ruffled the linen cloth, and crickets droned away tiresomely. Iced yoghourt was served by a young boy and, the girl in denims having departed, Susannah was the only woman present. She had fasted for thirty hours, barring only the peppermints, and now she set to hungrily.

Dishes of vine-leaves, nuts and black olives were presented to her; quartered tomatoes, cucumbers, auber-
gine purée, hummus, shrimps and artichoke hearts. She
ate with her fingers, as all did, and wiped them on the
cloth. The 'mezze' was replaced by broiled chicken,
and by minced lamb barbecued with onions. After the
meat a dried fruit salad, slices of *baklava, konafa*, and
sweet, thick coffee, accompanied by *ouzo*. Throughout
the meal the huge airships of Middle East Airlines
droned and whined and roared overhead. Lights were
gradually extinguished in the windows of the highrise
flats surrounding the camp. Refugee children crept out
of corners when the meat was served, and their faces
were like a circle of small moons shining faintly around
the horizon. The smell of mosquito repellent warred
in the air with the smell of the spicy food. It was just
possible to hear the Mediterranean.

No one addressed Susannah. They addressed one
another in a language which she failed to understand,
and they grew excited over the *ouzo*, and they sang
snatches of songs, and they laughed raucously, and
they picked their teeth. An old man, grizzled and lined,
stood and said a few solemn words, after which there
was a brief silence, before festivities were resumed.

Abu Khalil was the star of the show. Whatever he
said was a joke or a marvel or a tragedy. Whenever he
stretched out a hand to emphasise a point, the hand
returned with food or drink in it—but he was not spon-
taneous. His eyes were wary, his smiles slow to arrive,
swift to depart.

Susannah was content to be there. She ate and drank
what was placed before her to eat and drink. Indeed,
long before the candles had spilled their wax, or the
sun risen behind Mount Lebanon, her head had sunk
to the table, her eyes were shut, and she was dreaming

the fevered dreams of those who have fasted too long
and eaten too well.

She scarcely stirred when, towards dawn, a stocky
man with shoulders like an ox-yoke hoisted her up and
carried her off between the square white structures to
her modest accommodation.

It had been her bowels which roused her the following morning, and she had been surprised to discover
that a mattress, a blanket, a bucket and a handbag
seemed to comprise her entire inheritance, and that she
was locked in a room barely fit for habitation. Where
was she? She remembered a banquet and before that a
flight by air and before that . . . Soon she remembered
everything. But as to where she was, and for how long,
well, it was better not to exercise her mind on those
problems, because even that kind of exercise resulted
in another pilgrimage to the bucket.

"Mārheba! Queen Elizabetty? Mārheba!"

"Oh, do go away."

The 'Pastel Fawn' was useless to her in any case.
She had no mirror.

The heat was merciless. She watched as the bright
patch of sunlight sneaked across the floor and then,
losing something of its intensity, crept halfway up the
wall. Exhausted by her frequent trips to the bucket and
faint from the heat, she dozed intermittently, and was
asleep when her visitor arrived. How long had Khalil
been sitting there when she opened her eyes? He was
sitting very quietly.

"Somebody has stolen my watch," Susannah said. "It
was on my wrist last evening, and now it's gone. That
really is the limit."

Khalil smiled and offered her a cigarette. He held
out a battered case that looked as though it were made

out of gun-metal, then some book-matches over-stamped in English 'New Yacht Club, Beruit'. Susannah's hand was shaking when she put the match to the cigarette. Khalil's hand closed over hers to steady it. His was hard and cold, hers hot and sweaty. After a long, hard drag she said:

"It's just the sort of thing I find most objectionable. Senseless pilfering. I trust you'll investigate what's going on around here?"

Khalil didn't answer, but took the matches from her and picked at the phosphorous tip of one of them with his thumbnail.

"And while we're on the subject, might I kindly be provided with washing facilities, soap and water at the very least, a change of underwear, some aspirin, some writing paper and sanitary towels? I've not been well. The food last night didn't agree with me, and this sudden change of climate on top of everything else, well I can't take it. That's all I wanted to say to you really, because I know there's no point asking about your future plans for me. I'll not make trouble. But all I do ask is that you show me a little common courtesy. Not too much to ask really, is it?"

"Come," said Khalil, taking the cigarette out of her mouth and grinding it under his heel, "take your bucket and follow me."

Susannah was on the point of making a further complaint concerning the bucket itself, and the danger to her health arising from it, but Khalil had the door open, and the rush of cooler air was so welcome that she had taken her bucket and left her cell before she knew it. Her bowels heaved ominously.

"You fill the bucket, you empty the bucket," said Khalil. "Lesson number one, and you learn that lesson good." He pointed along a pathway of beaten earth.

Susannah followed the path, walking gingerly, averting her face from the bucket and breathing through her mouth. She was surprised to notice that the camp, which she could see for the first time in what remained of the daylight, was by no means as squalid as she had imagined. Low concrete huts with tin roofs had washing lines strung between them, and, in front of each, a tiny patch of garden. There were a few larger administrative buildings, and scattered stumps of trees. Wooden fencing in front of these contained huge-lettered graffiti, some in English: 'Drive the new colonialists into the sea'. Also photographs of Fatah martyrs, and Fedayeen slogans. Away to the North the balconied ice-cliffs of the modern blocks of flats, glistening gold in the rays of the setting sun, stared superciliously from a great height.

A large block set a little away from the other buildings appeared to be a communal wash-house and latrines. Once it had been clean and cared for, but it had grown dilapidated now that most of the refugee homes had running water. In her weakened state, Susannah stumbled and lost hold of her bucket while she was still some hundred yards from her destination. Faeces were all around her.

An hour later, washed and with a clean bucket, she was back in the cell, where Khalil was waiting with a portable cassette recording machine.

"You read this in front of the microphone," he said, holding out an index card on which some words had been scrawled in green Pentel. "Then I bring you what you ask for."

"My watch?"

"No, baby, not your watch. You never had no watch."

"Then I shall read nothing."

"Then you will eat nothing. And stay in your cell."

A long silence. Susannah said at length:

"This is exactly the sort of situation I wanted to avoid. Why can't we behave like adults? You think I can be useful to you, but you don't trust me . . . I don't blame you. But I'm in your power and I don't altogether trust you, especially after losing my watch. I was particularly fond of it as it happens. My father gave it to me."

"I shit on your watch!" Khalil shouted.

"Charming!" said Susannah icily. And then, speaking precisely, continued: "If I do what you want me to do, what will I get in return? Clean clothes, aspirin, Tampax, writing paper, and a little privacy to prove that you're not savages. Those are my terms, nothing less. As to the watch, that's between you and your conscience, if you have one."

"Read the card," said Khalil.

His expression was so pugnacious and humourless that Susannah could not restrain herself. She laughed. Khalil looked angrier still.

"I'm sorry," said Susannah, "I can't help it. This is all so melodramatic and absurd. I'll read your grubby little card for you, if you insist, of course I will. Why the hell not?"

And, when she finally read it, she did so in a voice that was flippant and high-spirited and quite out of keeping with the occasion.

Jethro concluded that if you had to be in hospital for anything, a bad leg was the best thing to be in hospital for. He quite wished that the doctors had discovered some complication so that he could have stayed longer in that peaceful green and white ward in which he was something of a celebrity and a great

favourite with the nurses, who played Scrabble with
him and had warm hands.

One Sunday morning he was invited into the hospital's Radio Control Room to introduce records requested by patients and the families of patients. The
regular DJ said that Jethro had quite a flair, a good
voice and an easy manner, and that if he wished to
make a career of it, he, Uncle Billie, would introduce
him to some Prominent People who would Get Him
Off to a Good Start. And then, on the air, Uncle Billie
asked him, without warning, if he would like to play a
record for Ruth because, as everyone knew by now, if
it had not been for him, that lovely little lady might
now . . . what record would he like to choose?
Daunted, Jethro stammered a little.

"I have just the thing—ting-a-ling!" cried Uncle
Billie winsomely, and played a raucous record called,
Them There Eyes. He interrupted the music frequently
with coy references to Jethro and Ruth, so much so
that Jethro felt obliged that afternoon to visit the
Women's Ward (even those iron-bound doors slid
smoothly open to admit such a famous little fellow)
and make his apologies in person. Unnecessarily, as it
turned out, for Ruth had been having her dressing
changed, and although she had heard *about* the requested record, she hadn't actually *heard* it, nor Uncle
Billie's over-jovial comments.

It wasn't easy for Jethro and Ruth. Everyone was
particular that they should be allowed to have an intimate *tête-à-tête*, and a crowd of nurses and orderlies
hovered just out of ear-shot, whispering excitedly
amongst themselves. Sister had been asked if it would
be possible to put screens around Ruth's bed for the
occasion—as though she were using the bed-pan or
being shaved or dying—but of course such a thing

could not possibly be countenanced in a well-run hospital.

As a result of their brave leap to freedom, and, since Ruth had the intense and languid good looks of a Joan Baez, while Jethro appeared loose-limbed and cool, the publicity tended towards romantically vulgar excesses. The newspapers would have a liaison between them— 'Back to Back but Heart to Heart' was one of the more tasteless headlines—and what made it all the sadder was that Ruth *did* feel more than just a flicker of interest in Jethro, so that the result of all the publicity was to put chains upon her tongue. As far as Jethro was concerned, he felt Obligation's heavy hand upon his shoulder, and Obligation drove away Affection. Thus, sitting by Ruth's bed, he was able to feel sympathy for the tongue-tied and bandaged girl, but, stronger than sympathy, an intense desire to be anywhere else at all. As soon as he decently could—and hospital routine admits of many pretexts—he left the Women's Ward and returned to his own bed, from which he was discharged the following day.

Discharged into a world of flashing cameras and intrusive questions—there were over a dozen reporters waiting for him on the steps of the hospital building— and they all wanted to know the same thing. Jethro and Ruth, a Love Stronger than Guns, a Romance Forged out of Fire, yuck! He was whisked away in his Dad's car with only one commitment, a night on the town with Ruth at the expense of the *Daily* ——, accompanied by a lady reporter from that journal. They told him that Ruth had already agreed enthusiastically, and would be broken-hearted if he refused, which was not entirely true. They were about to tell Ruth that Jethro had agreed enthusiastically and would be broken-hearted if she refused. So anyway he agreed, and she was to agree, but it would take a while before Ruth was fit enough to honour the obligation.

Jamie was granted six months' fully-paid leave of absence from the Synagogue; until his domestic problems had been sorted out, it was felt that he could not be expected to give himself whole-heartedly to the problems of others. A doe-eyed young rabbi from Brookline, Massachusetts was appointed in his place, on sale or return, as it were.

For a few days Jamie was pestered by newspapermen and by a number of obscene telephone calls from men who claimed to know where Susannah was.

"She's in my cellar, and she's got nothing on at all, Rabbi, and she can't get enough of it, and shall I tell you what she likes to do most of all? You'll be really surprised when I tell you . . ." There was a lot of this sort of thing, and a number of messages from self-proclaimed Nazis.

And then the story was dropped. With Jethro's release from hospital, and in the absence of further news of Susannah, any reference to the events in the Blackheath Synagogue on Yom Kippur was wiped off the front pages, then off the inside pages, and finally off the letter pages. The telephone no longer rang in Jamie's house and the rabbi was left to his own devices.

He should have been able to fill the time. He had plenty of urgent projects wailing at him like unfed children. His Collected Sermons sat in drawers uncollected. The book which the University of Pennsylvania had commissioned from him—*A Modern Midrash*—remained in outline. He bought newspapers obsessively, searching amongst all the platitudes and banalities for some clue to the unresolved mystery of Susannah. He studied the foreign pages, poring over them by the hour, leaving coffee rings on them, finding nothing, then half-heartedly filling in the anagrams in the crossword puzzles and tossing them aside. He subscribed to the news-sheets put out by Middle Eastern agencies, and to propoganda written by British ex-Army personnel who seemed to find in the Arab world and in the Palestinian cause a glamour and a magic that were no longer to be discovered in England. He was more than a little impressed by a booklet in which an organic chemist from Warsaw, an old boy from the Belsen school, argued the case for Arab/Jewish solidarity over the resettlement of the Palestinians in the Gaza Strip and on the West Bank. He wrote to the author but his letter was returned 'Not Known'. He fooled around endlessly with an old radio set on which he was sometimes able to pick up snatches of programmes from the Palestinian stations in Libya, Syria, Cairo and the Lebanon, but usually these snatches were in languages which he could not understand. He importuned the BBC Monitoring Station at Caversham, and the Greenwich Police Station, both of whom were becoming impatient and rather brusque with him. When he attempted to reach the Commissioner of Police, he was unable to hack his way through the defensive jungle of the outer offices. He had telephone extensions fitted in every room of the house, and flitted between them, dressed in an old pair of pyjamas. Several times a day a creaking door, or a shout from a neighbour's house or a car which seemed to be stopping directly outside, would convince him that Susannah had returned. As many times he would be disappointed.

During the long hours of the night, when he failed to sleep, he would catch glimpses of Susannah in the kitchen, on the bed, bending over the sundial in the garden. Hallucinations; and their effect was to lead him to suspect the evidence of his own eyes, and to become surly and confused. It was better, if he could avoid it, not to sleep at all. When he did sleep, dreams of Susannah dead, of Susannah being held to ransom by gunmen—on one occasion he, Jamie, was the gunman—of Susannah trying to reach him, trying to contact him, confused and upset him still further. He found himself wishing she were dead. He was growing hot for certainties.

He had little consolation in books, little even in Bonhoeffer or Büber or the Ethics of the Fathers or Torah. To come to terms with abstract ideas required more concentration than he could muster, and novels bored him. Imaginary stories of imaginary people. What a sterile exercise! To think that the country honoured fiction-writers with prestige and prizes and grants; why, they contributed nothing! Ocasionally he would take from the shelves Susannah's childish copies of Beatrix Potter books and into these he would dip, reading a chapter here, a chapter there, tracing the lines of the illustrations with the tip of his middle finger, slumped low on the settee.

His face had changed alarmingly. It was as though gravity had suddenly increased its pull; everything was being tugged downwards from the bones. The eyes were sinking back into their sockets. And he had as many grey hairs as black ones; and more than a few white.

Walking with a stick, Jethro called to see him the morning after his night on the town with Ruth, and, oh, what a grisly night that had been! Dressed up in a suit with studs and links and a tie with unicorns on it ("What an interesting tie!" the beaky lady reporter had cried effusively. "What is it, I wonder?" Jethro had glared at her and muttered: "A tie"), he and Ruth had been taken in a chauffeur-driven Daimler to the Talk of the Town, where a comedian of minimal talent was impersonating other comedians of minimal talents and where from time to time girls dressed as humming birds and air-hostesses and traffic signals gyrated hopelessly. That would have been sufferable (and the food was quite tasty) had it not been for the dreadful moment when the comedian summoned the young couple from the security of their ring-side table to join him under the lights.

"Well, Ruth and Julian," he had chortled, "how do you feel about this truly wonderful night out?"

This was the first of a series of questions he had oozed at them; and none of them could be answered the way questions should be answered, with a carefully considered and *authentic* sort of reply. And, whatever they said, the audience smirked and clapped until Jethro became entirely tongue-tied, and Ruth reduced to monosyllables. Not that this had discouraged the comedian; rather the reverse, for the less they said, the more he did, gurgling and grimacing and waving his hands around like feather dusters. Cameras flashed constantly. From time to time the joker put damp hands on the backs of their necks, and, as soon as he released them, the lady reporter got to work on them, fiddling with her tape-recorder and microphone, but not listening to a word they said in reply to her impertinent questions.

Once or twice Jethro had exchanged glances with Ruth, who seemed to find the whole experience as desperate as he did, but, by the end of the evening— and it had ended with a posed photograph of him looking up at Ruth's bedroom window, and Ruth blowing him a kiss from between the lace curtains—he had felt that enough was enough.

"Ah, to be young and in love!" were the last words
of the lady reporter as she drove off in her Allegro,
tapping cigarette ash into the pocket of the photographer who had wasted valuable interview time, she considered, with his pseudo-artistic nonsense.

But it was over now, or would be when the article
had appeared and been forgotten, and instead of going
to school—it was his last term and anyway they had
granted him an additional fortnight off for recupera-
tion—he had decided to visit Jamie, who had prepared
him for his barmitzvah three years previously, and
whose wretchedness, thought Jethro, must be overwhelming compared with his. For Susannah had been
really something, and the rabbi had lost her.

Susannah had been in the cell ten days, and it was a
week since she had recorded the message when the first
one came. She was able to record the passage of time
by the progress of the sun across the room, by the
meals they brought her at midday and at dusk. Pulse
at midday with a slice of melon; strips of meat or fish
with a honey-cake at night. Khalil had not revisited her.
She had had no change of clothing. No Tampax—although that, thank heaven, she no longer needed. No
aspirin, no writing paper, no privacy. No more visits to
the wash-house. They brought her a bucket of water to
wash in, and they took her other bucket away each
morning, returning it empty but vile-smelling. The heat
in the cell was oppressive, the hours endless. And then
after ten days the first one came.

She thought at first from the wild look in his eyes
that he was going to kill her, but she knew from news-
reels and articles about atrocities that they rarely killed
you indoors. They took you to the woods or the fields;
they put you up against a wall; they took you to a

stream or a quarry or a haystack; they made you dig a ditch; that was how it was usually done. He shut the door behind him with great care and locked it, so she thought it unlikely that he would kill her. But the look in his eyes was odd, and she felt sure that something was afoot.

The pistol remained firmly grasped in one hand as he unbuttoned and unzipped her with the other. When she understood his intention, she said:

"No, no, let me do it. I don't want you to do it. I should rather do it myself."

He spoke not a word, and evidently understood no English, but waited and shuffled his feet while she completed the undressing. Throughout this operation she kept her eyes fixed upon him. Just a boy.

"What's your name?" she asked kindly. He blushed a little but did not lower his gaze. Perhaps the wild look in his eyes, Susannah thought, was no more than embarrassment; there was no ambiguity in the pistol however.

"Well, there it is," she said at length. And made no attempt to cover breasts or groin, but even took a step towards him, staring at him all the time.

He opened the front of his dirty, white drill trousers, but remained fully dressed. It was hard on the floor of the cell and painful. Her back was sore and her heels grated against the stone flags. After a while she lifted her legs and put her heels on the backs of his thighs. It was less painful that way.

He did not take long. All the time it was happening he kept one hand on his pistol and, with the other hand, caressed her breasts, although there was no tenderness in the caress. Kneading dough, thought Susannah. He was quite small and found his way into her without too much trouble. She wondered what to do with her hands;

decided eventually that by putting her hands behind
her head she would not be committing herself. She was
not repelled by the boy, nor attracted by him, nor did
she detest him. She watched his skin while he was at it.
His neck was filthy—somebody should mention it to
him—and there was a scar on his elbow the shape of
the Isle of Man. Once she banged her nose against the
barrel of the pistol and apologised. What most disturbed her were those perfunctory caresses. She wished
that he had not found it necessary to undertake those.

When it was all quite over he did up his trousers
with the free hand, looking everywhere now except at
her, and left the cell. He'd uttered no word since he
entered, and only once made any sound, a deep and
rather sad-seeming sigh. He was gone.

It was late afternoon. A breeze had sprung up, and
she could faintly detect the smell of the sea. It was still
hot, but she shivered. She would not put her clothes
back on, no, she could not. She had washed them in
the bucket the previous day, and, if she put them on
now, they would carry the stink and stain of his sweat
and his . . . stuff. She took the rough blanket from the
bed, and wrapped herself in it, and sat on her haunches
in the corner.

An hour or so later they brought supper to her, and
she found that her appetite was unimpaired. The following morning she was able to wash herself in the
bucket, and make vigorous representations, as she usually did, to the man who brought it, that she *must* be
allowed a change of costume, but he was very old,
spoke no English, and seemed half-sharp in any case.
That evening, too, she received a gentleman caller, but
one less courteous than on the previous evening.

He was middle-aged. He took her twice, once from
behind. He gained much pleasure from it, evidently,

and hit her when she was slow in conforming to his wishes. His nose ran. He gave her some pleasure, a little pleasure, despite herself. Once she cried out, and he drew back his lips to disclose teeth at all angles, like buildings after an earthquake, in a sort of vindictive smile. It was odd, she thought, her being pleasured, and him being pleased that she was, yet the two of them such enemies and so cold with one another, conjoining like cogs in a machine. He had no gun though, this one, and would have nothing to do with caresses, perfunctory or otherwise.

She felt humiliated again after he left, but not so pernickety about getting dressed. She thought to herself, if it happens again I shall imagine it's Jamie, but when it did happen again—the following night—she forgot her resolution, or, if she remembered it, was unable to focus her mind steadily on Jamie, or anything else, because this one was huge and clumsy, and needed all the help she could offer him. What if she had not been prepared to offer it? Oh, it couldn't be doubted that he would have tried to force her; he was a very tough customer, notwithstanding one of his legs had been amputated at the knee.

And the next night, and the next, two more whom she had not seen before, a scarred one, and one who reminded her of an uncle in shipping, which was disconcerting, but she did her best.

She was sore now, and bruised, and waited for them apprehensively under the blanket, and when they had done with her, rubbed and rubbed at herself with what little water she was able to retain from her morning wash, rubbed until she was raw. If only it was not always a different man, if only she could build up some sort of a relationship, if only she was not just a *thing*. Being treated as an object, she began to regard

herself as an object. "You only want one thing," she
and her girl-friends at school had used to cry to their
boy-friends reproachfully, "you don't think of my feelings at all." But it was not true. The boys had been
the most sentimental of creatures, though smutty. They
had pleaded and ingratiated their way through layers of
clothing, and then stayed half the night, talking of God
and morality, but these . . . Even animals were not
subjected to this, or only rarely.

And the next night, and the next . . .

She no longer bothered to demand clean clothes,
she was nauseated by the food they brought her, and
yet she had no complaints; it was what she deserved,
no more, no less.

During the hours of daylight she sat on the floor
under the window and stared up at the sky. There were
few clouds, each one an event. And staring into the
blue void, she tried to find the top of it, the end of it,
the extent of it, and looked and looked until vertigo
set in and she had to look away; but not for long.
Sometimes she searched for certainties in the sky, but
found just one, that space went on for ever, and that
there was no room for God unless he floated about in
it, like that monolith in that spooky film, or unless in
some way she could not comprehend He 'contained'
everything. But not 'contain', that was not right, that
implied boundaries and limits; unless He 'was' everything. But that wasn't right either, and she grew giddy
at the thought, as her eyes grew giddy, staring into the
sky, so she focussed on a cloud, a tiny one with blown,
ragged edges—indeed it was little more than ragged
edges when you came to consider it closely—and
thought that that at least had edges, had boundaries
and limits, had a sort of reality, only of course it was
just gases, and if you were amongst them you would

be no more able to set limits to the clouds than separate the rain drops or count the stars. Which led, of
course, to a nocturnal vigil, sitting again under the
window, staring at the sky; but this was even worse.
The blueness of the daytime was bland, demanded
nothing of her, proposed nothing, resolved nothing,
but these damn stars! The more you looked, the more
they multiplied. And while you were trying to isolate
one, it would lose its brightness and another would
pop up behind, beyond, beneath it, and when you
looked back to the old one, it had vanished, or *had* it?
and three, no five, no *eight* had taken its place. Unlike
the blue sky, you could take your bearing from the
stars, this one must be a long way away, but the distance was measurable by astronomists with proper
equipment, they would know, they would be able to
tell. So many light years above you, so many . . .
Above? No, that wasn't right at all. You might as well
say Australia was beneath you. Was she looking up at
that star, or was she looking down on it, like a
reflection, like those crazy villagers who had emptied
their ponds in bucketsful to find the moon, and see if
it was really made of cheese. But if that star was beneath her, she could fall, she would fall, everything
would fall towards it, indeed everything perhaps was
falling towards it, and that's why it was getting brighter,
for it *was* getting brighter, unless perhaps she was
looking at a different star to the one she thought she
was looking at.

Why wouldn't they be still? They ran around the
sky like marbles!

And the next night, and the next . . .

And the longer she spent under her window by day
and by night, measuring, deducing, estimating the in-
finitude of space and the unrealiability of stars, the

more ridiculous her own situation seemed. What did it matter how many enemies she entertained in the parlour of her body? How many children died, and how many stayed alive? What she felt about her inadequate rabbi, and what he felt about his despicable and humiliated wife? What indeed did it matter which revolutionaries languished in prison, or which tribe inherited which strip of polluted land? None of it was of any importance. Let them all come and make free with her body; let them all come.

They didn't all come, but a dozen of them did. And then Salah came.

Abu Salah had soft, brown hands and beautiful manners. He padded his way through the door, unlike the others who had treated the door with no more respect than they had treated Susannah's body. He padded his way so softly through the door that Susannah had not moved from her observation post under the window before he touched her on the shoulders with his soft, brown hands. Then she turned and saw him, and he said: "Good evening to you," and she knew that her status had changed.

"This won't do," added Abu Salah with a voice like best butter, as he draped a white, woollen shawl around her shoulders. "From the stories that they tell me this won't do at all."

His voice was so kind, and the touch of the shawl so soft that tears welled up in Susannah's eyes and flooded down her cheeks. There was no staunching them, and Susannah didn't even try.

"I should think you've had enough of this pigsty, haven't you? I should think you'd welcome a few creature comforts like fresh linen and a warm bath. Am I right? Of course I am! Oh my, just look at those tears!

Have you ever seen such tears?"

Abu Salah took Susannah into society. Society was an elegant, white apartment in the Snoubra district of Beirut. Society began with the promised hot bath, and the new clothes which were beautifully tailored in contrasting shades of brown—a silk blouse and a linen suit. Even the shoes fitted. Society meant wrought-iron balconies, mathematical toys on low coffee tables, air conditioning and a long, cool drink made from yoghourt and crushed almonds.

"I was in Iraq last week," said Salah, "or I should never have permitted things to have got so out of hand. Believe me. A pointless visit, as it turned out. The French were there in force trying to sell Concordes to anyone and everyone. Champagne was flowing like oil. Toasts were drunk to Pan-Arabism, and to Chairman Mao, and to Al Saiqua, and to Colonel Quadhafi, and to the FAR, and then everyone got a bit the worse for wear and started to drink toasts to one another. All on expenses of course. But I must apologise for what has taken place, if words can be a comfort to you in your distress. Still, what's done is done, and, if it wasn't done with any great finesse, then that is to be regretted. To tell you the truth, they are a lot of Bedouins, most of them, and they've still got the sand in their navels to prove it. The most I can do is plead that it was done in your own best interests."

"My best interests?" Susannah's voice hovered on the brink of inaudibility. It was lower than the distant muzak from the restaurant down the street.

"I will explain. But over dinner . . ." said Salah. "Poor girl, she's so thin, she scarcely looks up to a set of tennis, let alone a seminal role in world revolution."

"The problem is," Salah continued half an hour later, as he dug the edge of his spoon into the yellow

flesh of a young melon, "that we've received no answer
as yet to the message we sent to England. And, under
the terms of that communiqué, we were obliged to kill
you if we didn't receive satisfaction, and, really, Susannah, to be totally ignored is most unsatisfactory. On
the other hand, of course, it's in nobody's interest to
kill you, yours least of all."

"I'm not so sure," muttered Susannah.

"So we thought what a good idea it would be if we
could have another little hostage of fortune, and no
sooner had we conceived the idea than we thought you
should be given the opportunity to do the same. But we
were afraid you might not see it our way, so we just
went ahead. Still, I accept wholeheartedly that things
could have been done more tactfully."

Susannah had eaten only a few spoonsful of melon,
when they brought her a lobster covered in cheese.
She watched Salah. He filled her view. He loomed large
in front of her. He was like a wall.

"It must seem barbarous to you, I know, but then
you can have no idea of how we've been treated. You
who played bridge, no doubt, to raise money for the
friends of Zion, you who dug deep into your dividends
to support our oppressors, you for whom Israel was a
shining beacon in a world of cynicism and treachery,
what do you know of our despair? Am I unfair to you?
Do I exaggerate?"

"You do exaggerate," said Susannah, "you exaggerate your despair as well." Her voice was still quiet.

"What we really need," said Salah portentously, "is
another bottle of this elegant wine. Then I shall tell you
a children's tale." Time passed and Susannah's head
was nodding forward on to her chest. Salah continued
to talk.

"I was twelve when the British withdrew from Pal-

estine. My home was in Safad, ancient city of the
Cabala. You have not visited Safad? It is on all the
tourists itineraries. A beautiful place on the side of a
hill, the houses blue, the sky blue, the olive groves and
the cypresses green. My childhood was like a child's
story-book, brightly-coloured, Susannah, too bright to
last. And then when the United Nations voted for par-
tition, my father and my elder brother went off to fight
for Abdelkader Hussaini. A real man, Susannah, the
like of whom I have not seen since, nor am likely to. I
asked my mother why they had to go, for what they
were fighting; and she said for me, they were fighting
for me. Why then could I not fight? They will take you
soon, she said. They will take you next time, she said.
But supposing there is no next time, I asked, and was
filled with foreboding that my strong father and my
brave brother would finish off the enemy before I
could get at them.

"Then we heard tales about a village called Deir
Yassin, where all the villagers had been massacred by
the Jews, and everyone said that Galilee was alive with
marauding Jew soldiers, and that no Arab would be
left alive. It started as rumour, but soon all believed it.
And my father and my brother did not return from the
fighting, not even to visit us, and we heard that Abdelkader Hussaini himself had been killed, and no one
was left to defend us. And my mother said that we
must leave at once. Everyone was to leave. There was
a bus going north across the mountains into Lebanon.
We packed our clothes and a little food, but nothing
else, 'for,' said my mother, 'when your father and your
brother come home, they will not want to find the
place quite deserted.' She would not permit me even
to take the radio. 'It will be safe,' she said, 'until we
return.' But I did not understand. '*Why* do we go? It is

our house. Who drives us away? Will not the British
protect us?' And my mother laughed, which she had
not done since my father went off to fight. And she
laughed so hard she started to cry. And then she would
not stop crying. Nor could I stop her.

"I remember the smell of that bus, Susannah. Even
in this restaurant, I can smell those refugees."

"What about your mother?" Susannah asked. Her
speech was slurred with wine and with tiredness. Salah
did not answer this question, but poured more coffee,
and continued in a lighter tone.

"We were talking about you last night, Susannah,
Khalil and myself. Of course he's the man of action; he
doesn't enjoy talking as I do. His kind are the aristo-
crats of the movement, myself, with my little sample
case of ideas, no more than a commercial traveller for
the cause, a leg-man. He had certain ideas about you,
I had others, but you remained an enigma. So languid,
so quiet, and inside maybe plotting to murder us all in
our beds. But what I feel is, if not you, it will very
likely be someone else; there have been five attempts
on my life alone. We have many enemies, and no
country where we can feel welcome. They threw us out
of Palestine and out of Jordan and they'll throw us out
of here as soon as they get the chance. And if it is to
be you who will plant the explosive, hurl the grenade
or press the trigger, don't do it in ignorance, Susannah.
Look around yourself, make judgements. Injustice does
exist. We are not all paranoid. You could be a great
friend to us, Susannah, a friend to many millions, if
you so chose. You would not be the first . . . Lawrence,
Glubb Pasha, even today we have powerful friends in
Britain and America, friends who do not at all see us
as terrorists and scavengers and refugees. An old culture, Susannah, something immutable, which will sur-

vive. You could return and tell them, Susannah, for they would listen to you. Forget what is past, think of the future. Perhaps you will look back upon this moment, this estimable restaurant, this wine which has been too long in the glass, this music, this strange, ambiguous town torn between past and future, between Muslim and Christian, the East and the West, the old empires and the new republics, myself clumsy and inarticulate but sincere, for you will not deny me that, I hope, Susannah, and you will see it as a moment of commitment, the decisive turning point of your young life. Are you asleep, Susannah? The world is full of sleepers, who dream that the world is as they would have it, and that is why we must constantly prick ourselves to make sure we are not asleep also."

Reaching across the table, Salah put a soft, brown hand upon hers. No sooner had Susannah's head jerked up, and her eyes blinked open, than there was the livid shock of a photographer's flash, and footsteps hurrying away down the hill.

Jethro was not prepared for the sight of Jamie in pyjama trousers and an old duffel coat poring over *The Pie and the Patty Pan*, nor was he prepared for the state of the rabbi's house. Every horizontal surface supported the remains of a meal or a chipped cup half-full of congealing coffee. The front door was open and Jethro walked in. Jamie looked up grimly.

"If you're another of these reporters ..."

"No, I'm not anything like that."

"Well, I don't mind telling you, you've called at a most inconvenient time."

"Don't you remember me? You confirmed me. And I was with Mrs Arnatt when—that is, at the Young People's Service on Yom Kippur."

"So what do you want?"

"Can I tidy things up a bit? I mean, I might as well make myself useful now I'm here." He waited for an answer from the rabbi, but none was forthcoming, so he leant his stick against a radiator and limped across the room, collecting a pile of crockery and cutlery as he did so.

"Is the kitchen through there? It doesn't matter. I'll find it okay. How would it be if I made us both a coffee? I could do with one myself."

He was wearing a white T-shirt with a Snoopy illustration on the front, faded jeans which wouldn't fade fast enough for Jethro's taste, and the tartan jacket he had worn on the Day of Atonement. His mother had wanted it burned, but Jethro insisted that it was returned to him after the bloodstains had been removed. Now he wore it every day.

"What's your name?"

"Jethro. Black or white? Sugar?"

"You've got a nerve."

Jethro left the milk on the stove and the coffee in the cups, and hurried into the living-room.

"If you really want to know, I'm probably as unhappy as you are," he said, "that's why I came."

"You're probably B'nai B'rith, or one of those other organisations who push old ladies across roads and wallpaper bathrooms."

"Had I better go?"

"You had better go, but there's an errand you can run first. Here's some money. Get me the latest edition of the evening paper, would you? There's a newsagent this end of the village."

Jethro glanced first at the sports page, then at the television programmes, then at the chess problem. It was not until he was once more outside the rabbi's house that the specially featured photograph—almost the whole of page three—caught his attention. The headline was facetious: 'Dinner For Two Please James', but the caption was less enigmatic:

'A smart Beirut nightspot,' it read, 'a handsome escort, coffee, a glass of wine, the caress of a friendly hand, everything a girl could dream of. But do you recognise her?' And then, inset, a copy of the picture from a few weeks back, Susannah with the gun to her head outside the Blackheath and District. 'That's right!' the copy continued cheerily. 'Susannah, the Rabbi's Wife from Blackheath!'

There was nothing more. The boy held the picture up to catch what was left of the daylight. She was much changed, he thought, but it was her all right. She looked tired, and the expression was a dazed half-smile, but there was no mistaking that mouth, those eyes. What could it mean? No question, he must keep it from Rabbi Arnatt. But the rabbi was already at the door, holding out his hand.

"Kind of you," said Jamie.

Jethro improvised wildly. "It's an old one," he said. "They didn't have today's in. There's a strike or something. I picked this one up in the street. But it's not today's."

Still Jamie stood, hand outstretched.

"Bloody hell!" said the boy. "It's for your own sake. All right, take your stinking paper!" And he crumpled it into a ball and threw it at the minister. All Jamie said was:

"You can keep the change."

"I'm off," said Jethro, and limped across the heath to the bus stop. He felt furious with himself. By his crassness he had drawn the rabbi's attention to what should have been kept from him, though surely he

must have seen it sooner or later. He felt better when
the bus arrived, for he loved to sit on the top deck at
the front and imagine he was driving. Vroom vroom.
He really loved buses.

When he reached home, Ruth was there. His mother
had invited her to tea. Her hair looked different, shinier
somehow, as though she had done it specially. She
wore a frock instead of jeans, and kept her hands
folded in her lap. She was thin, demure and pale.
Jethro's mum and dad were sitting either side of her,
looking like the lion and the unicorn, and all three of
them smiled at him as he came through the door. It was
creepy.

"The prodigal returns, eh?" said his dad, as he often
did these days, and Jethro said: "Yes."

His mother remarked: "Isn't it exciting, seeing Ruth
out and about again?" and looked at Jethro for his two-
pence-worth.

"Yes," said Jethro, and went upstairs to his room.
Ten minutes later Ruth joined him. Jethro was sitting
at his desk, playing with a toy bus, pushing it backwards and forwards, backwards and forwards.

"Jeth, what's the matter?"

"That poor bugger."

"Who?"

"The rabbi. Can you imagine? I feel awful about it."

"Not your fault."

"It's somebody's fault though, isn't it? S'got to be."

"Have they been bothering you again?"

"Who?"

"The newspapermen. They wanted me to go back
with them to the Synagogue and have my picture taken
where it all happened, looking out of the window, and
all that. They offered me a hundred pounds."

"That's not much," said Jethro, who had been offered nothing.

"Anyway I'm not doing it. But I've been asked to model nighties for *Honey*."

"What the hell have nighties got to do with the price of eggs? Honestly Ruth . . ."

"I haven't said whether I'm doing it or not."

"No, but you will, won't you? That's why you're so on the defensive about it."

"Well, I don't see why—"

"No, you wouldn't. Shit!"

There was silence between them. Ruth looked around her at Jethro's room. School photographs, Van Gogh reproductions, a piece of hardboard with newspaper cuttings and telephone numbers on it, a chess-set frozen in mid-game, a record-player, a rude poster—hands emerging from a lavatory pan—and a handful of classical LPs. Not many give-aways there, except maybe the bus which Jethro still pushed backwards and forwards, backwards and forwards. Ruth got the feeling that he hadn't taken much interest in the decorating of the room.

"It's nice here," she said. "Homely."

"You think?"

"What's the matter, love? Would you like me to go?"

"Well, it's my room!"

"Okay. I'll go."

"Listen, Ruth, it's best to say these things, don't you think? Well, when it was all happening, I mean, when we were wired together and I was next on the list, I could feel you trembling, and I chatted him up, you remember, and then I got this crazy idea, and off we went through the window, and all that way down— it was a hell of a way down, wasn't it?—anyway, all the time that was going on I felt like, I don't know, it mattered, we mattered. In a way it was good, Ruth, oh, not for the others, I know, but for me it was good, *things were happening*. They don't often happen, Ruth, you've got to make them. And since then that awful hospital and that awful night at the Talk of the Town and that poor fucking Jamie, and suddenly here you are talking about modelling nighties for *Honey*. That's not what it's about, Ruthie, that's not what it was for. That's rubbish, Ruth, really it is."

Ruth fumbled for words. She looked hard into Jethro's eyes, trying to find *him*, but he wasn't there. Then she reached out a hand to his hand, and her fingers settled on his, drew his away from that beastly bus, wriggled between his, each one of hers squeezing between two of his, tight and warm, and hoped that that would do, that that would be enough.

But Jethro did not respond as Ruth had hoped. If he had not responded at all, she would have been quite happy just to sit there with him holding hands. It would have been quite nice. But he did respond, that was the trouble: he hurled her backwards on to the bed and flung himself upon her and tore at her buttons (they were just show buttons anyway, they didn't *do* anything). In amazement and distress—he was so fierce and determined—she cried out to him to stop, and must have cried out louder than she had intended to, because there were feet on the stairs, and the door was flung open, and Jethro's dad was there before Jethro had a chance to compose himself.

"It's all right, it's all right, really," said Ruth desperately embarrassed and smiling reassuringly, but it couldn't have been all right for Jethro because he was out of the room in a flash, and down the stairs, and crash!—that was the front door—into the street. Ruth smoothed her skirts, picked the bus up from the floor and examined its damaged axle ruefully.

"I'd better go," she said. But all Jethro's dad said was:

"You and his mother between you. I hope to God you know what you're doing to the boy."

Jethro loved buses and there were buses to take him wherever he wanted to go. The West End was vibrant with possibilities. Nonetheless Jethro did not take a bus to the West End. There was only the one place to be.

From within the rabbi's house banging and tearing noises could be heard. Yet the doors were still locked and the windows curtained. Jethro's shouts were unacknowledged, so he made his way round the side of the house to the back garden, and found that the window of Jamie's study was slightly ajar. He slid his long frame through it like a ferret.

Enough light spilled into the room from the corridor to enable Jethro to see how Jamie had been occupying his time. A twisted sheet divided up the room, and a multitude of objects were distributed either side of the sheet. A pile of books one side, a smaller pile the other; records the same; similarly with letters, ornaments, pictures and so on. Bustling noises from upstairs encouraged Jethro to believe that he was safe to investigate further, and he tip-toed, one foot either side of the sheet, out of the study and into the adjoining living-room. Here the disruption was worse. Another twisted sheet indicated the demarcation line, but in this room the carpet had been cut back either side of the sheet to form a strip of bare boards. To the right of the strip the settee, to the left the matching armchairs, a tumult of books on both sides, to the right the television lying on its side, to the left the stereogram similarly humiliated. The pictures from the walls, the hessian wall-covering, the shelving, everything had been torn from its rigthful place and redistributed. In the dining-room the same; a handsome Pembroke table had had one of its flaps torn off, the electrolier had been wrenched in half, a canteen of cutlery had been disembowelled, its guts equally divided either side of the sheet. In the kitchen the distribution was quite un-equal; one side of the sheet had an immense pile of pots, pans, tins of food, utensils, plates and so forth; the other side only a few bottles of wine, a corkscrew, a pair of scissors, a tool-kit and electrical equipment. In the lavatory, the toilet roll had been torn roughly in half. It was evident that a very thorough madman had been at work in this house—and for many hours.

Jethro ventured a little nervously upstairs. When he reached the half-way landing he could see the figure of Jamie, a gloomy outline in the gloom, looking down.

"Come to pry, have you, or gloat?"

"I . . . heard noises."

"There have been noises, yes."

"I was anxious."

"How kind."

"I thought perhaps I could help."

"Help? Oh yes, certainly, come right upstairs. Come along, come along. If it's help you have to offer . . ."

Jamie led the way to the bedroom, and switched on the light. Partly prepared by what he had seen down-stairs, Jethro was nevertheless shocked and alarmed at the state of the room.

"What I am doing," said Jamie—and Jethro could see that he was wearing only pyjama bottoms—"is separating my belongings from those of my wife. Not you might suppose a very demanding task, but that just goes to show how little you understand of such things. When you have lived with someone as long as I have with Susannah, you will appreciate how tightly her life entwines with yours. You're not married, are you?"

"No," and Jethro smiled, "by no means."

"Well, there you are then. They smother you to death with their fine, fancy ways, women do, and all their clutter."

"I don't like women much," said Jethro.

"She was a fine specimen though, didn't you think so, mine, *everyone* thought so. What do they think now, eh?"

"They're suspending judgement, I suspect," said Jethro. Jamie roared with laughter at this, then Jethro added: "I thought she was beautiful."

"Maybe, maybe, but what use is that to us, now? We have work to do, especially if you were serious when you offered to help."

"I was quite serious."

"In that case, pay attention." Jamie frowned. "This side of the line is hers, that side is mine, so be careful where you tread, if you want me to trust you. Here take this blanket and these shears. Snip it up the middle, snip, snip. It was a wedding present, all wedding presents must be divided. Snip, snip, don't be shy."

"Weren't you given a pair? Blankets usually come in pairs."

"Yes, I believe we were. Good thinking. One this side, one that. What next? Pillows? Mattress?"

"You saw it in the paper. I feel awful about that. I would have kept it from you."

"I own the house, but we paid jointly for the car. That's a tricky problem, I do admit it. So, my little *meshuggah*, what do you suggest?" His tone had been and remained extremely genial.

"I think you should take a break, Rabbi. Let me make you a cup of coffee. I made you one before, but

I don't suppose you drank it."

There was a surprised pause, then: "After all, why not?"

They had trouble finding the tin of Maxwell House, and the kettle, and all the mugs were in piles on the floor, but in due course the coffee got made, and the two men sat together on the upturned settee to drink it.

"This was a sound idea," said the rabbi, hands cupped around the mug. "I can't remember when I last took any refreshment. And there's her in that smart restaurant, but let's talk no more of that. Pick up the pieces. Get things going. That's a healthy attitude, don't you think?"

"Positive."

"You're the boy from B'nai B'rith, aren't you? I remember you quite clearly. For years one arranges functions, one visits the sick, one makes onself generally available, then suddenly one day they're all doing it to you. Most disagreeable experience, I should imagine. I shall burn all her things, you know. A burnt offering unto the Lord. Make a huge bonfire and burn them all. Quite the best. That's what they used to do, the old Norsemen, when someone died, float them out to sea on a funeral pyre. Can't do that in Blackheath very well. Even the boating pond is hardly big enough."

"She's not dead."

"I said we would not discuss it any further. Anyway what do you know? A kid. You offered to help, right then, help, don't gabble. I've done the lion's share of what needs to be done. You take all her things into the garden and make a big bonfire of them. Not on the lawn, that was my lawn, but on the flowerbeds; pile them up on the herbaceous border, she spent a lot of time on that, that's the most appropriate place. I know what I'm doing despite appearances. Here's the key to the door. Okay? It's unconventional, my behaviour, perhaps, but I have logic on my side. Okay? Well, get a move on."

They worked all night, and, by the morning, had made quite a mountain of Susannah's belongings. Jamie was most meticulous about it, even down to Susannah's cosmetics and soap and the school exercise books. It came on to rain with the dawn, and their efforts to get the bonfire to light met with no success. They added fuel from the lawn-mower, but it came on to rain more heavily, and, after several abortive attempts, Jethro insisted on moving indoors (he was drenched and cold in his jeans, T-shirt, and jacket, although Jamie in his pyjama trousers apparently suffered not at all) and, with a last despairing look around him, Jamie trotted into the house. Jethro changed out of his wet things into a bath-robe of Jamie's and heated up a tin of baked beans which he'd salvaged from the bonfire, and this did duty for breakfast. Then Jethro spotted the chess-set.

They played for four hours, then slept for two. In the late afternoon Jamie repaired to the India House restaurant for two take-away Chicken Specials, and, after these had been consumed, they played a second game.

Jamie was an advocate of hypermodernism, that is to say, the secession of the centre of the board to one's opponent, followed by an outflanking attempt with pawns, knights and fianchettoed bishops. Jethro was a player of flair and impatience, hurling all his pieces forward centrally at every opportunity, disdaining all simplification. The two were thus well-matched, and, in their first game, Jamie was just gaining control when his concentration snapped and Jethro won a piece. It was a prototype of most of the games they were to play. Time and again Jamie was to survive Jethro's un-inhibited attack, slowly gain control, then blunder, and slump lower on the settee, the light fading from his eyes. Just occasionally he would win, but he never won twice running. And chess destroyed the reserve between them.

"Were you always going to be a rabbi?"

"I liked books and studying. My father was *fromm*. But my faith wasn't cabalistic like his, more common-sense supported by natural observation."

"Was that enough?"

"It was a reaction to my father's extreme orthodoxy. But he had seen *his* father lose everything in a pogrom, so maybe mysticism was the only way for him. In Edinburgh I had no need of such an escape."

"And now!"

"Don't hurry me," said Jamie, "I can't be hurried."

Then they spoke of Jethro and his religious up-bringing.

"At school we have comparative religions and un-denominational assembly and sex education and citi-zenship. We're very advanced."

"You've moved beyond the Bible?"

"They think it's a bit old hat."

"Maybe it is."

"They say it's marvellous literature."

"They're clever; that's damning."

"What I don't care for is all that theeing and thou-ing. It's as bad as scientists wrapping everything up in magic formulas and doctors writing prescriptions that no one can read. We never talk about God at school. I mean, that's a bit weird, isn't it? The scientists do, at least they're on about patterns and first principles and DNA and that. You'd have thought there'd be a meeting of minds between what the scientists reduce it all to and what you lot built it all up to, but there isn't, just a fucking great chasm! Hey, there was an astronaut on television the other night on one of the religious programmes, and he was saying about how he'd found God in space. It sounded like a load of cobblers to me, but at least he believed it. Well, if scientists and astronauts can be that committed, why can't rabbis and clergymen?"

"I'm sorry you think so little of us."

"What I think is, you should either admit that you don't know, or, if you do, explain it to us in a way that all of us silly buggers can understand. Hey, it's Friday night. Why don't you light the candles? Just the two of us. It would be *really* nice. Even if it is meaningless. And I'll get another curry."

The boy stood up to clear away the chess pieces. His bath-wrap fell away. Faced with an imposing cluster of genitals Jamie was confused and alarmed. Jethro turned away quickly enough, but the image remained.

"Go away, child, go away."

"What's this? What do you mean 'child'?"

"I wish you'd never come here. Now get out, get weaving, go on, get out."

"And what about my clothes?"

"Well, go and put them on, can't you? Good lord, it's a simple enough operation."

"I don't understand what this is all about. A rabbi should be pleased to conduct a Friday evening in his own home." Jethro was shouting from halfway up the stairs. Jamie was grinding a black queen and a white bishop between his hands.

"I'm no rabbi." Muttered not shouted. But Jethro was sharp of hearing.

"You may not want to be . . ."

"What are you doing yammering away on the stairs? Get into your clothes."

"I mean, if you're not a rabbi, what are you? All right, all right, I'll be out of your way in a couple of minutes. What a carry-on!"

But Jethro put Jamie's intransigence down to the strain under which he had been living, and returned the following day. And the volatile relationship which grew up between Jethro and Jamie was not dissimilar to a marriage. Jethro did the cooking and the housework. Jamie began to consider whether he might not get back to his writing, and indeed whether there might not be a suitable post for him in a grateful Synagogue somewhere a long way from Blackheath. And Susannah's possessions mouldered and rotted in a heap upon the herbaceous border.

1972 was dragging its weary length into a corner, where it might whimper and die. President Nixon was re-elected to the White House and celebrated his return with the biggest ever bombing raid over the civilians of Vietnam. Arab terrorists dressed in white ties and tails burst into the Israeli Embassy in Bangkok and took hostages, while the Queen of England celebrated her silver wedding quietly at home; it was the last year in which she would enjoy absolute sovereignty over her subjects. And in a hospital bed in Holloway Prison, Alia lay alone with her shame.

The bed was in the middle of the room, and there were no other beds in the room, just white curtains with lilies of the valley on them, and a basin, and a picture of an owl with a mouse in its beak, and a bedside cabinet, and an invalid table, and some hooks on the wall, and a light bulb which swung gently whenever the door was opened and around which at night flew moths and flies and the occasional maybug, and a bed-pan, and a bottle of lemon-barley water, and a stern-looking woman sitting on a chair. There were others, Alia knew, stationed permanently beyond the door, because she heard their voices from time to time, although she could not understand what they were saying.

Alia's thigh had been bad, even after they extracted the bullet from it, and it was only now, six weeks after the day of the mission, that the pain relented sufficiently for Alia to be able to concentrate her mind upon the shame. Shameful enough to have failed—and, despite the wide publicity given to the enterprise, the loss of her colleagues' lives and the refusal of the authorities to make concessions, had ensured that it was a failure —but to survive the débâcle was more shameful still. While she lay in a hostile bed, eating and drinking enemy food, her people's struggle was going forward without her. Once, when the woman on the chair was slumped in slumber, Alia had eased herself out of bed. She had no spectacular plan, but felt the need to make at least a defiant gesture. Her legs were too weak however to sustain her weight. In her hospital nightie she crumpled to the floor. Now they spoke of moving her. They did not tell her her destination, but inevitably it would be a place more strenuously guarded than this white bed in this white room. So—and this was the conclusion she had reached when they came for her— she must try to get away immediately, and, if no softer option presented itself, there was the unbarred window, for the room was three storeys up in the hospital block. Perhaps if she were able unobserved to twist the bottom sheet and attach one end of it to the curtains, that would help a little to break her fall. It might be necessary to silence her guard first—it *would* be necessary—

and that, to a girl with Alia's training, offered no
peculiar problems, but the most important thing was to
choose her moment. Darkness would facilitate her
getaway and, whatever obstacles awaited her beyond
the window she would do well to delay until after the
evening meal. Then, nourished by the food and dressed
in the guard's uniform (yes!) she would boldly undertake her escape. Death was the likely outcome. It
would be preferable to this continuing and shameful
inactivity. Her death would be reported. Word would
get back. An inspiration to others. Another step along
the road to liberation. An honourable end.

But then they came in with a white blouse and tights
and knickers and a bra and a blue dress and gestured
to her to prepare herself. They stood between her and
the window. They held up the dress. How pretty it was.
A bourgeois tear trickled down the shameful cheek.
Oh how pretty it was!

The photograph of Susannah and Salah *à deux*
caused consternation to others besides Jamie. In Down-
ing Street, in Whitehall, in New Scotland Yard, the
same questions were asked.

"Is it genuine?"

"Is it her?"

"Is it Beirut?"

Salah was readily identifiable. A potent, committed
and implacable terrorist. And, after many experts had
been called in, it was concluded that the photograph,
transmitted by a respectable news agency, who had received it through the post, was exactly what it pur-
ported to be: unnerving.

Salah installed Susannah in a suite in the Carlton
Hotel. She was encouraged to order anything she

needed from room service. She never saw a bill; indeed she had no money with which to pay one. From her bedroom window she looked across the Mediterranean. In the foreground a swimming pool, kidney-shaped and deserted, in the background the Oxford and Cambridge blues met on the horizon, silver flying fish hung motionless, it seemed, over a collage of boats and ripples. Even the speed-boats sliced open the mattress of the sea quite slowly and gently.

Susannah was impressed. Said Salah:

"We are not short of money. They fall over each other to give it to us. They would rather give us money than those things we ask for. They would rather give us money than the lives of their young men."

"Am I free to leave?"

"Do you wish to?"

"I might."

"If you wish to, you are not free. If you do not wish it, you may go."

"But I wouldn't get far?"

"No, not far. If you wish to see the sights, that we can arrange."

"I don't know."

"What matters is that you drink plenty of milk." Salah showed his teeth in a grin. He could afford to grin. And evidently he could afford the gold teeth, for Susannah watched him drive up and leave in a Mercedes. "You feel well?"

"Yes."

"You wish for dates, maybe, or herrings, or peppermint creams?"

"I have all I wish."

"Have you read the books?"

Susannah smiled apologetically: "Some of them . . ."

"You must persevere. When I was a boy I did not

always find it easy to study. I thought it was enough to throw stones, to creep out at night with a pot of red paint. It was not. Without study we become a rabble. We cannot identify our brothers, nor learn from yesterday the lesson for tomorrow. You read Kim Il-Sung? Read him first, Susannah, for, if you can read him, you can read them all."

"Salah, I will try."

"It is your duty as a mother-to-be."

"I will try." Truth was Susannah hankered after a Michael Innes or an Agatha Christie or a James Bond. Maybe if she rang reception . . .

"One day soon," said Salah, and grinned as he said it, "I shall take you to see the Lion Cubs. Not the ones in the menagerie, these are our own wild breed, who make those others tame."

"Salah, there is something I should say. You ask if I wish to leave and you ask if I am well and you ask if there's anything I want and you ask if I've read those books. Salah, I can't answer your questions."

She was not looking at him, but staring out across the sea. She was aware of him behind her, could see his shadow in the window-glass. She would have liked to have been able to explain to Salah, to anyone, her desolation, her lethargy, her incapacity to feel joy or express pleasure.

"How long have I been in this country?"

"Ten weeks."

"And I am to stay until—"

"Until the child is born, yes."

"Oh, but Salah, how will I survive? I mean, like this, just going on like this, how will I?"

Salah spread his hands wide and asked:

"Are you lonely?"

Susannah beat her head against the glass, gently to

begin with, then with increasing force.

"It is natural that you should be, but what can we do? Khalil is in Bangkok, and it would not be suitable for the others. I come when I can, but . . ."

Bang, bang, bang. The glass was smeared where Susannah struck it. Salah put his hands on her shoulders, pulled her gently away, and led her to a chair. She was trembling.

"You must not do such violence to yourself. If not for your sake, for the sake of the baby."

"Send me back to England," Susannah muttered, barely audible. "When I get to England I will do whatever you tell me."

Salah sounded quite cross. "In that case you will stay here in this excellent hotel and not be such a child in arms." Then he dialled room service and ordered coffee. "You scarcely seem to realise how lucky you are. Your death sentence was signed, you would have been shot, had I not intervened."

"You shouldn't have bothered."

"And not just kept alive, but here in such style, while others are dying, yes, and barely living in those foul camps."

"I never asked for all this."

"No, and nor did they, but that's where they were born and that's where they had to stay, having no land to go to since your friends took it."

"From all I hear, from what I have seen"—Susannah's voice was steadier and suddenly quite schoolmarmish—"the refugee camps are a great deal better than many of the Arab villages, and just as good as conditions in some of the kibbutzim." (This was a précis of a lecture given by a tame UNRWA Official at a Ladies' Lunch in Streatham.) "Furthermore the camps have been kept artificially in existence by the

various Arab Governments who are not prepared to
take the responsibility for assimilating the poor
wretches who live there. And by all accounts it suits
your lot too because you want to continue to breed
new recruits to your army of murderers and psycho-
paths!"

"So!" Salah was scarlet in the face. He bent forward
stiffly from the waist and overhung her like an outcrop
of rock. "You know all that, do you? You have heard
all that, have you? And from whom I should very
much like to know? From your London friends in their
Whitehall clubs, is that who? From your Harrods
ladies with their little dogs, yes? To whom you want to
return, I am not so very surprised. Well, now you shall
hear it from one who knows, from Abu Salah, born a
Palestinian and ready to die one, if need be. Let us
suppose that they take your country, your beloved
England, away from you, and fill it with your enemies.
And when you say no, no, this is not fair, they slap you
in the face and say if you want to stay in *our* country
you must behave yourself. And when again you say
no, no, why is this, I was not consulted, they say, very
well, go and live in Wales or Scotland or the Isles of
Wight and Man. And you say no, no, this is not just, I
shall fight for my home, so they put bombs in your
home, and bulldoze it to the ground, and say fight for
that by all means, you scum, and laugh and send for
more of your enemies, millions more from all over the
world, to come and take your place. And tear down
your ancient places, your Synagogues, and say, no,
you shall never come back here now, you shall go and
live somewhere else, and your children shall be refugees, and their children. And you look through the
barbed wire and you see them in your homes and
building on your land and tilling your soil. Does that

prospect please you? Do you then become good and obedient children? Do you then say: Oh please let me stay, I shall be no more trouble to you, oh thank you so much, you are very good to me! Is that what you say? I ask you, why do you not answer?"

Susannah was certain that Salah was going to beat an answer out of her with his fists, or tear one out of her with handsful of hair, when there was an obsequious knock on the door and a little brown boy came in with a tray of coffee and a dish of Turkish delight. The interruption was absurd but effective. Salah's momentum was broken, Susannah was not required to answer.

Soon afterwards Salah left, and, within ten minutes of his leaving, a porter arrived to move Susannah's effects—such as they were—into a much smaller room at the back of the hotel. If this was intended as a punishment it was not an effective one, for Susannah had felt herself to be an impostor in that grandiose suite, but in this dingy back room she could stare at the wall without being dazzled by so much space. The gloom was friendly to her. Nor was there the sea, nor were there those airborne silver fish to remind her of other places, other faces, other possibilities, Jamie.

She had not thought of him since she recorded that ludicrous tape; subsequently she had obliterated him from her mind. Until today when Salah had spoken of 'home', and she had remembered the meaning of the word. 'Home' was Jamie, no doubt about that. And what would Jamie say if she were to arrive suddenly on the porch with a cheerful: "Hello, darling, I'm home"? And how would he look? Smug and superior? Or kindly and forgiving? And when he looked lower, assuming that her condition showed by then, which it didn't but should soon, all hell would break loose. Or would he perhaps—men being curiously innocent in these matters—presume that he was responsible and that that was what had brought her home? Surely not. But if he did, she would have to disabuse him, wouldn't she, because he'd find out in the end, and how in the name of all that was miraculous would she do that? "It wasn't you at all, darling, but an Arab, well a Palestinian, well a Levantine anyway. No, I don't know precisely who. Well, you see, it's rather more complicated than that . . ."

It didn't bear thinking about. On the other hand if there were no guilty and inconvenient swelling of the waist, could she then persuade him that she had been held under duress and forced to make a tape and had managed—as she would have to—by a combination of undaunted courage and brilliant improvisation to escape from their evil clutches and come home—home! —where they both belonged. A happy ending indeed. No doubt the police would want to see her, lots of officials would, and she could say—yes!—she could tell them that she had stayed all these weeks because she was learning so much that might be useful, the names of those responsible, Khalil's whereabouts, information which the Israelis would be gratified to receive, if no one else would. And she'd be invited to lecture about her experiences, and she'd pick up where she left off, and only she would know The Secret.

Ah, but it was not so simple. Supposing she should snap her fingers and that little embryo—I mean, what was it at this stage, only like the bud on a tree, one couldn't argue that it had a personality—could be severed from its supply line so that it withered and died and was disposed of, why then it would all be possible. Escape? Why not? They couldn't watch her all the time. Indeed they scarcely seemed to bother to watch her at all. And there must be a British Embassy somewhere with a nice, plump, paternal Ambassador stumping off for golf most afternoons and wasting his evenings in the casinos. Put like that, it's simple. They must have considered the possibility. Well then, do they know me better than I know myself? If I'm as valuable to them as I seem to be—what must I have cost them in this hotel?—then surely they wouldn't risk, they wouldn't permit . . . And, if I undertake it, a tiny crime against this inconvenient little bud within me, a misconception from the start, originating in violence and despair, and they see that they have failed, will they not put me finally out of the way, as no longer valuable to them, merely an inconvenience and an expense? So I must undertake it soon, I must undertake it now. And if I wait I might grow sentimental and that would never do.

It was dark. Susannah had been lying on the bed for over an hour. There was no doubt that this small room was a comfort. Time passed more swiftly within its compass. Susannah spoke into the telephone.

"Reception?"

"Yes."

"Would you give me room service, please."

"I am sorry, madame."

"What?"

"We have had instructions that madame is not to incur any additional charges. We are most sincerely sorry that this should be so."

Susannah remembered her training, how she and her friends had used to complain about slovenly service in shops and restaurants, the casual discourtesies that were so infuriating to women of her class, remembered particularly Myra, the wife of that property man, whose voice raised in anger was sufficient to turn milk to junket. How odd to think of Myra now! How angry Myra would have become with all those men who had invaded her body, taken her for granted. Myra would have seen them off! Once Myra had taken her on a shopping expedition for linen sheets and a new winter coat, and she had listened in amazement and admiration to Myra in full cry. She summoned up the spirit of Myra.

"How dare you?" she and Myra's spirit cried together into the mouthpiece. "Who the hell do you think you are?"

"Madame, we—"

"I want none of your excuses. There can be none. Put me through to room service, or, if you want to make an issue of it, to the British Embassy."

"But, madame—"

"That's enough now, do as I say."

"Very well, but madame must appreciate the position. It cannot be allowed again. Putting you through."

"Room service."

"Two bottles of gin."

"*Two* bottles, madame?"

"Two bottles."

"Gin?"

"At once. Do you hear me?"

Gin. That's how it was done. That's what they'd said at school. Gin and a hot bath. And in all those books, and in all those films, it was a cliché, a cheap cliché, and, what's worse, according to all those books and films, it rarely worked. Nevertheless.

The gin arrived. A nervous boy with huge eyes held the two bottles out to her on a tray, like a pilgrim offering his all to a holy man. She wrapped the bottles in her towel and took them to the bathroom.

The water had to be hot. That much she remem-

bered. As hot as she could bear it. And constantly re-
newed. She turned on the tap, undressed, and studied
herself in the mirror until the glass misted over. She
didn't look like a woman to whom such things had
happened. Her skin was very white, her nipples very
dark. Darker than usual? Oh, yes. No other signs of
pregnancy. She looked . . . anonymous, and then the
steam obliterated her. She lowered herself into the
water.

It was too hot. The pain was frightful. She half-
raised herself out of the water; her skin was crimson.
When she could hold herself out of the water no longer
she lowered herself gently back in, and the pain clutched
at her again from all sides.

Well done, girl. Now for the reward. Perhaps she
should have started on the gin before she got into the
bath, that way she would have been bolstered against
the worst of the pain. She unscrewed the cap, held the
bottle-neck to her mouth and swallowed the alcohol as
though it were lemonade. At once she was coughing
and choking and tears flowed from her eyes. She
tossed her head back and took another swig.

If it worked, she would leave as soon as she was
strong enough to leave. They wouldn't be expecting
that. She would have to avoid the front lobby. They
would have someone there for certain. But there must
be other ways. Where the tradespeople delivered the
food, the fuel, the . . . babies! She laughed aloud at
that. Not much of a joke, but it was good to laugh.
Then she'd leap into a cab, not the first one—those
films again, the cabbie turns his head, and, as he does
so, we see with a shock of recognition that he is none
other than our old friend Carl, and in his hand there
sprouts a gat, a rod, a Webley automatic.

The bath water was cooling down; top it up. The

gin was only a quarter gone, and there was another
bottle yet unopened. Take another draught. The tips
of her fingers had started to pucker, she had been so
long in the water, but nothing else had happened, no
breakaway movements, no buds coming out, my Guard,
but she was witty tonight!

And sleepy. Goodness, that was something to be
watched for. Lying sleepily and mildly tipsy in a luke-
warm bath—and not a very full one, seeing as how the
water seeped away around the plug—would butter no
parsnips. More hot! More gin!

But nothing happened. After a while the water ran
cold and refused to run hot again. By then Susannah
had started on the second bottle of gin, but was feeling
so strange that she had difficulty finding her mouth,
and gin trickled between her breasts into the water. By
now the taste of the stuff nauseated her, and the whole
operation was degenerating into farce. She tried to pull
herself upright, but was overcome with dizziness and
slumped back into the water. She took hold of the
empty gin bottle and beat her stomach with it; water
splashed everywhere, and, at the third blow, the bottle
caught the side of the bath and shattered into fragments.

"Oh, but this is hopeless!" she exclaimed aloud,
and dragged herself over the end of the bath, giggling.
The room and the bath began to buck like a rodeo steer
and, although Susannah hung on as resolutely as she
could, she was soon tipped off on to the floor, landing
on some broken glass which lacerated her buttocks. At
once it occurred to her that this way salvation lay, and
she hunted amongst the green stained fragments of gin
bottle for a sliver that was long and sharp enough to
do the job. There wasn't one. After another gulp or
two from the remaining gin bottle, Susannah smashed

that one also against the side of the bath, and found
herself holding the ideal abortifacient. But it was not
easy. There was the problem of balance. Perching with
her legs apart on the bathroom stool would have been
precarious enough sober; in her present condition it
was out of the question. Glass littered the floor. The
edge of the bath was the only remaining surface, and
that would not be still. Susannah hung on grimly for
a while with both hands, and discovered that, by taking
deep breaths, she was able to control the bucking somewhat, enough at least for her to be able to let go of the
rim of the bath with one hand and grasp the broken
bottle.

Experimentally she opened her legs. It must be down
there somewhere, yes, there it was, sneaky old thing.
Ugly too. Why they made so much fuss about it, heaven
only knew. And—oh God, this was going to be nasty.
If anyone had told her that one day she was going to
find herself drunk in the bathroom of a Beirut hotel
doing this with a broken gin bottle, she would have
slapped their face hard, and they would have deserved
it, what's more. If we knew what was in store for us,
if only we knew . . . And look at the condition of the
floor! Just look! Broken glass, gin, blood; kindly leave
this room as you would wish to find it. And she had
always been so meticulous, hadn't she, prided herself
on that, and it was something to be proud of too, when
one saw the way some people lived—it was selfish of
them, all right so they didn't mind, maybe not, but
what about their husbands, their children? And there
was a lot of rubbish written and talked about housework, not such a chore, not if one was organised, not
if one didn't put the thing off. Do it now! That was
the secret. So what was she waiting for? She had the
broken bottle—'give us the tools and we'll finish the

job', who was it said that? Churchill. What tools, what job? Nothing like the one she was engaged upon now, she had no doubt. Couldn't imagine old Winnie sitting on the side of the bath doing himself a mischief with a broken bottle, but there you are, you never knew about people. Every bit as odd for her as for Winnie, just as out of character when you came to think of it.

In with it then, yugh, it was nasty, right in, yugh, and there was a banging at the door, someone banging at the door. How inconvenient! But no, it was *not* inconvenient, now she wouldn't have to go through with it, now she wouldn't have to do it at all.

The bottle fell from her hand, her head dropped between her knees.

"Come in," she whispered, but they needed no invitation, they came in anyway, they had a pass key, they came in. They stared at her humiliation. They took her away.

A new year was born. Or at least delivered, kicking and screaming, with premature teeth and a nasty, twisted expression on its precociously careworn face, into a disinterested world. And with equally little optimism was Great Britain delivered into the Common Market.

All the most optimistic could hope for as they welcomed in 1973 with raised and unbiodegradable cans of chemically constituted beer was that this year, please God, would be no worse than the previous year. But before the cans were lowered, the optimists recalled all the other new years, just as new as this one, when they had hoped the same hope, and seen it grinning back at them from the distorting mirror of history.

"Once," said Jamie, "when Tal was asked for his autograph, he signed Bobby Fischer's name in addition to his own. They asked him why. 'Why not?' he replied, 'I've beaten Bobby so often that gives me the right to sign for him'!"

Jethro smiled. He had left school at the end of the year, and was staying with the rabbi while he considered possible future careers. He wasn't considering very seriously, but his chess had improved.

Jamie continued: "Did you never think of chess as a career? Now that Jim Slater is offering all that money . . ."

"I've thought about it. Yeah. You know what attracts me? It's safe, isn't it? I mean, to spend my life playing games, that can't hurt anyone, can it? The violence is controlled. It doesn't mean anything, and it doesn't matter. Is there any other career in which I could keep my hands so clean?"

"Don't become a rabbi."

"I wondered about writing, but no one can live at that, can they?"

They were playing over the great Fischer/Tal Candidates Tournament Series. Jamie made the moves for Tal, while Jethro played for the scintillating seventeen-year-old Fischer. How like Fischer he was, thought Jamie, the elongated face and figure, the mournful, arrogant, Semitic manner, the nervousness and the loneliness.

"There's always mountaineering. I'd love that. That's clean. The cleanest thing there is. But the only way you earn a living from that is talking about it to people, and you should never talk about mountains."

"Moses found God in a mountain, and Jesus too, according to the New Testament."

Jethro studied the ticklish bishop and pawn endgame for a moment. Then:

"I wouldn't be a doctor either, that's what they all wanted me to be. I'd rather mix with healthy people than sick ones."

"No, not a doctor," said Jamie, "they go mad. They know that there are no cures. Rabbis go mad too. They know there are no answers. They suspect that there's no God."

"If I thought my chess was good enough . . ."

"It *is* an odd game. The king sits cowering in a corner, while the queen goes off and fights for him. Bishops move diagonally, keeping to their own colour, dogmatic to the last. Pawns may occasionally become queens, but more often they get sacrificed after spending their lives guarding more important pieces. They are dispensable. Sex, religion and class on sixty-four squares. That's it in black and white."

"I read," said Jethro, "where the game is a repressed version of Oedipal myth. You try to kill your father at the same time as protecting him from being killed. It's homosexual incest."

"They teach you such things at school?"

"One picks them up."

"What about the queen?"

"I'm not so sure about that." And Jethro scratched where he hoped his beard would be. "But I read in the same article that Bobby Fischer's mother's name is Regina, and that's the Latin for Queen. But the thing I never understand about Freud is—were people Freudian before Freud came along?"

"I can ask you a more difficult one than that. Did people love one another before they had a word for it?"

"Do they now?" Jethro retorted.

And Jamie, alarmed, recommended that they return to chess. Jethro was happy to do so.

"Remember Fischer versus Petrosian in '59? The four marauding queens?"

Jamie smiled. " 'An apocalyptic vision of a world gone mad.' Terrifying! Like Russian music."

"Let's play it over, shall we? That adjourned overnight position? Fantastic!" And Jethro's eyes sparkled.

It was at such moments that Jamie though that he might after all survive. But the two men were not to be left alone to make the best of things in the empty house.

Mrs Klein, Susannah's mother, lived in Hove. She did not make it her habit to visit her daughter and son-in-law, nor require them to visit her. There had been times when meetings were unavoidable, when Jamie's work took him to Brighton and Hove, and Mrs Klein could not resist inviting her worldly whist-playing friends to meet this personable young rabbi, in whose presence she too felt a little more of a woman. He was not the sort of son-in-law to be kept under drapes, and, though it was true that rabbis' pay was woefully inadequate and that Jamie could not therefore keep her daughter in quite the style which Mrs Klein had accustomed her to expect, nevertheless, even in this changing world, a rabbi was a rabbi, and one should be thankful for that.

So far as Jamie was concerned Mrs Klein was a Pharaoh. Every time he came into the presence of that imperious lady, he felt himself to be once more in bondage in Egypt. She had the ability, just by being there, to diminish him; his religious beliefs—never intense at the best of times—became a sham, his private life furtive and degrading, his marriage to Susannah a dishonourable flirtation. How such a woman as Mrs Klein could have excited admiration—let alone passion —in the breast of the dedicated intellectual whose work he had so much admired and for so long, was inexplicable. Equally mystifying was that such a woman could have spawned the delicate and sensitive creature whom he had courted with such joy and wonder. Physically you had to recognise that there were similarities. Both women were tall, long-legged, with the same dark hair, the same brown eyes, even at unguarded moments the same gaucheness of gesture, a sweep of the arm to indicate helplessness in the face of the world's demands, a lowering of the head to indicate obstinate resolution not to be deterred. But spiritually and aesthetically what light years between them!

Jethro was shopping and Jamie was sitting on an upturned box, staring at his notes for *A Modern Midrash* when Mrs Klein came calling. The energy with which she flung wide the door—Jethro had left it ajar—started a current of air, a miniature whirlwind which cascaded Jamie's papers on to the floor. The rabbi, who had stood up when Mrs Klein entered, less from formality than to avoid having the woman tower over him, sat down again. Mrs Klein was waving a newspaper in the air.

"You read this newspaper? Sure you read it! Everyone reads it. You read where they call her a traitor, where they say she drove off with that man, where they say she was—how you put it?—with that Arab? Sure you did. How come people are saying such things? Why do they not regard a mother's feelings? You think *I* do not have feelings, James? You think she is a tiresome middle-aged lady, what does she count? Go on, deny it! You would not, I think, dare to. Well I for one do not believe such stories, and my opinion counts for something surely? So where is she? I do not think you are ignorant, so I come to you, I come to my son-in-law, and I ask it again: where is Susannah, my daughter? Tscha! If you were a man you would have gone after her, why do you not now do so? There cannot be a reason.

"And from all the men in London she would be choosing this man, this man who sits at home and lets them all say such and such terrible things. You believe that she is a traitor? No, that is surely going too far."

Jamie sighed. There was nothing to say. He recognised that there was some justice in her accusations, but he would admit nothing. Best to sit tight, and let her blow herself out. She moved closer to him, towered over him, he could smell her excitement. She seized hold of his hair and tugged it, while he grabbed her wrists and attempted to ease the pressure on his scalp.

"This isn't any good," he gasped, "this sort of thing is useless. It won't undo what's done. It won't bring her back."

Mrs Klein broke away from him, slumped down on a water-logged chair salvaged from the garden, and stared gloomily at a few tufts of black and grey hair in her clenched fists.

"They have killed her. There is no doubt in my mind. Them and you between you. What does it matter she is someone's daughter? She is inconvenient, we will do away with her. Who cares? That is how I think it is."

"No," said Jamie.

"He speaks to me *again*!" cried Mrs Klein triumphantly. "Oh, we are making good progress! He speaks to his mother-in-law, although he does not care to offer her a drink after her long journey. And I see now, looking about me, that all Susannah's things are gone from the house. No doubt you have sold them. No doubt you have got good money. Ah, but that is going too far!"

The telephone rang. Jamie made no attempt to answer it.

"The man is mad," Mrs Klein made mad illustrative gestures in the air. "He's just going to sit there and let it ring."

"Yes," said Jamie.

"Oh, that *is* nice. That *is* considerate. It may be his wife. She may have news for him. She may be at the airport. But he won't even speak to her, that's how much he cares for her. He sits here, having sold her few possessions, and then, if she should wish to speak to him on the telephone, he turns his nose in the air. But I shall speak to her, to my daughter, if you please . . ."

She answered the telephone, but it was a wrong number. She spoke severely to the caller.

"You are like all the rest of them—you have no feelings." And then, replacing the receiver, inquired of Jamie: "Well, what now?" as though he had deliberately engineered the interruption. "What do you propose to do now?"

At which moment Jethro appeared at the door with a shopping bag, and mumbled something about free-range eggs. Mrs Klein clapped her hands together mockingly.

"My! So we have a new Susannah, do we? At once all is clear for those who have eyes to see and a nose to smell. My my! Come and sit by me, my dear, and we shall have a nice chat about James. Do you find him a good husband to you? And your mother, poor lady, does she hit it off with him?"

"Oh Lord," muttered Jethro. Then to Jamie: "I couldn't get any pears, at least not any ripe ones."

This sent the widow into peals of laughter. She put one hand on her chest and gasped for air. Then started laughing again more modestly.

"Ripe pears!"

Jethro said: "I'm off," and went.

"What a charming boy," chortled Mrs Klein, and examined her reflection in the glass of her compact. Jamie would have followed Jethro, but his mother-in-law rose up in front of him like Frankenstein's monster, reactivated by a flash of lightning. "Oh, that is the easy way out, to go after him so, and talk to him about that foolish, middle-aged lady. Besides, my dear, we must not keep this exciting news to ourselves. A religious minister who works always for the young, that he is to get married to one of his boy-pupils, why this is such news to shout from the rooftops! To shout perhaps so that my darling Susannah may hear . . ."

She continued in this style for some time, until she had convinced herself that what she was saying was true; and then became vindictive. Jamie did not defend himself against her attacks but put his hands to his head, as if she were still tugging at his hair. She threatened him. She would, she said, write to each member of the Synagogue Council separately. She would appear on radio and television (she had been invited to do so already, she claimed) and announced that her daughter's behaviour deserved pity and not censure when one considered her tragic domestic situation. She would sue for the furniture and effects. She would drag Jamie through every court in the country. He would not dare to show his face in society. His career would be at an end.

Eventually she left, slamming the door. Jamie remained seated, grinding his teeth.

In the Synagogue Library a Council Meeting was in session, and Item Three on the Agenda—the adminis-

tration of the Day of Atonement Fund in memory of
the child victims—had been reached. In the aftermath
of that appalling day money had poured into a hastily
opened bank account, but there had been no debate as
yet about the use to which the money should be put.
It was generally held that, although the wishes of the
bereaved families were naturally to be considered, the
money should not go directly to those families, who
were not impoverished. More appropriate would be
the erection of some sort of permanent memorial. The
bereaved parents had been invited to attend the Council
Meeting, and Mr Pereira, Jack's father, had come
along as their spokesman. He was a youngish man in
an orange shirt, who ran a small chain of Do-It-Yourself shops in the Rotherhithe and Peckham areas, and
appeared rather overawed by the formal nature of the
proceedings since Old Jacob, in the chair, was such a
stickler for protocol.

There were £80,000 to spend. Old Jacob expressed
the hope that things should not become acrimonious.
The children's memory should inspire them all with a
feeling of brotherly accord, and a determination to do
their duty in the highest traditions of Anglo-Jewry.

The energetic, prematurely grey, doe-eyed rabbi
from Brookline, Massachusetts was the first to come
up with a practical proposal. His name was Lewis
Stronheim, and he fancied that he was to the Liberal
and Progressive Movement what Bernstein was to
music, or Warhol to art.

"I see before me in my mind this room. Just a room.
But such a room! A place of sanctuary, a place of quietude and tranquillity, a place to sit and meditate, away
from the throb and pulse of the global metropolis. It
will not be a purposive, functional-type amenity, as
other rooms are, but a macrocosm of the still, small

voice within the breast of each one of us, a microcosm
of the silent splendour of the spheres."

Impressed, the Council considered this proposal in
quietude and tranquillity while Rabbi Stronheim glowed
before the warmth of their approval. Judith, who had
been taking minutes, and offering surreptitious peppermints to her immediate neighbours, coughed nervously.
People beamed encouragingly at her. She stood up,
moved her pencil a little further from the side of her
shorthand book, moved it back.

Eventually: "I shouldn't want the Committee to
think that I'm in any way . . . that is Rabbi Stronheim,
em, *Lewis's* idea of a *room*"—this word with enormous
emphasis—"is, of course, a super idea, and would be a
valuable addition to our, em . . . and we have, I know,
a *very* considerable responsibility towards those who
find themselves . . . in short, perhaps, something a
little more practical, perhaps? Like, maybe, a *swimming pool*, for instance? That children could swim in?
or something of the sort." A nervous giggle. "Thank
you so much for your attention."

"And thank you, Judith," said Old Jacob, "for your
useful comments. Is it possible, I have to ask myself,
for a swimming pool, if I understand you, Judith, to be
in the true sense a memorial? If I could find an answer
to that one—and it's a knotty one, I admit—then I
feel sure that Judith's criticisms—"

"Oh, I didn't intend any *criticisms*," muttered Judith,
and crammed an anxious peppermint into her mouth.
There was more quietude and tranquillity then, until
the Chairman called upon Mr Pereira, who stood up,
glanced a little defiantly at the Committee, a little un-
easily at the notes concealed in the palm of his hand,
and began:

"Ladies and gentlemen, I am here on behalf of the

mums and dads, on account of they've asked me to
represent them, and, as it were, express their thanks
for this opportunity to, so to speak, perpetuate the
memory of our little kiddies . . ."

For a moment or two he was overcome with emotion and unable to continue. Hattie poured him a glass
of sherry and passed it across the table, but he shook
his head, blew his nose, and, returning his handker-
chief to his pocket, took the opportunity of referring
to his notes.

"Some of us feel, and I don't mind saying that I
count myself amongst that number, that our kiddies
died in vain, on account of we read our papers and
watch our tellies where there's just as much violence as
ever there was. Definitely. And so what we thought
was—though, mind you, a swimming pool would be a
very nice amenity, and so too, I'm sure, would a, em,
room be—that the money should go to the Palestinian
refugees. Oh, I don't want you to get me wrong, we
want the money to go towards rehousing them, because
if the kiddies growing up in those camps don't find
themselves nice places to settle down in, then they're
going to grow up just like the others, hijackers and
that, know what I mean? And then we thought, specially if they knew where the money had come from
and why, if you're with me, then in years to come they
might not bear such grudges in a manner of speaking.
So that's what I've been asked to put to the Committee,
on account of I'm representing the mums and dads,
you understand, not just yours truly, and I hope I'm
not out of order if I say that I hope you'll give it your
full consideration."

Smiling and nodding his head to the Chair, now that
the ordeal was over, Mr Pereira sat down. It was Old

Jacob who took it upon himself to answer for the Committee.

"No, Mr Pereira, you were by no means out of order, and I'm sure we all tender our thanks for your most interesting proposal. I feel certain that I speak for all of us when I say that it was not one that had occurred to us. It is the expressed wish of all the bereaved parents, I am right about that, am I? That is what you said?"

Mr Pereira smiled and nodded and mildly replied:

"We thought, all in all, it would be a good thing to do with the money."

"Well then, it must engage our most serious attention, although I feel myself bound to say—speaking now in a private capacity—that the gift of £80,000 to hoodlums and murderers, those dedicated to the extinction of the Jewish State and prepared to use any means towards that avowed end, seems a somewhat paradoxical gesture to put it no stronger."

"Just to build homes for them, you see," Mr Pereira added, "so they've got a little bit of something to be proud of."

The door opened. Mrs Klein, avenging angel, stood on the threshold.

"They told me you were in Committee," she said, "so let them be in Committee, I said, that is good news, for then all shall hear together what I have come to say. Although I cannot help but notice that my son-in-law, the rabbi, is not present. No doubt he is a little out of sorts." And, although ruled out of order by Old Jacob, she proceeded to tell them about her son-in-law, the rabbi, who, it was plain to see, was no longer fit to hold any post in, goodness knows, a Synagogue.

As a result of Mrs Klein's intervention the matter of the Memorial Fund was referred to a working sub-com-

mittee. All the heart had gone out of the debate. But
under Any Other Business Old Jacob raised the issue
which Mrs Klein had brought to the attention of the
Committee in her engaging way. Lewis Stronheim was
asked if he would mind taking no further part in the
meeting and leaving the Library, since inevitably the
matter of his own future would figure in the discussion.
He did as requested with a spring in his step.

"It is for Jamie's own sake that I feel we should re-
move him from the responsibilities of office. His six
months' leave are almost up and it would be flying in
the face of all the evidence to suppose that he's any
fitter for office now than he was on Yom Kippur. Much
as one hates to heed such a ghastly woman's advice, I,
for one, can see no future for James Arnatt in this
Synagogue."

Jack Cowan, who had been silent during most of the
Committee meeting, except when he presented his
Treasurer's Report—an alarmist report calling for a
tightening of belts all round lest the fabric of the Jewish State of Israel and the fabric of the Synagogue
should simultaneously crumble to dust—requested that
he be allowed to visit Rabbi Arnatt and find out from
the man himself whether or not he wished to continue
to associate himself with the Blackheath and District.
How much more agreeable it would be, he argued, if
Jamie were willingly to resign his position; and, if he
did not, then perhaps after all he should stay on. Who
knew but that news of Susannah, or her reappearance,
would work miracles on the rabbi's state of mind? He's
like the City of London, added Jack surprisingly, he
cannot flourish in a state of continued uncertainty. Old
Jacob nodded his head at that. He had felt for some
time that his own portfolio was top-heavy with specula-
tive equity shareholdings.

Judith supported Jack and thought to herself that she would bake Jamie a cake. However down in the dumps one might feel, it was very difficult not to respond to a well-baked cake with plenty of cherries in it. In her experience, when one had Trouble with Men one could do a lot worse than bake a cake. To tell the truth, the technique had never entirely solved Judith's Troubles with Men, but who was to say that the troubles might not have been overwhelming without cakes?

So a cake was baked, and there never was a cake with more cherries in it, and Jack bore Jamie a gift too, Oistrakh and Stern bowing away like the troopers they were on the Double Violin Concerto. Jack believed that anyone exposed to such music was bound to see some light at the end of the tunnel.

"It's no use," said Jethro, receiving the delegation at the front door, "he'll not see you. He'll not see anyone. He's become very suspicious of visitors."

"Oh dear," said Judith. "I've brought him a cherry cake too."

"Will you tell him we're here," said Jack. "Judith and Jack from the Synagogue."

"It'll do no good, there's no talking to him."

Judith looked around her and spotted the wreckage in the herbaceous border.

"Have people been using this beautiful garden as a dump? What a shame. What a terrible shame! It was Susannah's pride and joy."

"Would you tell him all the same?" Jack asked.

Jamie's head peered out of an upstairs window. Judith was appalled at the ravaged face, the stubble, the neglected hair. She nudged Jack, who glanced up.

"Why hello, Jamie, how have you been keeping?"

"I've brought you a cherry cake, Jamie, nothing like

a bit of home cooking, I always say."

"You're wasting your time," said the rabbi, "the kindest thing to do would be to leave me alone. The boy is looking after me. I think it would be best if you go now." The window shut.

"I told you," said Jethro.

Judith asked anxiously: "Is he always like this?"

"Not all the time. He has good days and bad days. This is quite a good day actually."

"I brought him a record," said Jack. "I thought perhaps music . . ."

"Can't play it," and Jethro gestured towards the radiogram mouldering in the flower bed.

"This is awful," said Judith, "don't you think perhaps a doctor—I mean, I'm sure you're doing your best, but . . ."

"There's nothing a doctor could do. He's not ill. He wouldn't see one anyway. There's only one cure for his trouble, and, if he doesn't hear anything from her soon, I don't know what'll happen." Jethro's voice dropped as he added: "I wish the bloody woman had died in the Synagogue."

"Oh Jethro," said Judith, "is that kind? For all we know she's being held captive somewhere."

"I think she's probably dead," was Jack's view.

"It's awful to think of that lovely young couple . . ."

"Then don't," said Jethro. "And if you'll excuse me, I've got a hell of a lot to do."

"Why aren't you at school?"

"School? It's a bad joke, isn't it? Dead kings . . . I left as a matter of fact. Now go, *please*."

"Will you take the record," Jack asked.

"Okay. Thanks."

"And the cake?"

"No. Not the cake."

To Rabbi Lewis Stronheim, who had never met his predecessor, Jamie Arnatt was a figure of some mystery, almost romance. There were so many conflicting reports. Jacob was uncharitable, declaring that the man had no backbone, no moral fibre, that what one didn't look for in a rabbi was self-indulgence, and that Jamie wouldn't last a week in a merchant bank. Furthermore anyone who made a fool of himself over a pretty woman deserved all that was coming to him. (Jacob spoke as one who had once made a fool of himself over an ugly woman, but that was in the past, and besides the wench was dead.) Jack's theory was that Jamie was a man without a sense of humour, unable to recognise the ridiculous, and therefore particularly vulnerable to tragedy. Judith thought him more sinned against than sinning, and spoke of Achilles in his tent, and Job in his ashes, while Hattie thought it all too sad, and refused to speak of it at all. Obviously he was a man attractive to women, and Lewis, who fancied himself to be similarly advantaged—and had numerous little conquests in Blackheath and District to prove it —identified and sympathised with the unseen Jamie. However, it was chiefly curiosity which impelled him to try his luck where Jack and Judith had so notably failed.

In any case the situation was most unsatisfactory. Until he knew whether or not his contract was to be extended he could make no plans for the future, put down no payment on a house, pay serious court to no English girl. He felt himself to be the understudy going on for the star in the first act. He could put little spirit into his performance if he was not to be playing act two, and the audience, that is to say the congregation, shared his unease.

Having tried without success to telephone for an appointment, he sent Jamie a card suggesting that he visit him the following week "to discuss matters of mutual concern", and hoping that his visit would not be inconvenient.

He was to meet with no greater success than Jack and Judith. Certainly he was admitted into the bare and, to his taste, bitterly underheated, house. He was even brought by Jethro face to face with Jamie, whom he was surprised to find—knowing him to be a youngish man—haggard, unshaven, pouchy and without any of the charisma he had been led to expect. This man was a phantom-rabbi, and you only had to see him to realise that he would never stand in front of the Ark of the Lord again. Poor guy. He really should take himself in hand. Oh wow!

"Who are you?" Jamie asked, and when Jethro explained that Lewis was his temporary replacement and that he had written to say that he was calling added:

"How's it feel to be stepping into a dead man's shoes?"

Said Lewis: "I came here to extend the hand of friendship," accompanying his words with the appropriate gesture.

"Friends," said Jamie, "do not force their friendship upon me. I know why you came. Are you satisfied? Or did you hope to see me confined to my bed, being fed through a straw or something like that?"

"Oh *no*, by no means, Mr Arnatt." Lewis seemed hurt and horrified. "Is there not some little thing I can do to help? I guess this must be an awful time for you."

"Just one thing," said Jamie. "Mind your own business." And stumped off upstairs leaving Jethro to apologise, which the boy did with skill and tact.

"He's not always like this."

"I had no expectation that he would take things so hard. He seems to feel that I have usurped him. It's a tough situation. But, if I may say so, Geoffrey—"

"Jethro, actually."

"You seem to be doing a grand job. You're not falling behind in your studies, I hope? Book-learning is a wonderful thing, and I can't help thinking—though you may consider this controversial—that an active mind is every bit as important as physical fitness. Gosh, when I think of the hours I wasted poring over the funny papers . . ."

There was plenty of this sort of thing, more than enough for Jethro's taste, before Lewis made his effusive farewells.

At Pesach Jamie and Jethro held their *seder*. The mattress did duty for a table, a clean sheet for a tablecloth, and upon the sheet they piled all the traditional Passover props, the lambbone, the *matzos*, the *maror*, the roasted egg and so forth.

For one who had recently come to regard himself as an agnostic, Jethro had been meticulous in his preparations for the occasion. He bought all the provisions with his own pocket-money—he returned religiously home to collect that each week and indeed Jamie had no money to give him—he collected two curries from the India House restaurant, and he even brushed his hair in honour of the Exodus from Egypt.

Jamie sat on the floor in prayer-shawl and hat and solemnly intoned the benediction on the kindling of the sabbath lights, while the smoke from the candles spiralled gently to the ceiling, where it mingled with the spicy aroma arising from the India House curries.

When they reached the passage containing the four questions to be asked by the wise son, the wicked son, the foolish son, and on behalf of the one 'who is unable to inquire', Jethro could not help but feel himself overcome with sadness, partly for Jamie, whose Passover had diminished to this poor travesty, and partly for himself, who knew now that he would never again be a part of a family celebrating such a family occasion. What do *you* mean by this ceremony, asks the wicked son, distancing himself from the family circle and the Jewish tradition. Jethro felt very distant, and wondered if he was therefore very wicked.

There was a repeated knocking at the door.

"Shall I answer it?" asked the boy, but Jamie continued to read as if unaware of the disturbance.

As the tradition required, the door had been left ajar in case Elijah cared to come and claim his glass of wine, but it was not Elijah who marched into the hall, nor did they come for wine, but for Jethro, their son.

"Are you there, Jethro?" shouted his mother.

"Where are you, son?" shouted his father.

And the lawyer, whom they had instructed to accompany them, whispered a word of warning. If they would permit it he would like to handle the situation, which was fraught with intricate legal possibilities, and he advised them (and they were paying heavily for the advice) to do just that.

"I'm sorry," said Jethro in the bedroom to his friend.

"Don't apologise. I expected something of the sort."

"No, but it's humiliating, it really is."

"It's not your fault," said Jamie. "Besides they're quite within their rights. Shall we continue?"

"Perhaps I'd better lock the door. I think I'd better." The rabbi didn't answer and the door didn't lock, but Jethro wedged a chair against it. "Let them do their worst. I don't give a shit."

"They've come to fetch you away from the leper-colony," said Jamie, "away from the walking dead."

The boy smiled. "I've still got my nose and my fingers. I've a good mind to put the two of them together, so they'll know what I think."

Downstairs the lawyer and the parents wandered disconsolately from bare room to bare room, ready for anything, but disheartened by the delay.

"Bloody cold!" exclaimed Jethro's father.

"Imagine him living here," exclaimed Jethro's mother. "And he's always suffered so from chilblains. I do hope he's not taken cold."

The lawyer merely swung his arms about and slapped his sides. Moving upstairs, the trio found all doors open but one. This jammed door, behind which they could hear voices, confirmed their worst fears, although the smell of the curry was confusing.

"Let's hope they've not got squatters in," said Jethro's father.

"Do something," Jethro's mother insisted with such urgency that one might have supposed that whatever it was Mrs Klein had suggested in her letter could happen to Jethro was actually happening at that very moment behind that very door.

"Open up in there," cried Jethro's father, tapping quite gently on the door panels with his knuckles.

"Please leave this one to me," said the lawyer in a hopeless tone of voice.

Jethro's mother was speaking to the door as though it was animate and filial. "We expected you home for the *seder* at least. Uncle Dick and Auntie Jo came specially, and Auntie Meg, *and* Phil Edwards. He came all the way from Waltham Forest, just imagine. At least I think it was Waltham Forest. Anyway it took him a long time because the traffic was so bad, and he's been having clutch trouble."

"I'm not coming out," cried Jethro from the bedroom, "as far as I'm concerned you can whistle for it!"

But the rabbi told him: "It's no use. You'll just make things worse. Better run along."

"But . . ." the boy was close to tears, "but what about the food?"

"I'll eat some of it."

"Promise?"

"Yes. And you can take some of it home. Don't fret. Take one of the cartons. Off you go now."

"That's enough of this nonsense," suggested Jethro's father, kneeling down to spy through the key-hole and feeling a sharp rheumatic twinge in his right knee.

"It's all right. The boy's coming out," said Jamie.

"I'm a lawyer," insisted the lawyer in a loud voice.

But still Jethro was reluctant to go. "It seems like a betrayal. It worries me. You might do anything. You might do something stupid."

"I usually do," said Jamie, "but you'll not be to blame. I exonerate you. You've done your best, God knows."

"Please look after yourself, Jamie, *please*."

"I may. It depends. I may."

"Ruthie said she might be looking in later on," said Jethro's mother. "She's missed you, I expect."

"I really must insist," pleaded Jethro's father.

All the lawyer said was: "This is a crazy way of spending an evening." And Jethro opened the door and emerged on to the gloom of the landing.

"I'll never forgive you," he said.

It was a lethal spring. A Libyan Boeing 727, piloted by a Frenchman and seriously off-course, was shot down by Israeli Phantom jets over the Sinai Desert and more than a hundred people were killed. Said the Israeli Minister of Transport: 'Israel acted in accordance with international precedures, defended its air space and did what was required after serious consideration.' Added General Dayan: 'These are not normal days.'

A week later in Khartoum Black September guerillas, acting without the authority of the Al Fatah leadership, killed one Belgian and two American diplomats before surrendering themselves and their hostages to the Sudanese. The killings were a reprisal for the Israeli devastation of the Cold River refugee camp in North Lebanon.

In London two Pakistanis, just eighteen and twenty years old, forced an entry into India House in the Aldwych and were shot dead by two constables of the Metropolitan Police Special Patrol Group. Constables Canley and Burrows were armed with .38 Webley revolvers, and these proved more efficient than the Pakastani's Super Bangs, brought for 58p from Woolworths. A third Pakistani youth of fifteen, armed with a sword, was overpowered. All were hailed as heroes in their home town of Jaipur.

And two weeks later, on a wonderfully and prematurely warm March afternoon, London had its first licks at the car bomb lollipops; the Old Bailey and the Army Recruiting Office melting tastily to the flavour of gelignite. London, which had swung its way through the swinging sixties, hopped and skipped in the early spring of 1973.

As atrocity succeeded atrocity (and there were others, for the language of gun and bomb was universal), the affair at Blackheath faded into the distant landscape of blurred memory. "Wasn't that the one in which all those children . . . ?" "I thought that was at that school on the West Bank . . ." "No, no, it was in Londonderry surely . . ." "Anyway it was an awful business, no question about that." "Awful, too awful."

Some days a curious knot of spectators would gather outside the Synagogue and point to the celebrated window; if the weather was clement quite a little group might form, but, with the passage of time, things reverted more or less to the way they had been prior to the Day of Atonement. Blackheath and Anglo-Jewry was itself again, suburbia and diaspora.

Jamie was relieved to be on his own again. The chess-games had been a pleasant diversion, but had meant nothing. The endless cups of coffee, the obsessive nosey-parkering, it couldn't have continued, and, on the whole, the rabbi was grateful to Jethro's father and mother for making the divorce absolute. The boy would naturally feel resentful against his parents, which was as it should be, but he would harbour no grudge against Jamie. He would probably leave home, and work things out for himself, and remember Jamie with affection and a touch of embarrassment. Most likely he would move on to college or university, find a role, find a girl, find some peace of mind. Jamie hoped that he would continue to play chess.

The rabbi had no visitors now. Mrs Klein had returned self-righteously to Hove, where she chatted to herself about the boy she had rescued from a fate worse than death. The gulls cackled gleefully, and Mrs Klein hurled hard little lumps of biscuit at them.

Lewis's permanent appointment at the Blackheath and District was confirmed, and he celebrated by proposing marriage to two local girls, finding their English accents and compliant habits irresistible, but both were too startled to consider accepting such an offer, whereupon Lewis fell ever more in love with them. He wrote home that English girls were 'proud'; he did not understand that they would have been satisfied with a great deal less than he was prepared to offer.

Ruth might have been sympathetic, but she studiously avoided the Synagogue, and all functions which it sponsored, for fear that she might meet Jethro, who, coincidentally had no wish at all to see her. Since posing for the *Honey* photographs, Ruth had received several offers to pose for other magazines, and, through the good offices of a kindly photographer, she came to specialise in 'erotic schoolgirl' postures, for which she was generously rewarded. She added two years to her age, acquired an agent and a split personality, for at home and at school she could not have been more demure. Ten per cent of her earnings she sent anonymously to Oxfam, and she started a novel, set in crusading days, whose heroine was haughty and heartless, and refused to entertain any of the romantically inclined Christians who came to call.

Jack and Judith made no attempt to repeat their disastrous visit to the rabbi's house, and, since the police and the press had other businesses with which to concern their busy little minds, Jamie properly considered that the enemy had been thoroughly routed. Only trouble was Jamie found himself increasingly subject to uncontrollable fits of weeping. Everything made him weep. A bird on a twig, a cloud in the sky, a half-empty corned beef tin, and off he would go, blubbing like a child. He would be lying down or sitting or standing up, doing nothing in particular, and the tears would start to flow, and he could do nothing to staunch them. The tears had motives of their own, it seemed, and in due course he let them plop on to the floor, for they were harmless enough.

He tried not to think about Susannah, but one night he dreamed that she was dying and needed a blood transfusion, and his blood was the only blood that would do. Only trouble was that whenever the nurses tried to take the blood from his veins, it splashed all over the floor and couldn't be collected in the take-away curry cartons set aside for the purpose.

He woke up (crying of course) convinced that Susannah was still alive. And there was no reason why she should not be; a dead hostage is poor currency. He hoped that she was not distressed or in pain, and hoped moreover that she would not return to trouble him. She might have gone mad, and he would not like a mad woman about the house. Yes, she surely must have gone mad, and, since she had not been mad when he met her—a perfectly sane intermediary between her dotty mother and himself—or when he married her— apprehensive, as any girl would be, and highly strung, and charmingly romantic in a world of bottomless cynicism—it followed that he must have driven her mad.

She had been considered fortunate, he knew, by women in the congregation, whose husbands drank and gambled, whored and flirted in the office; yet most of these women had retained their reason. They had cooked and run their houses and raised money for charity and children for their old age in the manner of sane women. Would he have driven them mad if he had married them? If so he was a monster, and mon- sters must not be allowed to live. Well, he had not been a willing monster, but he was just as destructive a mon- ster for all that. Indeed few monsters were willing ones, most of them being handsome princes under the spells of wicked fairies.

He turned to the Bible for instruction. It opened at Numbers, a page full of begetting. He tried again:

> "Who can find a virtuous woman? for her price is above rubies.
> The heart of the husband does safely trust in her, so that he shall have no need of spoil.
> She will do him good and not evil all the days of her life.
> She seeketh wool, and flax, and worketh willingly with her hands.
> She is like the merchants' ships; she bringeth her food from afar . . ."

(He remembered with a pang Susannah's cooking; not just the intricate flavours, but the presentation of it. She could make a feast out of mashed potatoes. And when, since Jethro left, had he eaten except from a tin? The tears flowed and plopped on to the fine Indian paper of the Bible.)

> "She openeth her mouth with wisdom; and in her tongue is the law of kindness.
> She looketh well to the ways of her household, and eateth not the bread of idleness.
> Her children arise up, and—"

Was that it? Had she wanted them so much, and never said? Had it been secretly with her for all these years, nibbling at her when she was busy with other things, biting at her when she was lying awake at night? Was that it? It was just the sort of thing that could drive a woman mad. There were plenty of cases of it. The cheap papers were full of them, baby-snatchers and foster-mothers who wouldn't let go. If it is that, thought Jamie, then it is not entirely my fault that my wife is mad. But she never hinted, never for a moment suggested . . .

> "Her children arise up, and call her blessed;
> her husband also, and he praiseth her.
> Many daughters have done virtuously, but thou
> excellest them all.
> Favour is deceitful and beauty is vain; but a
> woman that feareth the Lord, she shall be
> praised."

And then Jamie thought of that other woman, the one about whom he had preached with such fervour in the Synagogue on New Year's Day.

"Blessed above women shall Jael the wife of Heber the Kenite be, blessed shall she be above women in the tent."

Susannah had accused him of hypocrisy; she had claimed that he was striking attitudes, that he did not believe in revenge. She had insisted—and this was what had stung—that he had written his sermon so that she should approve of it.

". . . with the hammer she smote Sisera, she smote off his head, when she had pierced and stricken through his temples."

And now that she had shown him so clearly what she thought of him, it was up to him to prove that she had been wrong, that he had merely been biding his time until an opportunity presented itself. Well, well, there had never been a better opportunity than now, never had he had less to lose.

"And the land had rest forty years."

He had been born unlucky. Too young to fight against Hitler, he had swung his little fists against those of his school-mates who had sent him to the concentration camps of their contempt, and then had turned and run (though they crept back with reinforcements later, and beat him into a more Christian frame of mind). But it was no substitute for war, and he would have willingly risked his life in defence of Israel (Susannah had been wrong about that. She should never have suggested that he had been dilatory, nor implied that he had been cowardly), only the war had been over in six days, and would have been concluded just as satisfactorily even if he had not led the prayers for a successful outcome. Born unlucky, and punished for it, but now granted the astonishing opportunity of a second chance. It was like waking up and finding yourself ten years younger. He was resolute.

And as soon as he made up his mind the tears stopped. It was cold in the house, which he now saw to be pitifully neglected; the cupboard was bare. He entered the garage and sat in the Volkswagen. The engine fired at the first time of asking. When even machinery fell in so tidily with his plans, there could be no doubt that he was acting for the best. It was strange nonetheless that the course of a man's life should depend upon such a whimsical thing as the retentive juices of an old car battery—a man's life and a woman's. Had we so little control to direct our own destinies? He had been trained to believe otherwise. But every day men, women and children, even children who had had no chance to direct anything, were being blown to fragments, or shot to pieces, or burnt to ashes, simply because they happened to be in the wrong place at the wrong time.

He drove down Shooter's Hill into the gloom of New Cross. Even there the sun emblazoned occasional grubby bushes of almond and double cherry. But in the Old Kent Road a cyclist had been knocked down by a bus. They had rested his head on his saddle-bag and covered him with a woman's overcoat from a nearby second-hand clothes shop.

"Let's get this thing done," said Jamie aloud, "with as much dignity and despatch as possible. That at least I have the right and the obligation to do."

There was Salah, and there was Khalil, and there was another she had not seen before. They were angry with her. Khalil was surly as he always had been, but Salah was scarcely recogniseable as the smooth-talking charmer she had once known. The other one was swart and fresh-faced with dark-rimmed glasses and a habit of running his tongue over his lips. He looked pleasant.

They were angry with her because she had told them she didn't want to visit any more refugee camps. (They always expected her to look shocked and make appropriate comments, but she had seen much worse in Gateshead and Glasgow.) And they were doubly angry because when she advanced tiredness and swollen feet as her excuse for not going, as she had done on this occasion, they had to concede defeat. In fact, her pregnancy, now thoroughly self-evident, had been a trouble-free affair, as though the embryo thrived on Susannah's distaste for it. Like a tiresome house-guest, who made Susannah aware of its presence every minute of the day, the sprouting creature caused her no physical inconvenience or discomfort; it was just a nuisance. And apparently it enjoyed hot baths and gin, welcomed a bit of knockabout fun with a broken bottle.

Since that interrupted débâcle Susannah had been closely supervised; she was accompanied even when she bathed, slept or defecated. And she was removed from her room in the Carlton to a first-floor flat with shuttered windows.

A few days after her gin-sodden evening she had been visited by an Arab doctor who poked and prodded, peered and pried, and pronounced her quite fit, and her baby apparently flexing its biceps and ready for anything. Other visitors had been infrequent.

When Khalil returned from his exploits in Bangkok, he visited her, but made no attempt to socialise, simply handing her three sheets of paper, messily typed and clumsily stapled. It was a list of the names and addresses of eminent Britons, and it did not take Susannah long to realise what it was that this store magnate, this merchant banker, this press lord and this Member of Parliament, this bookmaker, this furniture manufacturer and this racehorse owner had in common, besides money.

"Well?"

Susannah had studied the list more closely. Old Jacob was on it. A youngish cinema producer who had once escorted her to the première of a classy erotic film (and learned little from it to judge by his behaviour in the taxi on the way home—so clumsy, so crass!) was on it. A tame psychiatrist and an elder statesman noted for his patronage of homes for spastic children was on it. The Chairman of a huge chain of stores was on it. A television actor, who specialised in characterising policemen and had begun to imagine that he was one, was on it. Bankers were there, and city men in profusion. Eventually Susannah had commented:

"I don't think much of the typing." And Khalil had been predictably angry. He had left the list with her, instructing her to tick off those she knew slightly and put an asterisk against those she knew well. She had

not done so. She had done nothing. And here was
Khalil returned with Salah and the young one.

It was evening, and rain was beating against the shutters. The central bulb was the only source of light in
the room and it seemed rather to absorb light than dis-
tribute it. There were mosquitoes. The faces of the
men were shadowy, the whites of their eyes shone,
and their teeth glinted when they smiled, which they
did rarely. They handed round a packet of dates, and
wedges of bread with goats' cheese. They did not offer
Susannah any. The young man unfolded a copy of *Al
Hurriya* and drew the attention of the others to an
article on the front page. Salah explained to Susannah:

"Your Israeli friends grow bolder and bolder. There
have been raids on the camps at Sidon and Chatila.
President Frangié does nothing. The cartoonist here
pictures him in bed with Golda Meir and Hussein,
while Nixon is spying on them through the keyhole. To
tell you the truth, we are losing our patience . . ."

Khalil said abruptly: "You know what we've come
for, baby?" Susannah knew well enough, but said that
she didn't.

"You gotta earn your bread now. Those people on
the list . . ."

"I don't know them. They're just names."

"The President of your Synagogue, just a name?"

"Oh, is he there?"

"You've had the fucking list a week, right?"

"I'm no use to you, Khalil. What can I tell you?"

"This Lawrence Harris, you know him?"

"No."

"And Roy Lippmann?"

"No."

"And Sir Michael Cohen?"

"Everyone knows about him."

"We don't. We would like to, but we don't."

"Well, he makes ice cream, and he's on the board of Covent Garden, and he collects porcelain or jade or something like that."

"You met him?"

"Not to speak to."

"How many kids?"

"I don't know. Two or three."

"Four," said Khalil contemptuously, and muttered something to the young man, who licked his lips and nodded vigorously.

"Sir Simon Green?"

Susannah remembered Sir Simon Green. Jamie had conducted his eldest son's barmitzvah when he had been on attachment to a very grand cinema (a joke of Jamie's; the rich luxurious Synagogues he called 'cinemas') in the West End. Sir Simon had been impressive in vicuna. Very relaxed for such an important man. They had visited his country place. Rose gardens, Blue Rider paintings, and a thoroughbred stallion which snorted disdainfully at the nervous rabbi and his solemn-eyed young wife. Sir Simon had canvassed Jamie's advice about a proposed business take-over; he hoped to be reassured that what appeared ruthless to the world at large would be acceptable to God. Jamie duly reassured him—what was the history of the Jews if not one grand take-over?—and returned home with a Coutts cheque made out to the Friends of Zion.

"Did you meet him?"

"A long time ago." (He had had this huge wife, and a daughter who was getting ready for a dance, and wearing a Gina Frattini dress which glowed like the wings of a giant butterfly.)

"And you'd recognise him?"

"Probably."

"And he'd recognise you?"

"I doubt it."

"Your picture has been in the papers." She had not considered that. And, if Sir Simon had seen it, Jamie would have seen it, and everyone, and they'd all have been discussing her, and . . . Her picture in the papers, no, she had not thought of that.

"Then I suppose he would."

"Kids?"

"Three, I think." Yes, three. Jamie had been impressed with them. Very natural, he had said, whatever that meant.

"Ages?"

"The oldest would be . . . maybe nineteen."

"Good. Keep right on."

She told them more about Sir Simon. When she had told them all she could remember, and they still seemed dissatisfied, she invented things. She gave Sir Simon a chauffeur-driven Mercedes. And a reputation for sharp practice at the backgammon board. Then she moved on to other names. Some she knew and admitted knowing. Some she pretended to know. Some, whom she knew, she denied knowing. She hoped they would not ask her to go through the list again. She would never remember what she had said. When they were halfway through the list Salah handed Susannah the packet of dates. They appeared pleased with her. It's like charades, Susannah thought. The swart young man licked his lips; Khalil made notes on the typed sheets of paper. The rain assaulted the shutters. Susannah ate dates.

And the gunmen moved in.

These gunmen were not like the other gunmen, and yet there were similarities. They were young, their skins were toughened by exposure to the sun, their sensibilities by ruthless training. They wore no marks of identification, and knew little of each other's backgrounds, although they knew a great deal about each other's strengths and weaknesses. Three of the gunmen had been Nazi-hunting in Latin America, a strenuous sport requiring improvisational skills, because Nazis are not as easy to identify as other big game, more adept at concealing their tracks, though just as dangerous at bay. Like tigers and elephants and bison, they are a doomed species, nor is there any pressure group dedicated to their preservation. One of the gunmen was an agent from the West; or at least he had been trained in Arizona. And several of them were patriotic Israelis who found life on the kibbutzim a little slow, and the contribution they were making as fruit pickers and canners to their country's survival unfulfilling. They were as a group more sophisticated than those other gunmen, but their task was simpler, for their presence in the Lebanon was not entirely unwelcome to the French-speaking Maronite authorities, a body of men as rich as they are pragmatic. Nonetheless these sophisticated young gunmen did not think it politic to advertise their entrance into the country. The rules of the game were there to be observed, and these rules included the forging of Dutch and German, British and Belgian passports, and the authenticating of detailed personal biographies. They arrived in Beirut over a period of weeks, stayed in fancy hotels, visited the casinos, hired cars, tasted the excellent food available in that tastiest of countries, in other words lived most unobtrusively before coming together for a final briefing in a chic winter sports centre on the slopes of Mount Hebron.

They relished the easy life for as long as it lasted.

Such treats were not available in Israel, at least not for the residents, and it was, no question, all in a good cause. So they ate and they drank and, unlike those other gunmen, they were merry, as only those who expect and maybe intend to die young can be merry, and then most of them made for the Headquarters of the Democratic Popular Front for the Liberation of Palestine in the refugee camp of Sabra, where they made their killing. But a smaller splinter group, two of the Nazi-hunters and a young kibbutznik, drove coolly along Verdun Street, past the army barracks where a bunch of students with placards proclaiming in Arabic: 'The Lebanese Security Forces—in collusion with the Enemy!' were keeping themselves warm with nips of alcohol and shouted slogans, to the house which contained Khalil and Salah and the young man who licked his lips and Susannah Arnatt, rabbi's wife from Blackheath.

And they shot the door down, and there were the three Palestinians, one each, and there was no mistake about it. Khalil's eyes were on Susannah as he lurched over. Was he recalling another occasion eight months ago to the day when he and his storm-troopers . . . when Susannah . . . when . . . ? Ah, but it had been tougher for Khalil than for these glamourous young Sabras. Had he been permitted to shoot and kill, it would have been child's play. Or did he recall, before his sad eyes glazed over, more recent events in Bangkok? Shots had been fired there too; straight and lethal. Having lived with death for so long, Khalil should not have been so reluctant to die, for he was reluctant, and angry it seemed. "Shit" he muttered as he went down, and "Fuck" venomously before he went out. Strange how fiercely this freedom fighter fought against eternal freedom.

Salah went down in style with a smile on his lips, and a twinkle in his eyes. Or was it just an illusory smile, a reflex twinkle, caused by some muscular contraction, some physiognomical quirk? His right hand went to the place where the bullets entered his chest—the urgent gesture of a man who fears that his wallet has been pinched—and blood poured out between his fingers as he fell, soiling the tweed jacket with the side vents, of which he had been so vain. And the smooth skinned, swart young man with the spectacles, who was so new to the business of killing and even newer to the business of being killed, did he die well, bravely, savagely, ironically, wistfully, or with hatred in his heart? He was only just a week out of training and, in all his fifteen years, he had never seen a corpse. He was an intellectual. He liked Camus particularly. He licked the blood from his lips just before he died. He looked fed up.

Susannah was separated from the three doomed Palestinians by the width of the room. The killers glanced at her before they shot down their targets. She was in half-profile to them; they could clearly see that she was pregnant. What she saw was their bleached jeans, and their open-necked shirts with the white T-shirts under them, and the expression on their faces, intensity like the intensity of a pianist wrestling with a testing passage in a big concert hall or the intensity of a tennis player striving to make an impossible shot. They looked handsome. And a little surprised, for evidently their briefing had led them to expect nothing of this sort. Their guns wavered, but then did their duty. As soon as the shooting was over—and it was over in a couple of seconds—Susannah said absurdly:

"I'm English," and stretched her arms out wide to show she was. One of the gunmen muttered something

to the others in Hebrew, and they were gone. Susannah
was left with the dying and the newly dead, her arms
absurdly apart.

To reach the door she had to step over the body of
Salah. As she did so she said "Sorry", before continuing on her way. Her teeth were chattering, her body
was shaking convulsively, and she was muttering:

"Oh God, oh no, oh God, oh no," with violent in-
halations between the words. Reaching the street she
was violently sick. People glanced at her and passed
on. She began to walk, then to trot, then to run with
the wind and the rain in her face. She ran downhill,
carrying her great burden clumsily, past hotels and
restaurants and brightly lit shop-fronts; at length she
reached the sea.

"What's up?" asked a middle-aged American in a
blazer with naval buttons. "You look done in."

"I'm fine," Susannah gasped improbably, "but can
you direct me to the British Embassy?"

"Sure thing. I'll walk you there myself."

"No!"

"As you please, ma'am. You just keep right on."
And he pointed along the cliff-top. "Are you sure
you're okay?"

The Prison Governor at Holloway—they would
have called her the Governess only that conjured up
images of cosiness and crêpe—had been reluctant to
let Alia go.

"A girl like that," she explained, "has had so little
in her life. I believe we could make something of her
given a chance. I should like to take her around a bit,
introduce her to an *alternative* way. It is only we, the
lucky ones, who can afford alternatives. What chance
will she have in Gartree? And regarding the security

aspect, she is safe enough here, indeed I very much doubt whether she would want to leave, at least for a while longer. And in any case which one of us *is* safe these days? There are no longer warrens and burrows, you know, to be had anywhere. If you take that poor girl away from me to Gartree it will be equivalent to taking an arsonist to an arsenal. Maximum security they call it, I believe. Maximum risk would be nearer the mark. And does nobody but me consider the girl's soul?"

Despite all the Governor's protestations, the Home Office had its way, indeed there never had been any doubt but that it would. The Governor had tried it on, but ultimately had had to content herself with choosing Alia's pretty blue dress from Richard Shops and smiling her on her way.

Jamie had supposed that the girl was still in Holloway and, after buying himself a sober suit of clothes and a rabbinical haircut, repaired thence. The Governor received him with the courtesy befitting a religious minister, offering him home-made Swiss roll and a cup of Earl Grey tea in her sitting-room before inquiring his business. He had prepared his story.

"You heard about my wife, Susannah? You saw her picture in the papers? Rumour insists that she defected to the Palestinians. Well, one can't live all those years with a woman and not learn *something* about her, and I am as certain as anyone can be that Susannah would not have behaved in such a way. And that is why I came to you. It was no use sitting at home all day and feeling sorry for myself."

"Well, I'm very *flattered*," remarked the puzzled Governor, wondering what was the correct way to address a rabbi and anticipating a request for permission to do some prison visiting. It was commonplace for public figures to approach her with such requests. The Governor of Wormwood Scrubs had told her that he too was badgered in this way, but not to the same extent as she was, "unless we have a particularly notorious inmate". There seemed to be a glamour attaching to women in prison—indeed they had frequently been made the subject of highly suggestive films—and she had learned to accept such offers philosophically. No doubt the visitors derived benefit from the exercise, and it rarely seemed to harm the prisoners, who only took exception in the case of one well-meaning peer. He bored them so acutely with tales of his benevolence and their essential worthiness ('*Nobody* is beneath my notice!' he would cry, fixing some unhappy shoplifter with a beady but hypnotic stare) that it was rare indeed for a prisoner to enjoy more than one visit from him without raising shrill objections.

At first the rabbi did not disappoint her.

"You have a prisoner," he said, "in whom I have a particular interest."

Was it the baby-snatcher, the Governor wondered, or the sex murderess? Odds on it was one of the two.

"She is bound to have information regarding the whereabouts of my wife. I ask permission to visit her and see whether I cannot elicit some information from her which will simplify my search."

"You must be referring to Alia," said the Governor, mentally ticking herself off for cynicism, "but I'm afraid you are in for a disappointment. The girl has been removed. She is no longer with us. And furthermore she speaks scarcely any English, so you would find an interview with her rather fruitless. Another slice of Swiss roll?"

"No, thank you!" the rabbi cried with great vehemence, "but you will kindly tell me where she has been removed to."

"I'm not at all sure I can do that. You must understand that this is a matter of top security."

"It's a matter of my wife! Have I got to go down on my knees to you?"

Alarmed that he was about to carry out this threat, and extremely sorry for the nice-looking young man, who was obviously having such a time of it, she suggested that he make his request to the Home Office, and gave him a letter of introduction to Stewart-Taylor, who would help him there if anyone would. The rabbi took the letter and was gone, leaving the Governor so concerned over his abrupt behaviour that she trotted off to spend a restorative evening with her favourite prisoner, a compulsive prostitute of notable hideousness, who would reassure her that she had behaved in a Christian manner, and regale her with lurid anecdotes of Soho nights.

Sir Bertram Kidlington, British Ambassador in Beirut, had been playing golf. He was a heavy, dozy man, born into a political family, but too idle, or perhaps too humorous, to take politics with a proper seriousness. Even his relatives had to pull out all the stops to have him adopted for a somnolent Shropshire constituency, and he found the whole business of getting himself elected vulgar and enervating. Rejected in Shropshire, Bertram found that the Diplomatic Corps was less particular, and he was sent to Geneva where he headed a League of Nations committee inquiring into the white slave traffic in the Middle East. In those days he sported an opulent ginger beard—shaving was *such* a shag—but, by the time he was appointed HM Ambassador to the Lebanon, the beard was tinged with

grey. The Lebanese mistook his indolence for wisdom
and were moved almost to tears by his girth and his
benevolent, hirsute presence.

When his golf was over, Bertram changed out of
his drenched and odiferous plus-fours into an old pair
of corduroys and hurried back to the Embassy to check
whether the telex had yet recorded the result of the
Stone's Ginger Wine Steeplechase, and found instead
a grubby, bloodstained and eight months pregnant
English woman sitting in the lobby. The poor thing
was white as a sheet and shaking all over in a most
distressing manner. Consequently Bertram, who would
normally have left such routine matters to his highly
responsible underlings, invited Susannah into his office
for a chinwag and a whisky mac.

"Damn," he said, glancing at the telex as he passed,
"second is no bloody good." And then to Susannah:
"Now don't tell me, my dear, let me guess. You've
lost your ticket and you're out of funds, and England
seems a long, long way away. Am I right, eh?"

Susannah nodded. The story was just as probable
as any she could have concocted, and she was in no
mood to contradict. Images of the dead and dying
filled her head; the smell of blood and the taste of
vomit.

Bertram, who had defeated a wily, Beirut antique
dealer on the last green, was chuffed with his expertise
at this game too.

"Well, don't let it upset you, my chicken, England is
not a long way off, in fact you're already there. Just a
few formalities and we'll have you home in a jiffy.
Husband called back to England on business, was he?
Heartless old sausage what with you in your—oh,
pardon me, pay no attention, I'm just a tubby old
bachelor, I don't know a thing about all that. You

shouldn't be in bed, should you? I mean it's not, em, imminent, is it?"

Susannah shook her head, and managed a wan smile.

"Thank God for that," Bertram exclaimed, pouring two more drinks, "not that I don't like babies, but . . . Now let me see, here am I rabbitting on, and no doubt you're thinking who's this fatty I've landed myself with, when what I should be doing is getting you to fill out some forms and all that sort of rot. When in doubt, fill up a form, that's what they teach you out here—oh Lord, where *has* Crispin put them, he is such a ninny, but his mother was the toast of Ludlow, although what that has to do with the price of eggs is a different matter. Where was I? Ah yes, *bumf*. No sooner said than done." And he handed her some dog-eared papers in his huge, hairy paws.

There was nothing for it but to do as he requested. Only trouble was that she had the greatest difficulty in focussing her eyes, and her hands were shaking so violently that she could scarcely grasp the pen. She did the best she could, writing anything, while the Ambassador rattled on.

"I'll just make a call to some chums at the airport, see if we can't fix you up for tomorrow, old fruit, and then, if you feel up to it, I'll take you to a place where they serve a really smack-up steak and kidney pud, one that coats the tummy, if you're with me." But suddenly behind the beard the face sagged. "Or at least they did once, but now I remember the manager left, and God knows what sort of grub they're serving now. Can't trust anyone these days, and all this talk of food's got the old juices going, don't you know? By the way, I've suddenly thought, what about passports and all that balls, you do have yours, do you? Some kids, well, you wouldn't believe it, but they sell their

passports and they sell their blood and that's not all
they sell if half the stories I hear are true, which I
dare say they're not. But it's a bit off, selling your pass-
port, I mean, don't you agree?"

Susannah said faintly: "I lost mine. With the tickets."

"Well, you are a silly old chicken, aren't you, and
no doubt I'm a gullible old goose, but, oh—give me
those!" And he grabbed the forms without looking at
them. "And we'll get ourselves a bit of grub."

He took her to Uncle Sam's and ordered her a ham-
burger and a milk-shake, but she could neither eat nor
drink, being haunted still by the images of death. She
saw Sir Bertram's jolly, chewing face as through gauze,
and his words were blurred and indistinct, as though
his battery was fading. She lurched forward on to the
table, and brought it, and the food upon it to the floor,
where she lay amidst meat and milk and relish. To an
observer it must have appeared as if the top of her
head had been blown off or that she had been the victim of some similar assault, so much more gruesome
was the metaphor than the reality of death.

With the help of his Muslim housekeeper Bertram
nursed her. She lay in bed for a fortnight, during which
time the Ambassador asked her no questions, but was
content to sit by the bedside and reminisce about
scandalous happenings in the corridors of power. One
evening he played her selections from Ivor Novello on
the untuned embassy piano, whose white keys were
yellowing with age and neglect, singing the words to
her in a flat but sincere baritone:

> "Fly home, little heart,
> Although the way be long,
> Your wings are brave and strong
> Fly home where you belong.

I know, little heart,
How lonely you must be
So far across the sea.
So fly, little heart,
Fly home to me."

On other evenings he would pour himself a scotch and soda, make Susannah a cup of cocoa, and read to her from *Persuasion*. Against all expectations Susannah found herself entirely involved in Anne Elliott's progress. Far from finding her small-mindedness irritating and her confusion—for what did it really matter which of these wet young men she chose to spend her life with?—ridiculous, she found herself greatly touched by Anne's misery and much concerned for her happiness. "How much more straightforward," she said to Bertram, "it is to care for imaginary people than for real ones." But Bertram would not accept this. His view was that caring for people was the easiest thing in the world compared to being cared for.

"All the same," he added, "I think I will have a doctor in. We can't be too careful." And the doctor reported that Susannah should return to England, and that the sooner she travelled the better.

"Problem is," said Bertram, "this is no country for women who're preggers. We're all of us sitting on a bloody great bomb, any moment now there could be civil war. My instructions are plain, old fruit. All British nationals who are free to leave are requested to do so as soon as poss. That's what they've told me, and, although I don't want to lose you, my little duck, I don't seem to have much choice."

Susannah was extremely reluctant. She had no wish ever to leave her bed or the company of this fat, old

man. Never had she felt so secure as in the leathery old
Bentley of his personality.

"We get a lot of hippies out here," said Bertram,
"funny, dirty little creatures; I like them myself. Had
a niece who was a hippie, but the silly sausage had to
go off to India and meditate herself to death. Poor
child! But it seems that you're not one of those hippie
things at all. Truth to tell, I've been receiving a most
alarming series of messages from all sorts of boring
and important people. The telex has been ticking away
like billy-oh. They all think you're rather a notorious
lady. I told them I thought they'd got it all wrong,
that you like cocoa and Jane Austen, but I'm only a
fat old ambassador, and what I say counts for nothing.
They've insisted on putting a guard round the Embassy—well, isn't that dotty?—but they wouldn't do
that, I suppose, unless they were pretty sure of themselves. You're Susannah Arnatt, aren't you? Oh, don't
answer if you'd rather not, but you'll have to tell someone sooner or later, won't you? and you might as well
tell old Bertram."

"Yes," said Susannah, "I'm afraid I am."

"Good girl," and the Ambassador patted her hand
in a pleased sort of way. "When in doubt admit everything, that's my motto, but you did tell me some
whoppers. Still, tomorrow the RAF will have you, so
here's what we must do tonight. I'll make you a nice,
hot cocoa, and then we'll polish off *Persuasion.*
Wouldn't be fair to leave Anne at sixes and sevens,
now would it?"

*"In half a minute Charles was at the bottom of
Union Street again, and the other two proceeding together; and soon words enough had passed between
them to decide their direction towards the compara-
tively quiet and retired gravel-walk, where the power*

*of conversation would make the present hour a bless-
ing indeed; and prepare it for all the immortality which
the happiest recollections of their own future lives
could bestow. There they exchanged again those feelings and those promises which had once before seemed
to secure everything, but which had been followed by
so many, many years of divison and estrangement.
There they returned again into the past, more ex-
quisitely happy perhaps, in their reunion than when it
had been first projected; more tender, more tried, more
fixed in a knowledge of each other's character, truth,
and attachment; more equal to act, more justified in
acting."*

"Have I got to go home?" asked Susannah.

"It may not be so awful."

"It may be worse."

Stewart-Taylor ran the Department. He had seen
Ministers come and go, each one with an enthusiasm as
touching as it was misapplied, each one with something
of a social conscience, each one nervously ambitious,
and unsure whether this Ministry was a corridor to
power or something rather more like a fire-escape.
Stewart-Taylor gave advice to each incumbent minister,
and was quite used to having his advice disregarded;
at first. Later they came round to his way of doing
things, and, since he always took the precaution of
putting his advice in the form of a memo, he was regu-
larly on file as having been 'right'.

'Memos and minutes,' Stewart-Taylor wrote in his
journal one night, 'these are the modern chariots, the
modern gunpowder. With them a man can take his
elephants across the Alps, with them a man can—
could—lead a revolution. If our young radicals were

to master the art of memos and minutes, there would
be no stopping them.'

Since Stewart-Taylor ran the Department, he was
more highly paid even than the Minister. He also had
security of tenure, a generous pension scheme, and
free car-parking at the office. The power was his too,
and the Minister was welcome to the glory. He had
few enough perks.

'A political career was never built on glory,' another
entry in his diary assured whichever biographer got
there first. 'Glory is either vulgar or transient, and often
both. The true politician seeks from those around him
grudging respect. It was grudging respect which swept
the Fuehrer to power. The man who has the grudging
respect of his peers needs nothing else.'

Stewart-Taylor welcomed Jamie with a glass of
Oloroso. A letter from the Governor of Holloway (who
had once danced the last waltz with the civil servant in
younger and more care-free days; on the lawn at
Spindles, underneath the Chinese lanterns, ah!) ensured that. But Jamie thanked him and declined.

"You must be a busy man," Jamie said, "and I
didn't come here to drink your sherry."

"You're the only one who doesn't," said the Department man.

"You read the letter?"

"I did my best. Her handwriting is . . . I did my
best. You want permission to visit an inmate in Gartree? I'm a man of few words, in this case four:—It
Can't Be Done."

"You know who, I suppose, and why?"

"That's it, you see. Train robbers, wife-murderers,
no problem."

"Wife-murderers?"

"Why yes. Did you have an interest in one of them?"

"She comes into that category."

"She is a Palestinian terrorist. It's a fair bet that there are a couple of thousand people in this country would like nothing better than to see her dead. An equal number or more are prepared to go to any lengths to have her sprung. What would you do in my shoes?"

It was a fine office. Persian rug, photographs of wife and offspring, abstract sculpture, mathematical toys; like all the best offices, it gave little away.

"I'm a rabbi," said the rabbi. "I do not, I never have, dealt in deceptions. I will tell you the truth of the matter. My wife was kidnapped. This girl must know by whom, and where I can find her, through what channels get a message to her. This girl has been moved to Gartree. I wish to see her, speak to her. Now is that unreasonable?"

"No," said Stewart-Taylor.

"You are married. How would you feel if your wife disappeared? Would you not do everything in your power to get her back?"

Stewart-Taylor was startled. His wife had left him two days prior to this interview. He had done nothing to get her back, nor, for the moment, did he intend to.

"I'm sorry I can't help you," he told Jamie firmly. "I respect my old friend, the Governor of Holloway, and I respect you in your dilemma, but all the respect in the world won't make the blindest bit of difference. The girl can have no visitors for the moment. And that's that."

Said Jamie: "Has she been interrogated? Has she told you anything?"

"Everything is in hand. These things take a bit of time, of course. Well, it's been nice—"

"That means you've got nowhere," cried Jamie triumphantly. "Don't you see that our interests coincide?

She has information which we both need. Your boys haven't been able to obtain it. I think I can. What is to be lost by letting me try?"

"Why should she talk to you?" Despite himself Stewart-Taylor was intrigued by this fanatical little rabbi and felt inclined to be persuaded by him. In his journal he had written:

'Slogging hard work, friends in high places, discretion and diplomacy, none of this will help a man in public office if he has not the ability on rare occasions to "play his hunch".'

The rabbi had been correct in assuming that the girl Alia had proved utterly intransigent. The interrogations at Holloway and Gartree had been farcical. An interpreter had had to be found who was trustworthy, and that, so far as Arab interpreters were concerned, narrowed the field more than a little. Even so, there had been no way of checking that the questions had been properly comprehended, nor the replies accurately interpreted. It had been concluded that on the whole the sensible thing to do was to teach her English. This was undertaken through a series of tapes supplied by the BBC, so that Alia was becoming qualified to go shopping at the supermarket, to inspect a house in the country in the company of an estate agent, and to take her young children, Michael and Fiona, on an outing to the zoo. But she was still either incapable or, more likely, reluctant to answer questions about her organisation, about the Synagogue affair, about anything that mattered.

Jamie did not answer Stewart-Taylor's question directly. He stared at the mathematical toy, at the abstract sculpture, and then at the Home Office man.

"You've nothing to lose," he said at length. "I'm not begging, you know, I'm offering a service. I hoped you would have welcomed my contribution."

"You've not convinced me," replied Stewart-Taylor, "but then I don't convince easily. Ministry men don't, unlike politicians. Nevertheless I'll give you a chance. My secretary will let you have a letter to Brinton, the Governor of Gartree, and also a list of questions to which we would like answers. We shall see whether our interests do truly coincide. The girl is a sulky little thing, and I wish you well of her. But for Christ's sake, tread carefully."

Alia preferred the atmosphere of Gartree to the effete home comforts of the hospital at Holloway. The checks and counter-checks, the armed guards and the noctural flood-lighting seemed entirely appropriate in a war context, and much more suited to the dignity of a freedom-fighter. But she was sad when they took away her blue dress. She was kept apart from the other prisoners, and the isolation was not disagreeable to her, nor did she experience any difficulty in continuing to outwit the interrogators, whose gentle techniques she despised and whose limited stamina was soon exhausted by her obdurate refusal to cooperate.

Jamie knew little of Alia beyond what Stewart-Taylor had hinted, and what he had read in the papers. He had not seen her at the Synagogue; his eyes had been all for Susannah. And when at last he was escorted into her presence, the defiant brown eyes and chunky body, so absurdly out of place within the floppy prison costume, disconcerted him. This was no monster, or a very subtle form of monster. And the warder retreated discreetly behind a copy of the *Sporting Chronicle*.

"Do you know who I am?" asked Jamie. He was sitting knee to knee with the girl, who was on the bed.

The broken head of a snapdragon rested in a tooth-mug beside the pillow.

The girl did not answer. The cell smelt of disinfectant.

"I am a rabbi. I was at Blackheath when . . . when you were there." (It sounded ludicrously like party chat.) "My wife, Susannah, was the woman your people took hostage. Where is she? I have a right to ask that question, don't you agree?"

"Pardon?" said the girl. "You have to speak slow." She had a deep voice for a girl, thought Jamie. Her eyes never left his; he was too close, he had to look away, at the warder, at the snapdragon, at the chamber-pot. His hatred for her gave the relationship an unnerving intimacy; his intentions towards her made the intimacy more profound.

"I am looking for my wife, for Susannah," said Jamie, spacing the words out. "Where is she? Do you know?"

A slight narrowing of the girl's eyes convinced Jamie that she well understood, and intended a cunning reply.

"I know not anything," she said slowly. "She is your wife, she is not mine. You do not do so good to ask me."

Jamie glanced away from the girl at the snapdragon, at the chamber-pot, at the warder, whose eyes were spying over the top of his paper. Hastily they returned to the Stratford runners and riders.

"I can ask you anything," said Jamie, suddenly angry. "You're just a stupid, vindictive little girl and I hope they keep you here until you learn more sense. I shan't give up, you know. You'll be sick of the sight of me by the time you're done."

Almost certainly Alia was unable to follow this rush of words. But the gesture she made as soon as he had finished speaking was unequivocal. She pulled the hem of her faded uniform several inches up her thighs and opened her legs. As she did so she smiled, although her eyes remained fully on his, with an expression of total contempt.

"There's obviously no point in pursuing this now," Jamie remarked, his voice hoarse, "I shall return when you're a little more tractable."

"Pardon," said the girl, still using her brown eyes relentlessly, "you have to speak slow."

"Would you mind letting me out?" Jamie asked the warder. "I think we'll not progress any further today."

"That's all, is it, sir?"

"For now."

Susannah left Beirut on May Day. Sir Bertram escorted her to Ankara, where she was helped on board an RAF Trident supplied by Stewart-Taylor, who did not inform Jamie of her reappearance. The 'plane contained a midwife and a complete medical team.

The day following Susannah's departure, as Bertram had predicted, war broke out in the streets of the capital, and, in the Cercle Hippique, racehorses, terrified by the shooting, reared and foamed. Embassies, but not the British, came under artillery fire and government jets made strikes against the refugee camps, whilst on every corner Falangists waved their brand new Russian automatics at anyone who caught their eye. Within a week there were well over a hundred corpses unburied in the streets. And Israel celebrated her twenty-fifth birthday.

Susannah was brought into Lyneham airfield, and everything was done that could be done to ensure that the news of her homecoming remained secret. An ambulance swept her off to the Middlesex Hospital where a private suite had been prepared against her arrival, and there she lay, huge, exhausted, and obstinately silent.

One thing at a time, she thought to herself, one bloody thing at a time. First Jamie. Then the baby. After that they could do what they liked with her. Everyone else did.

The night after his visit to Alia's cell, Jamie dreamed of Dorset, of Golden Cap, of the top of the world, where he and Susannah had loved one another. "I will lift up mine eyes unto the hills; from whence cometh my help." In his dream it was just the same as it had always been. Once, before he met Susannah, he had revisited a favourite place in Cornwall, where the green baize cliffs rolled down to a crazy, rock-bespattered beach. It had still been there, but guarding it was a high chain fence and a board which proclaimed: 'Ministry of Defence, Strictly Private, All Passes Must be Shown'. He had asked questions of the publican, was told awful stories of monstrous mackerel pulled from the sea—you couldn't eat them, you wouldn't dare—and, when the wind was from the North, smells which made you bring up your beer just by smelling them. But in his dream Golden Cap was still a most notable crag, quite majestic against the rags and tatters of the sky. He woke up in the night and thought that it was once again the old days, that Susannah still lay obediently beside him. He bundled up a hotel pillow, and clutched it to him.

He could not get back to sleep. He lay and made plans. Plans were a comfort at such moments. Everything depended upon being alone with Alia, just for a minute or two. He planned it.

She was a menace, of that he had no doubt. Vicious,

perverted and cynical, it was all there to be read between the lines of that tawny face. Not many lines yet.
How old would she be? In her teens still, half his age,
less than half. And he, to whom the welfare of the
young had been specially entrusted, he to whom violence had always been abhorrent—yes, Susannah had
been right, his sermon *was* hypocritical, *then*, yes, but
no longer, not now, he had changed—he was to inflict
violence upon this *girl-child*, he was to bully, and
batter, and kill. *He* was? No, no, that was no way to
look at it. Think of the children who had been specially entrusted to *her*, the ones she and her friends had
bullied and battered and killed, and would again given
half the chance; think of that and there could be no
question that his resolve was courageous, his determination just. "And the land had rest forty years." And
think of Susannah, lost to him, lost . . .

"You wish to interview this girl alone, Rabbi?"

"Indeed I do."

"You realise how dangerous she is?"

"Well, naturally. You seem to forget that I was there,
that my wife—"

"No, no, I don't forget, but you must appreciate my
position. My first responsibility is for the security of
those within the prison."

"And you are seriously suggesting that I would in
some way threaten that security?"

"I fail to see why it's necessary for you to have this
tête-à-tête. Preston reported to me that you appeared
to have very little in common with the girl."

"We have little in common, that is true, but I don't
go to see her to make friends. All I need is information.
Stewart-Taylor—"

"Would it help if you were to see her in my office?"

"Where is immaterial. I believe that half an hour

with her alone would do the trick. It's only natural that's she's suspicious with a warder present."

"He's discreet, is Preston."

"He filled the damn room!"

"A half-hour would be sufficient?"

"I believe so, yes."

"Very well, I shall have you escorted to her cell. There will be someone outside the door should you need help. And I shall have to ask you to undergo a body-check."

"I'm most grateful," said Jamie, covering up his excitement as best he could. "I'm sure you'll not regret it. The girl will be quite safe."

"It was not the girl I was concerned about. Good luck."

It was best in the cell. That was the proper place for it. A pity about the search. His hand had been tight around the handle of the strong, steel knife in his pocket, the one he had carved the silverside of beef with almost a year ago. He abandoned it in the lavatory cistern.

They searched him. They showed him into the cell. The heavy door was pulled tight behind him. Bolts and keys. Take a while to open that lot.

And there she was. Alia. Young enough maybe to be his daughter. Lying on the bed. Reading. Didn't move when he came in. No respect. Turned her head, no more than that, but there were the eyes again. They had haunted him, those insolent, calculating eyes. Never seen eyes like that on a Jewish girl.

"What's that you're reading?" he asked, feeling impelled to break the silence. "Some slushy rubbish, I expect."

Since she didn't answer, he took the book out of her hands. It was *Alice Through the Looking-Glass*.

"You know why I am here?"

"Oh yes."

"Why I am *really* here?"

"Yes."

She made a movement, swinging her legs around, as though to sit up, facing him. Jamie had this sudden notion that she had a weapon of some sort concealed about her, and leapt upon her, attempting to pin her arms back against the bed. He lay against her body. She lay quite passively, not wriggling, breathing a little heavily, that was all, her eyes always on his, her mouth slightly apart in that contemptuous smile.

"Ah!" she sighed.

He moved his hands to her throat. He throbbed. He was aroused. He had never felt a sensation as powerful even in the early days, even with Susannah. He tried to tighten his grip. He had his knee forced between her legs. He drew it upwards. He was trembling so violently that his movements had lost all cohesion. She lay passively still, mustering her strength.

"I shall kill you," he said. "It's what I came here for."

Her eyes were still on his, mouth smiling, perfect teeth, faint smell on the breath, spearmint toothpaste, Susannah had used that. The warmth of her body, that dreadful smile, the softness of her throat . . . An uncontrollable surge of love, and then his fingers went suddenly limp around her neck.

It was a simple matter for the girl, trained in such a hard school, to arch her back and thrust him over the side of the bed. His head made a loud thwack as it struck the chamber-pot. He was conscious of her looking down at him, blouse gaping, and those eyes just as before. No question but that she was smiling openly now as she lunged at him with the side of her hand.

His last chance gone. He did not deserve to live. *She* did, because she had the strength and the will and the ruthlessness, but not him. The foot came in, down there where he was most vulnerable, most Jewish.

He'd bungled everything.

Then keys and bolts and shouts. Feet and hands. Humiliation and laughter. He shut his eyes. There was panic in his head.

Alia was still smiling as they pulled her away.

In the Middlesex two of Stewart-Taylor's men interrogated Susannah, if you could call it an interrogation.

"Come on, love," they said, "we've got a job to do, nothing personal. Play ball with us, and we'll put in a good word for you when the time comes. Just a few questions. Name, age, place of birth, that sort of thing will do to begin with, nothing to worry about."

"I wish to see my husband," was all Susannah would say.

"And so you shall. Don't worry about a thing. Would you care for a cup of tea? No? Would you rather we typed out a questionnaire and left you to fill it in by yourself? All we're concerned with are the formalities. So you can pick up the pieces, and we can close the file, as it were. You won't help us? We're your friends, you've no enemies here. Not at all?"

They kept her at it for a while, and then the attendant doctor warned them against tiring her excessively. She was in shock. She was forty weeks pregnant.

"Do us a favour," the men replied, "*she's* exhausting *us!*"

"Perhaps," said the doctor, "she is not prepared to speak to you for no more sinister reason than that she has nothing to say. What information does she have that is of such importance that it can't wait a few days?"

A psychiatrist who saw her briefly, said:

"You may call the subject's mutism bloody-mindedness, or you may call it a cry for help, but to me it reads like a rejection of the sort of help you're prepared to offer. Is it so strange that she wishes at such a moment to speak to her husband? Of course not. This is no sulky child, but a woman."

"So there's nothing we can do?"

"Did I say that? Don't expect miracles, but if I can treat her for a few months, we'll have her singing the Hallelujah Chorus yet."

"We don't want the Hallelujah Chorus, and we can't wait a few months."

"I'm only human," muttered the shrink tetchily, as though someone had suggested the contrary.

Susannah was closely guarded. Plain-clothes men were posted outside the door and wasted much of the orderlies' time demanding sweet, milky tea and custard creams. Inside the door a policewoman sat and read Galsworthy.

Said the nurse, a blonde girl with big, white arms, to Susannah, lying on her back and feeling as vulnerable as a splayed tortoise:

"Be positive. Think of the joy the child will bring you. Do you want a girl or a boy? Girls are nice, with a girl you can be girlish again yourself, girls can bring you a new lease of life, but a boy, well, the fathers are always best pleased with a boy."

Susannah shut her mind to all but painless things, such as the intricate pattern on the ceiling. If you peered at it, you could make out that it had once been wallpaper and they'd painted it over; you could just make out the whorls and curlicues of the design. She

put her hands on her drum-tight belly and felt bitterly
sorry for the baby. This was the first time she had
imagined it as a separate entity, something which would
have been perfectly capable for some weeks of sus-
taining life independently of her. Poor baby! Might
have been better off in an incubator. She could antici-
pate little joy for it. For any babies being born anywhere.

Stewart-Taylor was losing patience. He was angry
that Susannah was proving so intractable, and furiously
angry that Jamie had been permitted to visit Alia un-
chaperoned. The press were bound to get hold of the
story; they were utterly irresponsible, and would print
anything, often, it seemed, less to boost their circula-
tion than to embarrass responsible people and to under-
mine the authority of the leaders of the nation. Even
the Minister was beginning to stir a little, to stretch
and scratch in his burrow. He kept on about "holding
a press conference" so that "the official position" could
be put. Stewart-Taylor wrote him a couple of memos
on the subject of press conferences and the need for
secrecy in cases involving internal security, and insisted on another twenty-four hours before any sort of
statement was made. He had decided to bring Jamie
and Susannah together at the Middlesex and monitor
their meeting. (From his journal: 'Unconventional
problems require unconventional solutions. Many a
mariner has been wrecked because he failed to consider
using his shirt as a sail.')

Jamie had been taken, bruised, in distress and se-
dated, to a cottage hospital near Market Harborough,
so pretty a hospital that a sentimental old dame, coming round after her operation there and looking out of

the window, is reputed to have remarked:

"Whatever the Almighty has in store for me, he'll have to shift a bit if he's to improve on this."

But Jamie was put in a bed with screens round it, and though he spoke of the same God (give or take a heresy or two) he spoke in a different language:

"Figgaddal w'jis kaddasch sch'meh rabbo b'ol . . ."

"What's he saying?" Sister asked, in a tone of voice suggesting that anything she could not understand must be either subversive or obscene. Mr Berghof, the apothecary and known as a linguist since he wrote things down in Latin, was in the hospital for gallstones, and was summoned to give his views.

"He's praying," said Mr Berghof.

"Funny sort of prayer," sniffed Sister.

"It's in Hebrew."

"You mean he's an Israeli? Well, that's the very last thing we need here."

"No, no," said Mr Berghof, "he is very probably not an Israeli, just a Jew, as I am, and one in great need of comfort."

Sister was not entirely reassured, and was more than a little relieved when important people arrived to take Jamie off to London, where, by all accounts, all manner of eccentricities were tolerated. Like Corby, only worse.

And thus it was that Stewart-Taylor, improvising bravely, engineered at last a meeting between husband and wife in a private suite in the aptly named Middlesex Hospital, where a microphone had been secreted in a vase of bluebells, just in case Susannah should let anything slip, which might be turned to advantage.

Jamie, in hospital pyjamas and robe, and unaware of where he was or with whom, muttered away busily to himself.

"Surely he hath borne our grief, and carried our sorrows; yet we did deem him stricken, smitten of God, and afflicted. But he was wounded by our transgressions, he was bruised for our iniquities; the chastisement of our peace was upon him; and with his stripes we are healed!"

("Can't do much about the quality," submitted the audio-electronic engineer, sitting in front of his dials in a van parked behind the hospital, "if he won't speak up there's no equipment in the world can make him.")

"Yet it pleased the Lord to bruise him; he hath put him to grief; when thou shalt make his soul an offering for sin, he shall see his seed, he shall prolong his days, and the pleasure of the Lord shall prosper in his hand. He shall see the travail of his soil, and shall be satisfied; by his knowledge shall my righteous servant justify many; for he shall bear their iniquities." And he slept. And his pulse was very faint.

To Susannah it seemed as though in that white suite in that grey hospital there was no more time, neither past, present, nor future. The weights had been moved along the scales until her life was perfectly balanced. It was her birthday, her thirty-first. She had forgotten.

She had not anticipated that Jamie might have become physically wrecked. For nine months while she had grown both fat and bonny, he had become not just middle-aged but *old*. White-haired and emaciated, and his eyes had retreated further and further into his skull, as though terrified of what they had seen and might see. But why? He had been in Blackheath. What apocalyptic visions had haunted him there?

He stirred, turned towards her, opened his eyes.

"I've been having such dreams," he said in a thin surprised voice. "You've got fat." And at once was asleep again. A little while later he opened his eyes once again, and said:

"Nurse."

"I am not a nurse," Susannah replied severely.

"Could I have a drink?"

"Look, I'm the one who's meant to be in bed," Susannah sat up and craned forward. "But, Jamie, while you're awake there's something I've got to explain." Although Jamie's eyes were closing slowly, like a dog's, she continued. "I've wanted so much to be able to explain, but it's hard."

A doctor came in, young but tired-looking, with dark hair curling down to the top of his white coat.

"Excuse me," he said, and sat down beside Susannah on the bed, putting his fingers lightly on her wrist. Then, unpacking his rubber tubes and pressure gauge, he strapped up her arm and pumped away at the bulb.

"Mustn't get too excited," he said, "must we?" Susannah did not answer this; another question followed immediately. "Little fellow doesn't seem to want to come out, does he?"

"Who can bloody blame him?"

The doctor left after a brief examination. Jamie made grunting noises in his sleep and twitched violently several times. Susannah could just reach his hand, which felt very dry to the touch. She studied it intently. It had been neglected, that was evident, there was grime in the nails, which were broken and split, and cuts and scars along the surface of the skin. Jamie had been so proud of his hands. He slept for a long time. Susannah watched the rectangle of light slide across the wall. Traffic in the street. Tyres and taxis.

"What a pair of old crocks we have become," she said aloud, and smiled. "We who were such a handsome couple. No one would think it now, him so old-looking and me so fat and disgusting."

(In the van this sudden speech after such a long silence awoke the recording engineer, who asked his colleague: "What was that? Did I miss anything, Trev?" "Go back to sleep," said his colleague, "this is the craziest job I was ever on.")

"You know something, Jamie, something I've just remembered about my father. He told me once, he said: 'You've got a great gift, Susannah, you can bring people happiness. You just have to be there, that's all. It's a great gift.' And I could with him. And I could with you, Jamie, couldn't I? Sometimes? Dorset was nice. I'll have the baby adopted, Jamie, there's people desperate for them, or, if you'd rather, we could keep it. You only have to tell me what you'd like. Whatever you decide, I'll not mind, really."

His hand in hers was growing cramped. She released the fingers with some care, then, on an impulse, put his hand inside her nightdress, against the distended breast.

"I don't expect to salvage much from all this, Jamie. It would be nice, though, to be together for a while at least to sort things out. And I should think you'd need a bit of pampering after all you've been through. Not that they told me anything about you, just that you'd disappeared. When this is all over, perhaps you could write your books . . . . You're rather cold, Jamie, perhaps you'd better have your hand back. I'll cover it up."

Time passed. Susannah looked at her sleeping husband, who was so sadly changed. Her happiness evaporated, and in its place a sudden terror of being alive.

"After all," she muttered, "I was only doing what they told me to do. That was the worst I ever did."

There was the noise of a disturbance in the corridor, a nasal, raucous voice raised in anger, others placatory and persuasive. Then the loud voice domineeringly and with finality:

"You show me the law says you can keep a mother from her daughter, you show me such a law? I think you will have to look a long, long way to find such a law, which I doubt very much you will find."

Thereupon the door was flung open and Mrs Klein swept in, dangling a bunch of grapes by the stalk. The policewoman stood up, dropped Galsworthy, stepped forward, stepped back, sat down and retrieved Galsworthy, which, in any case, wasn't a patch on the TV series.

"So many people, Susannah, and for what do they need all these very rude people? I should like to hear them when I ask them what they mean by such things, I should indeed. Well now, Susannah, let me have a look at you. Tscha! The first thing I have to say is that you do not look at all well on it, it doesn't suit you, my dear, that's the first thing I have to say, and the other is that your fine Jamie certainly took his time. For what was he waiting so long, I ask myself, or could it be that he is not like other men, your handsome rabbi?"

"Mother, please—"

"They should open the windows in here. This place is like—what are those places in Rome where they left their loved ones? Ach, it is not so easy to remember so many things—but anyway air we must have!" And she flung open the window, and the sweetly scented evening air wafted into the sick room. "And those bluebells, what a thing! No water in the vase at all, my dear." And she took the bluebells to the hand-basin, and held them under the tap for a moment.

(The recording engineer swore fiercely, as a spluttering sound, much amplified, was followed by silence.)

"So now we can talk, yes? At last we can talk. Darling, why did you not write to me? Such a long time it was, believe me, such a long time to be without news, that was not kind."

"I couldn't send cards to anyone, you don't understand."

"No, I do not understand. As a mother I do not. There are many things which I do not at all understand. And darling, I have to talk to you, about *him*." Mrs Klein glared disapprovingly at Jamie. "But what is wrong with him? He looks terrible."

"He's tired," said Susannah.

"So he's tired? I should think we are all tired. Such a journey I had you would never believe!"

Then suddenly inside Susannah a violent muscular spasm, and a flood of water from between her legs.

"Mummy," she said, "it's starting!"

Sister took charge.

"Clear the room!" she said. "Now I want *everyone* out. Him and her and particularly *her*."

Mrs Klein refused to leave. Eventually she was bundled into a police car, gesticulating so violently that the vehicle swerved and narrowly missed the headquarters of the Family Planning Association opposite the hospital.

Jamie was put into a spare bed in the neurological ward where he was no trouble at all.

And Susannah gave birth to a daughter, and called her Alison.

Epilogue

———————

"Our God and God of our fathers, as evening casts its shadows over the earth, ushering in this most solemn of days, we join with our fellow Jews throughout the world . . ."

This Day of Atonement in the Blackheath and District Progressive Synagogue had peculiar poignancy. During the course of the previous one almost everyone in the small congregation had lost a relative. And although Rabbi Stronheim, who was clever—but not infallible as the Vatican had just reaffirmed that the Pope was—had stated quite categorically that the season of penitence represented the start of the new year, and not the end of the old one, one could hardly ignore the armed policemen outside the Synagogue, nor escape a thorough search on entering the building.

The services were a triumph of organisation, and

Judith and Hattie, who shouldered the main burden, deserved the congratulations which they shyly received. Old Jacob preached about the giving of tithes, and Rabbi Stronheim was unrelenting concerning the controversy between Rabbi Yohanan ben Nuri and Rabbi Akiba over the Seven Benedictions of the Amidah, a controversy conducted with some passion in the third century CE. And the little choir sang out sweetly, and the people stood and sat obediently, and the gates of the ark were opened and closed, and the *shofar* was blown, and God, if He existed, was there.

Of those held hostage in the Synagogue the previous year only Harry and Gerry attended this time. Harry took his water-pistol with him just in case, but Gerry said that that was silly, they wouldn't try the same place twice.

"Just let them!" cried Harry fiercely, but his mother looked at his father in dismay. Jonathan would have been there, but he was celebrating the settling of the Thalidomide dispute with a visit to his sister, who had found a blustery man in the Windy City, and decided to stay. Jonathan wrote home that he liked Chicago, but that it wasn't as windy as Blackheath.

Ruth was modelling in a school blazer and nothing else, spreading her legs at the photographer's whim, and earning so much money that the thought of it all made her dizzy. When she had amassed a thousand pounds she intended to pay the premium on a little flat, and give a house-warming party, and invite Jethro, and be very cool, and leave some sets of contacts about the place, and see what he had to say about *that*. She missed him. Only problem would be how to explain the money to her parents who believed that her frequent absences were due to the demands of her A Levels.

"I have to go to the Library," she would explain, "it's quiet there."

But they were most upset when she said that she would rather not attend the Synagogue on Yom Kippur.

"It would be awful, Mummy, after last year. I shouldn't be able to concentrate on the services at all. Please don't make me. *Please*."

As for Jethro, he had taken up residence in a mind-expanding commune in Chamberwell where a shiny brown guru, with the ingratiating trick of turning his tongue inside out, brought his 'love-children' to a fulfilling state of rightmindfulness, if they concentrated hard and were generous with their fathers' money.

On Yom Kippur morning from the window of the dormitory in Queen's Road, Jethro observed a group of Jews in black coats and bowler hats on their way to make peace with their maker; he thought they looked quaint and out of place in the modern world.

And that afternoon in a different kind of ritual a Jumbo Jet was hijacked from the main runway of Manchester Airport, and the lives of the passengers were bartered for the surrender from Gartree of a single girl, terms which the Prime Minister, the Home Secretary and the Commissioner of Scotland Yard considered unacceptable, but which Stewart-Taylor recommended them to accept, because the girl would be a constant temptation to terrorist groups to come to Britain, and in any case she was a sullen and unhelpful creature, more trouble than she was worth. He wrote a memo on the subject, and Alia was flown home.

And on the same day war broke out in the Middle East, a war which historians and economists of the future were to point to as the end of an era, a war after which things could never be the same again, the Yom Kippur War.

And a few days later Jamie and Susannah took
Alison home to Blackheath. The little girl was sturdy
and brown and intelligent; no trouble at all. Jamie
and Susannah spoiled her outrageously. They hoped,
and it was a modest enough hope, that through Alison,
they might one day find a way back to one another,
that they might again be friends.